GIRLS GHOSTS AND GUILT

VOLUME I

GIRLS GHOSTS AND GUILT

VOLUME I

TROY DECKER

ISBN:978-1-964452-25-8(hc)
ISBN:978-1-964452-24-1(sc)
ISBN:978-1-964452-26-5(e)

Library of Congress Control Number: 2024925251

The contents of this work, including, but not limited to, the accuracy of events, people,
and places depicted; opinions expressed; permission to use previously published
materials included; and any advice given or actions advocated are solely the
responsibility of the author, who assumes all liability for said work and indemnifies the
publisher against any claims stemming from publication of the work.

Rev. date:
05/17/2024

CHAPTER ONE

Seated on the edge of the bed, my body shook as adrenaline rushed to my brain. I remembered dreaming; dreams that were vivid to my mind, as if reality was nothing but a delusional reaction that my nightmare bore upon me. As I reached for something to wipe the intense trail of fear that ran down my brow, burning the flesh that lay beneath it, a voice caused distraction. The vocal tone brought ease to my skeptical thoughts and added comfort to my misconceptions.

"Hey Zippy," Tina whispered from around the corner, which forced my eyes to leap in her direction. My shoulders shrugged, and a lonely foot garment that was in reaching distance became the main tool that would relieve the misery from my brow. My forehead was sticky, and the foot warmer left evidence at the scene.

Tina had a way of showing up every time a bad dream haunted my mind. It did not matter where the image in my head occurred; she always found her way. It was a curse through my eyes; she viewed it as a gift.

A poor excuse of a smile appeared amongst my face. My insides tugged at the corners of my mouth, not letting them out of their grasp; it wasn't proven if the feelings I had were fear or pure confusion. My motives were to act in a sociable manner; however, it was uncertain that the words that would leak from my lips would be appropriate. My head moved in an up and down motion to show awareness of her presence.

"Would you rather I go?" Tina added to Zippy. Her face showed wrinkles that were formed from pure exhaustion. Her eyes were not as ornamental as they were years ago. The color somehow dissipated throughout the time she spent roaming the world, a world that had brought many frustrating events for the two of us.

We have had our share of misery, some experienced together and some dealt with separately. I often pondered on the days that were filled with agony and depression as I walked through life very slowly. When Tina was involved with one of my nightmarish tales, it was easier to feel at ease. We were meant to be together, in one way or another. In no way would my frail limbs still be moseying the earth if there was not such a remarkable human, who was referred to as Tina.

Female relationships did not come easy for me. Who was I kidding? All my relationships came with great difficulties. It did not matter if it was a romantic situation or merely friends; it didn't matter if it was family or foe. I did not have an acceptable rapport with people because my personality was not easy to understand. It appeared as if I was a decent person upon a first meeting, but then again, after the sun and moon continued to play their never-ending game of tag, it would become obvious that there was more than meets the eye. It wasn't that I was a horrible person, it was the fact that my secrets forced society to turn against me.

The struggle with trusting people was an ongoing battle; the mere sight of humans filled my mind with disgust. It truly felt as if evil surrounded the world, and most humans were weak and fell into a life of betrayal and selfishness. The hardest type of person to trust were those who only thought of themselves. The epidemic was rising fast, and the fear that someday the earth would be over-crowded with greedy, self- consumed humans that would definitely destroy each other for the lack of understanding that everyone… had feelings, was on high alert.

I was a person who had lost sight of living a happy fulfilling life and began to see the dark of the world. Tina somehow kept my hate controlled purely by supporting me no matter what foolish predicament I stumbled into. She had a smile that melted away my loathing; it was true love that I felt for her. It did not matter if we had an intimate connection or if we were close friends. Throughout my life, we've been known to have both styles of relationships. My adoration for her had been strong since the first day my eyes were blessed by her beauty; it didn't matter if we were considered to be a couple or simple acquaintances.

Gazing at Tina, I tried to let the images of my dream disappear back into the treacherous realm from which they came, however, it appeared as if they had nowhere else to be. Torment overwhelmed my overly sensitive mind. A section of my brain, where well-being was lacking, was consumed by impure thoughts that were draining all of my energy. For what lurked deep inside of my soul, showing itself in my weakest moments, were structured images that my mind was not ready or willing to ponder. An ultimate fantasy would be to go back in time and keep life stable, nevertheless, I was afraid my days of stability were far from my reach. I saw, heard, and even tasted the events that took over my mind while sleep was in action. Days, months, years went by, and their memories were still prominent in my brain. Somehow in my head, there rested answers to other beings' problems. The dead tried with all their power to pry the information from me, however, my stubbornness would not release it. Even though the data that was in my head was difficult to decipher, it was mine, and no one else was allowed to have it until I was able to interpret it. Understanding would have been an easier task if the problem at hand was actually one of true reality and not a piece of the messed-up world inside my mind: a complex conundrum in a world filled with so many complications.

"I've been trying to get you to move on for how many years now?" I muttered out of pure frustration.

"Who's supposed to be counting?" She said sarcastically as she loosely sat next to my shaking body.

"The only memories of us that I kept are those of joy. The bad... I discarded them. Only when my mind is clear do I retrieve our good moments. Unfortunately my mind is quite cluttered. A most glorious day is to come before us and show me the way back into a time that was most incredible," my thoughts were passed through my lips as the wiping cloth was tossed away. It left a mark on the wall from the sweat it obtained from my forehead.

"I had to leave. No good would have come from me staying," Tina added as she desperately tried to put her hand into mine. She disliked the fact that we were no longer as close as we were in the past. Her hands used to caress mine in a way that would cause bumps to cover my entire body and bring about happiness to shiver amongst my spine. Unfortunately, I couldn't feel her touch any longer; the distance between us was far too great to ever regain any intimacy that we shared in the past. We were well aware that we could not hurdle the obstacle that stopped us from being one, so we gave in to the fact that we were to be apart. We were still able to have each other in our lives, and that was the most important element.

She sat back, looking at me with the softest gaze. Her sadness was evident. Tina had a life that was by far not a simple one. She was one of the strongest people to ever walk the earth.

"What do you think our lives would have been like if the circumstances were different?" I asked as I turned my vibrating body towards her.

She attempted to express emotion as her lips quivered, struggling to form a smile of comfort.

"I wish you would stop destroying yourself with thoughts that you know were never meant to be," she said as she slowly rose to her feet; she needed to escape, and as she left, loneliness bled from her orbs of sight.

My attitude upset Tina; it aroused confusion in most people that were aware of my presence. I did not enjoy making her feel anger, however, no matter how hard I pressured myself to live in a more positive manner, the more negative my thoughts became. My head shook with disgust. My stomach was churning from the scene of a pompous ass; that ass was me. Tina was the last person that deserved to feel pain, nonetheless, my negligence allowed me to think of her as a superior being, which brought up the notion that a poor mortal such as myself, would not be good enough for her.

There was a sweet aroma surrounding my apartment; Tina always left a piece of her behind. The smell drifted across the furniture to make sure that my thoughts were of her. It was a pleasant fragrance that, unfortunately, brought an uncontrollable sadness. Tina and I came from a time not so long ago: a time that would never rejuvenate. I was a lost lad with a dream, an all-American dream: to be cherished by another; Tina was that other. We met through a mutual friend, a woman who had many interesting qualities. My body relaxed upon my bed and my mind was refreshed with the memory of how the lovely Tina entered my life.

The air was still; the chill was so immense that it froze the breezes. It was a quarter past midnight as I began to bring my vehicle to life. My mind was drawn to images of a life with no worries: to be lazy, do absolutely nothing, and have no reason to feel regret. Such thoughts often flowed through my weary head at the end of a long workday. My goal was to head home and smoke some herb on the way to let the high calm my chattering nerves. All sounded fantastic until my car hacked up fluid onto the frozen pavement underneath, which forced me to pull to the side of the road. It wasn't the end of the world as I knew it, but certainly it was a pain in the nether region. A little on the depressed side, my mind fluttered with the possibilities of what to do next when a squeak from the passenger side door caught my attention. As I turned to inspect the noise, the door opened all by its lonesome. A tiny waist upstaged everything in my sight line. The hips swung in a diagonal circular motion bringing a remarkably cute young woman into my gaze. She cheerfully hopped into the vehicle slamming the door behind her.

"This sucks!" the mystery brunette exclaimed as she watched me with amusement, "I thought my day was going real crappy until witnessing your bad luck; I now realize that mine is not so bad." She expressed her thoughts as she released the door and sprung to her feet. She smiled, waved, and with a slight push, the door clanked back to its original position.

Confused, but very enlightened, I began to gather my things for a long journey to a place of rest. Fumbling through my possessions, it was soon discovered that there was not one item that would provide warmth, so off I went with my hands desperately trying to stay above the rim of the sleeves hanging over them. After one block, my toes began to scream out in agony as the blood-flow slowed immensely. A corner approached and around the bend sat a small car with someone sitting inside smoking a large, distorted version of a pipe. It was made out of glass, and formally known as a bowl used to smoke marijuana. I peered up with a diligent smile creeping upon my face. The figure began to roll the window down when a gust of wind took me by surprise. My feet shifted slightly and managed to get footing on a plate of frozen water. Needless to say… I was no longer on foot. The person opened the door and came to my assistance. "So, I see your night just keeps improving," a female laughed as she held out her hand.

It was the same young lady who paid no haste to ridicule me a few minutes earlier. I accepted her offering.

"Nice to see you again," I muttered as she participated in my standing. "I was going to offer you a ride earlier, but I didn't," she said with a smirk upon her face. She had a definite cuteness to her whole act: a sexy little schoolgirl who wanted to piss off her parents, every boy's dream. We gazed into each other's frozen faces, waiting for the other to respond somehow. It seemed as if we were forever lost with amusement. I then held out my hand.

"Put your hand down and get your cute ass in the car," she exclaimed while pointing to her vehicle. She proceeded into the rust bucket and we drove a few blocks.

"I'll tell you where to go," I said, striving desperately to warm my hands.

"I know where I live. If you don't want to come, you may exit." "That won't be necessary. Could I get your name?"

"My name is Sydney," she answered. "And your name would be Terry," she added.

"You know of me?"

"My friend works with you, and I asked her about you." "Are you stalking me?"

"Don't flatter yourself," she remarked. "I work at the factory where your car took a crap; I was on my way to mine, when I noticed you."

"I'm sorry, I didn't mean it like that,"

"You shouldn't be sorry for what you say. You meant what you said, and I took it a different way. So, I should be sorry, not you."

"Good point. So where are we headed?" I inquired as we pulled up to an apartment building. Sydney rushed out of the car and made a mad dash to the entry way. She then waved her hands in a motion that led me to follow. I strolled to the door, wondering what the hell I'd gotten myself into.

We entered into a domain which appeared to be her home. The place gleamed as if no one actually lived there. Everything was in its place, no dust, no garbage… obviously a woman's station.

Following Sydney into the living room, we found three absolutely gorgeous women scattered in various places throughout the housing. It felt as if we stumbled into a beauty factory. Quickly, Sydney dragged me towards a door down the hall without any introduction whatsoever. As she reached for the doorknob, a squeak from the other side of the hall caught my attention. Turning to check out the noise, we observed a figure step out from the not-so-silent door. My jaw declined and my chin brushed the carpet. What stood in front of me at that very moment was a creature that was, by far, not made by the same maker that made me or anyone else.

"Well, hello new blood," remarked the amazing body of nature.

No words found the right path out of my mouth. I stood in absolute silence, detecting a waterfall displayed amongst my forehead. Sydney grabbed me by the waist and flung me into a dark room, which more than likely belonged to her. I heard her tell the other girl my name and she made every intention to let her know that the stranger was claimed. Sydney then entered the room, turning the darkness into a fabrication of a bad acid trip. A strobe light flashed as it revealed posters of drugs, parties, sex, and other extracurricular activities.

"So… who was that in the hall?" I asked excitedly.

"That was a woman who is never to have anything to do with you." "Does she have a name?"

"Her name is unavailable," she retorted with irritation in her voice. "If you are going to stay here you are going to be with me. If you don't like this offer you may disperse yourself immediately."

"I don't have a problem with that at all," I stretched the truth. The reality was that Sydney was a gorgeous girl, and in no way was my fascination with the lady in the hall going to mess up my chances with her. I awoke the following morning and took a short period of time to figure out the strange surroundings. After my memory was restored, I rolled out of Sydney's bed and went on a search for a source of water. Guessing which room to enter was quite an ordeal. My hand grabbed ahold of the second door knob my eyes located. To be quite honest, it was difficult to not walk into the wrong room, portraying it to be an accident only to get one more glimpse of the stunning stranger. That was not the type of person I was going to be. The room of refreshing liquid was entered and the water that splashed upon my face was more than gratifying. As the wet substance plastered my skin the door swung open.

Standing on the other side was the woman who would forever be enticing my mind.

"Oh, I'm sorry," she said.

"Don't be sorry, I'm the intruder here." "I'm Tina," she said with a smile.

First thing in the morning, she looked unbelievable. She had a glow that surrounded her entire body, and, that very instant, my brain described her as flawless. It was known that she was a complete stranger, nevertheless, it became necessary to make her a part of my life.

"I'm Terry," I said as I searched for something to wipe my dripping skin. She gently persuaded me to move aside as she opened a cupboard filled with wash towels. A smile crept upon my face as my shaky hand reached for a towel. Tina held my nervous limb as she picked up the cloth and wiped the liquid from my brow. Her touch sent shivers up my spine. It was hard to believe such a woman existed.

"I was told who you were last night. Sydney has had a little thing for you for quite some time," Tina replied as she moved her eyebrows quickly up and down. "I hope you made her fantasy come true."

"I'm feeling a little awkward, however, I did my best under the circumstances."

"Oh yeah, and what circumstances would those be?"

"That doesn't really matter. So, who all lives here?" I asked as I pulled myself onto the sink to get a more respected view of the lovely Tina.

"Sydney, myself, and the three girls that you saw last night," she politely answered my question. "So… am I going to be seeing you around?"

"That depends."

"Depends on what?" she asked as she headed towards a different room, motioning me to follow. I was in a trance and would have followed her anywhere she led, no matter how terrible the circumstances could have been.

"Would you enjoy seeing me around?" My voice cracked as the words left my throat.

"You are an interesting person. Something about you seems intriguing. Nevertheless, you are now involved with Sydney. Sydney is my best friend in the entire world, and I would not do anything to change that. Also, I have a certain somebody in my life. I've been with him for two and a half years now, and it is still going strong. Maybe all four of us can become friends," she recited as she sat upon her bed.

"He treats you the way you need to be treated?" My reasoning for the question came from pure jealousy.

"How am I supposed to be treated?"

"As a goddess," I confidently announced.

"Well, isn't that bold coming from someone who has only begun to see me for who I am?"

"I already know who you are."

"How could you possibly know who I am?"

"I can feel your purity. From the moment I laid my eyes on you I felt safe. I felt as if I had nothing else to gain in life unless somehow you were a part of it. I don't give a damn what anyone thinks, when I have a feeling, it is what it is," I quoted as I left her room.

As her door slowly closed, my mind took a few minutes to calculate what took place. Being as direct as I was with Tina was not a normal part of my personality. The usual manner for me was to let the woman call the shots and my pitiful mind would follow her lead. Tina was different, and she needed to know how I felt even if it was not the right moment. Eventually I would find the right time and bring the opportunity to an enlightened parallel universe where we would be together. No matter what the consequences may be, no matter who I would have to step on to get there, someday she would realize that the joy in her life that she was missing… went by the name of Terry.

That was the first time that my eyes bore the view of an angel.

Back amongst the present, I stood staring at a mess of a boy. Bitterness overtook my every thought; the reason why remained oblivious. There was a garden positioned in front of me, and, hovering directly over the vegetation, was a body. While my eyes gazed deep into the picture show, the entire scene began to transform. The green was consumed by a dark red liquid that soon took over the entire landscape. Rage engorged the inside of my cranium and a scream belted through my lips. The portrait was wiped from the mirror by my unsteady hand, and the closest garment in reach was used to cover my dripping body. I then dashed into the living quarters, throwing anything and everything that came into my path. The reason for the sudden outburst was unknown. Grabbing metal objects from the counter, I escaped the newly found burden and hopped into the machine that would need the shiny objects to bring it to life. The automobile purred once the metal implement was shoved into its opening, and I headed for the one place in the entire world that would provide me with the opportunity to get the disturbing image to move along.

CHAPTER TWO

fter arriving at a place of refuge, I slowly pulled my weary body from the vehicle. Not being able to reach realization of why a garden of red interrupted my morning shower was a definite nuisance. The confusion was thick and caused the blood to slowly flow to my brain, which allowed my limbs to become weak, and I tumbled face first onto the ground below. Dirt and grass were spit out of my mouth as a familiar voice cluttered the distant airwaves.

"I see were having a wonderful day, so early in the morn," the tone shrieked out to my ears. "I'm happy to see that you arrived safely. I had a few minutes with the bleeding garden myself and I've been expecting your company," Frank indulged me as he approached my fallen body.

Neither my body nor my mind was acting sociable. I gave up trying to cope and just let the strange emotions evade my every thought. Frank became irritated when I allowed obscure feelings the ability to frustrate me. He was a man of outrageous knowledge, knowledge of the unexplainable. Without Frank, my world would have complete power over me. There was no urge to fight at times and Frank was the man who spread the desire to learn and grow from my experiences. He often told stories of cheaters; he believed I was always in control, just a man with an ability to act as if he was lost. He felt that I had the ability to cheat people into thinking they were associating with an idiot.

As my mind started to return to a half normal state, energy began to resurface among my limbs. Frank held out his hand to provide assistance, and his polite gesture was waved off, which assured him that the tenacious boy on the ground was able to stand without aid. Once I rose to my feet we moseyed into Frank's domain where his sofa comforted my aching bones.

The couch was so familiar with my body that its cushions held my impression even when it was vacant. My stare pointed upward, searching for answers that could calm the trembling organ inside my head. Frank's humble home was a place that allowed flashbacks the ease to enter my brain. All the stories that were recited from my mouth, while lying on the sofa, would fly through my head, keeping their memories alive and every word that left my lips forced Frank to nod with enthusiasm. Frank was curious about the fact that there was another human roaming the world that reeked of torture and agonizing pain. He was my biggest fear; I did not want to become an old man without anyone to share my remaining days with. The problem was that my future was heading directly in the direction of isolation; the fault was my own. Frank was familiar with my fear of solitude and swore, if it was the last thing he did in life, that he would teach me to fill my mind with peace, which would allow me the ability to not push others away.

Frank was a man who was lost in unreality; the same misfortune surrounded my atmosphere. While gazing into his dark brown tunnels of sight, one would sense the strength that could only be felt through his wisdom. One look into his pupils would show any living thing that he was like no other. He often spoke of a young lad with words that served the same purpose. The youthful boy he was referring to was a boy named, Terry and every time he verbalized about his insight, I would rebut. My beliefs were that it was not possible for me to provide assistance to anyone; my so-called knowledge was good for nothing. My own well-being was in danger by my mind's thoughts, not to mention those poor individuals who found themselves caught up in my mess. In another life I'm presuming that I was nothing more than a mere peasant, an unimportant mortal whose only reason for surviving was to gain acceptance from others. My current life was spent fighting to separate the madness from the truth, which was becoming difficult to distinguish the difference.

Frank did not comment on those particular thoughts. He would shake his head with frustration and mumble nonsense as he left me to concentrate on what was important. We did not share the same beliefs about what was vital. His determination to open my eyes and view life the way he did was never ending. The sweetness of Frank was what drew me back over and over again. He was someone I could always trust no matter how uncontrollable the situation may have been. Frank was there to lead me down another path. I was not sure if the second path was any safer, however, it sure eased my perception just enough to push me to the next unexplainable tale.

"Would you like some tea?" Frank questioned as he had a seat next to the sofa of survival. With only one saucer in his hand, he began to slurp at what he called a drug for the mind. He was well aware that I did not indulge in the formality, yet he was of kind heart to always ask. His corneas drifted in my direction, and he smirked with an expression of unwillingness to even let the saddest of the sad interfere with trying to ease a troubled mind.

"So… any answers or should I respond with any solutions?" I asked as I pulled myself to an upright position.

"Your so-called solutions are only sodalities to let yourself run and hide.

You need to search for the cause of the problem at hand. Not run from it."

"I know you think I'm a coward; how can I ever figure out a situation when even you are kept up by my thoughts? I believe that even a wise man such as yourself is confused by what my life tosses in your general direction."

"Of course, I'm puzzled. Your thoughts do flow through me. Every time they do, I doubt everything I've ever learned or seen in my lifetime. You are definitely not a normal weirdo!" Frank said as he burst into a contagious laugh. The laugh visited us quite frequently. I'd noticed that it was the best way for Frank to relax when his mind started to run away from him. When a mind such as his, went into thinking mode, it was a perfect chance for anything that was trying to get his attention, to take control of his mentality. He had to keep his head clear, or he would lose sight of reality altogether.

"Tell me about your vision of the garden," I said as I returned to my original position.

"It was beautiful; seemed familiar nevertheless, I couldn't quite place it. The picture was a little fuzzy. The sky was clear, and the day seemed gorgeous, then out of nowhere, clouds interrupted the pleasant scene. When the sky blackened, I heard your voice screaming of forever darkness. I watched the green bleed to the soil, leaving the darkest red stain known to man. I then witnessed you standing on top of the lake of blood motioning me to leave."

"Come on… where's the philosophy in that? What the hell does it mean?"

"Who the hell knows?" He exclaimed as he took a moment to clear his head. "All these visions come from your mind. There is no way that I will ever make sense of them. I am only a part of this because you let me see parts of your visions, the parts that your mind does not have occupancy for. I let you in on the secrets that you keep from yourself. Now… tell me your version and be precise."

"I saw a man lying on the edge of a garden. I could not tell if he was dead. The sky drew dark, and the lifeless body moved towards the darkness as the vegetation was stained red by a lake of blood," I rambled through my version, completely ignoring his plea for great detail.

"Was the man a familiar or unfamiliar?" "Unfamiliar," I answered. "You dreamt this vision?"

"The show was seen upon my mirror after I showered."

"You now see them when you're awake? This is news to me."

"I'm to the point where I feel as if I am sleeping all the time. I can't separate reality from fiction anymore. To me, it is all the same region of pain and suffering."

"Nonsense, that's only the coward in you."

"I am a coward?" I questioned. "Try tired, depressed, lonely, and sick of losing precious time, a coward through your eyes."

"We've gone over and over this. I lived that life; you don't have to. Whatever you feel is the easy way out, you need to ignore. Choose the alternate way; it's the only chance to give you a half normal life. No one really wants to be normal anyway," he smirked as he took another sip of the steaming mind juice.

It was odd that such a man still walked the earth. To anyone's knowledge, he was a man above men. His stories told of humble voices in the wind. They reeked of visions of an old, rusty brain, visualizations of a future, a future that desired to be heeded by the myth; the myth was Frank himself. For what he saw were diagrams, bits, and fragments from other living minds. The diagrams were pieces of someone else's memory. So, Frank tried to get the message to those poor unsuspecting miscreants. He had much success; his failures… I knew nothing about. I knew he was burdened by them, and I didn't think he would ever be free of their haunting memories. I did not want to become one of his nightmares.

"I don't see myself being any help in these situations," I said as I let my eyes roll into the back of my mind.

"The man in the garden has to stand for something."

"They all have to be something. Problem being I waste my life searching for things I never find," I enticed him. "Am I supposed to go to every garden? You know I don't see visions of people who are presumed to be of the living. I only sense the afterlife."

"You saw the garden scene while you were awake. That is a new quality for you. Maybe your gift is improving."

"I never said it was new."

"Why hide this information!" He shouted as he leapt from his chair of tranquility. "Of all the people you lie to… why me?"

"I did not lie; you never asked, and I didn't feel that it was important until now."

"It's all important. Any bit of information is quite critical. Your mind is confused and cloudy. An open mind on the subject may see it in a different light."

"An open mind. Do you really think that your mind is open in this situation? Your brain is full of information that makes absolutely no sense whatsoever, and the pressure inside your skull is about to force its way too freedom. I feel the negative energy that you're giving off. Open- minded would not be the first words that enter my thoughts; confused and afraid would better describe," I responded revealing another secret that I had kept. It was not an everyday occurrence nonetheless, his thoughts appeared in my head from time to time. To Frank, I was a revelation, his next mission; unfortunately, we both knew his current assignment might also be his last. Frank had wandered this planet for many moons. It was certain that he'd already worn out his welcome, yet something inside of him would not let go.

"You feel me?" He asked with a puzzled look upon his face. The disappointment he was feeding left a bad taste in my mouth. He was sincerely upset with the fact that I held the truth from him. It was not normal for us to keep secrets from each other, nevertheless, we were both changing our ways unknowingly. Protecting Frank was my main concern, and if hiding information was the route to take for his safety, then so be it.

"I feel your confusion."

"I'm starting to feel disloyalty between us."

"Who are you trying to fool? We both know your time here with me is coming to an end."

"Don't you go and patronize me. The only reason I still walk this damn earth is to see your outcome."

"I have caused an extreme amount of harm to people that tried to help me in my so-called quest through life. Guilt runs through my veins every minute of the day. I have to stop causing disaster to other people. I didn't want you to know that I have powers that are similar to yours, because your heart is old and tired and would be missed dearly if it was to stop beating."

"I choose to let your thoughts into my life; I am an adult. You cannot stop me from making my own decisions. You need to help me understand your problems or I can't help you," he said with frustration in his voice.

Frank and his cup left the room. The sofa continued to support my body; it was uncomfortable. It was obvious that he was right, however, my selfishness wouldn't let him fall into my trap. My subconscious was a pitfall that found every good Samaritan in the world and tortured them with confusion, made their minds such a mess that they would lose total control of their reality. My situation drew them near, and their curiosity overwhelmed their spirit and drove them to a whole new way of thinking.

It was too much for a normal human, for it would drive anyone mad. I was neither an example nor a solution; merely a lost deviant searching for unity among his peers. If and when a being similar to my own would cross my path, I would jump in full force and try to rip answers from the poor individual's mind, strip them of all their pure thoughts, and in the end, they would become naked and reborn to the world in a way they would not be able to comprehend; hence, I failed.

Frank sauntered back into my range of sight. Holding a picture in his free hand, he emerged towards the sofa. His expression was one I had not yet been blessed with. His eyes filled with a small stream, a stream of the most magic, for sadness would turn into the most furious river if you did not dam it. The scent of guilt was thick in the air; it was definitely not my own. Sympathy dripped from my pores for the unfortunate being that was stuck with such a burden. A steady gaze into my old friend's eyes soon revealed that he was the one with the heavy stench. Reaching to an unnerved limb, I politely freed Frank's grip of the mystical tea. Lurking over the shoulder of a man who obviously had something to leak, I caught a glimpse of a picture of a young girl. She couldn't have been more than ten years old, but then again, her eyes were glowing with wisdom. For this young woman had witnessed scenes that no one should have had to ponder. After gently helping Frank seat his weary body, I took his place on the chair; it was his turn to weild the power of the sofa.

"The girl is your daughter. She loves you; she has no bad memories of your struggles. You are not to blame for her demise," the words poured from my mouth without any thought.

Frank's daughter was kept a secret from me; we immediately locked eyes. We both knew that what just occurred was not a typical incident, even for us. I cleared my mind to let the child feel welcome. Frank sat on the edge of his seat glowing with anticipation of what was to come. Within seconds, my face burned as trails poured from my eyes and launched themselves off my chin to another realm. They were most definitely not normal tears. I sat in horror, for my face was on fire; the river was acid from hell. It ran down my cheeks causing incredible amounts of sorrow. My body panicked and tumbled to the ground. My mind was lost with utter desperation. I had never experienced sorrow to be so painful. The girl was trying to break into my mind and I didn't know how to let her in. A groan dispersed through a small crack between my lips as I reached my trembling hand towards Frank. A feeling of numbness flowed throughout my brain. While fighting for control of my thoughts, blackness crept up and I spun around as the darkness caused suffocation.

"Quite a day we seem to be having," Frank simply stated.

I discovered my weary body had been placed upon the sofa; Frank was back in his trusty chair. I was not real positive of what truly happened or how much time had passed, nevertheless, it became certain that my ass would not find its way to his chair any time in the near future.

"It gets better every minute," I commented.

"Do we want to have this conversation right now?" Frank nonchalantly asked. I was in no condition to try to figure out the gritty details of the haunting experience we just faced. My eyes ventured shut, and my mind dreamt that when they opened, a reflection from a mirror would show a different person. Dealing with drama was not one of my strong suits; it was important that I learned how to cope, because my life was not going to get any easier.

"I'm thinking nap time."

"That sounds wonderful," he replied as he gently covered my body with a blanket. My mind tried to seek times of happiness while Frank made himself absent. I was not too sure what was going on. The ordeal was modified by moments that had no immediate meanings. The thought of what was to come was eating at me and I drifted into mental pictures of the past.

My mind recalled an incident that occurred years earlier. I was stretched out on my back in a corn field that I often escaped to. It was a place that sheltered me from my demons. I was a cannon loaded improperly, for when I was to blow, I would self-destruct and bring anything and everything that was in my sight with me. I often had to escape to a secluded place where I wouldn't cause harm to anyone else. After departing the nonjudgmental field, a burst of emotions darted through my veins and bounced off the walls inside my skull. The sudden surprise came to me as a certain home came into view. The old, wooden obstruction was one that visited during times of rest. The familiarity was so unnerving that an investigation was more than necessary.

Reaching the destination, an elderly man was discovered standing in the archway of the front porch. He smiled and waved, then motioned for me to join him. He did not bear a normal face; he had wrinkles that should not have been there. He was obviously a man who had struggled. "I've been waiting for you. Five long years I've been waiting for you," the lonely man spoke.

"I'm not sure how to respond to that; I feel so at ease here that I can't think of anything else, except the fact that I am at ease."

"Feels pretty good, doesn't it?"

"Damn good! This is a feeling I wish was more constant."

"Your life is a mess and by conversing with the likes of me, we may be able to lessen the tension that surrounds you."

"What is this shit? I'm definitely not ready for this," I pronounced my fear.

"Of everything I get from you, fear is my biggest concern. You are a strong young man. In my long years I have not come across anyone that even comes close to the situations that control your life. Control seems to be the problem you're having. You need to maintain command of your thoughts. You've been doing it alone for many years and that proves to me that you have great strength. I only know half of your stories, quite frankly, being funny because my name is Frank, I am struck by a force that I have not seen in my lifetime. You are unique."

"Nice to meet you, I am Terry if you didn't already know this," I spoke as I reached out my hand to show acceptance; that sounded funny to my ears. There I was at a complete stranger's house. My reason for being there was that I felt at ease, yet I was searching for *his* acceptance.

"I do know your name," Frank sputtered.

"Is this a common occurrence for you? I mean, strangers showing up at your porch?"

"It happens from time to time," he responded. "The only exception is you are no stranger."

"Tell me what you know of me and why I feel safe here. I have seen many different people about the madness that surrounds me and found that no one could help or really understand."

"Neither one of us can be considered normal. Obviously, you experience things that most people do not. I also have the same gift you do."

"Wait! What happens to me is no damn gift," I rudely interrupted. "What would you describe it as?"

"A curse," I enlightened him.

"It all depends on how you view it. A curse, it may be. It may also be a gift," Frank tried to describe his point of valor. "I see pieces of your life. You and only you can put all the pieces together to make sense of them. I can help you by letting you in on the ones you've been blocking out."

"So, you're trying to tell me that what my mind can't handle, I feed to you somehow?"

"Not necessarily. Your thoughts are out there not just for me to pick up on, but for anyone who has the ability."

"There are other people who can sense me?"

"I'm not positive. Nevertheless, I would tend to believe that there are."

My head was full of information that did not seem comprehendible. A tiny man or woman was pounding their drum inside of my head.

"I'm sorry… I desire some time to myself," I nervously pronounced. "Take all the time you need. I will always be here for you, Terry," he added as he held out his hand. I paid my respects and sauntered away, even more confused than before.

That was my first meeting with the infamous Frank. The thought of Frank's daughter continued to fight for my attention, and it was becoming difficult to hold her back. Concern was invading my thought process. How, over the years I had known Frank, could he keep such disaster from me? After making my way to the washroom, it became evident that the burning tears were not tears at all. Astonishment was the next emotion that lurked upon my face once I discovered that my pale skin was stained red. Soap, hot water, a cloth, and extreme force were used to make the blood trails fade however, nothing worked.

Flustered, I walked back into the room for living. To my surprise someone was sitting on the chair of mystery. It was not Frank, instead it was a small child. Her identity was acknowledged, however, communication was not something my weary mind was ready for. Hoping to escape confrontation, I quietly crept around the figure. As my hand stretched out for the doorknob, which led to freedom, a sensation that she was staring a hole directly through me… was overwhelming. My utter ignorance would not let me leave. I slowly turned my head in her general direction. My heart, mind, soul, and every part of me were urging me to run however, her force was too strong to refuse.

My head cocked to face her. The horizontal blinds that protected my sight were in closed position. The anticipation filled my body with regret and the regret forced my lids to pop open. At that very moment, my earlier attempt at escape seemed to be the best idea that I ever had. For what stood before me was a horrific sight. A loud scream relinquished through my lips as my eyes caught a glimpse of Frank's daughter. Attempting to put more space between us, my feet stumbled over each other, and my face found the hard wood floor. The poor girl had no eyes, only deep ruts that seemed to have no end. Once again, my own eyes welcomed the trails of misery. The burning brought visions, visions of non-acceptance, a sad, trite little girl running from things that were not real.

My shaking hands covered my eyes, demanding that she let me be. I then heard Frank return to the room. With all my strength I pried my hands from my bleeding bulbs of sight to see Frank standing over me with pure dismay written upon his face. Without any words, I grabbed his arm to pry myself from the floor. I looked at Frank with complete panic as a mad dash to my vehicle was made. Frank did not follow; he knew better.

He did not witness what happened, however, all notions say he felt the aggravation.

I leaned against my port of salvation and glanced at the house of impurity. Frank stood in the window casting a shadow along the lawn. He was motionless. As we locked vision streams, ignorance filled my mind. An explanation for my behavior seemed appropriate, nevertheless, fear froze me in place. Hopeless feelings of sorrow punctured my pure thoughts; no longer did I want to think. I slowly opened the door, and with a nonchalant nod, I erased myself from the terror that embarked in my being. At another time I would want an explanation from Frank; that would have to happen another time, for it was my instinct to run.

CHAPTER THREE

fter a drama filled morning, it was certain that my mind was in dire
need of quiet. There was one place that would offer the peace of mind
that was required. Hidden directly in the middle of town, there was
a large rock that sat upon a riverbank. Behind the massive boulder was a
small forest that provided shelter from any passer-by that held a curious
eye. Once on the stone structure it became impossible for anyone in the
city to know that the rock had an occupant. The best part of the rock of
tranquility was the fact that it was close to home. The occasional young
drunk and his buddies would appear from time to time however, if they
noticed that a stranger was present, they would rapidly find a new spot
to continue their under-age debauchery. My aching body was thrilled to
discover the rock was vacant. After a few moments of watching the water
slowly flow in front of me, the scenery was changed by leaning onto my
back and gazing out into the great big sky of blue that appeared overhead.
The wide-open ceiling to the earth acted as a magnet, and my thoughts
turned to metal. Every idea and theory that had ever crossed my mind
was sucked out of my head and taken into the atmosphere to be observed.
I concentrated upon the views that were about me, and how I perceived
myself. Over time it had been proven that people change. Some change
drastically while others seem to transform so little that the after product
isn't much different than the original. Modification has been a vast part of
my life. My opinions transformed daily, even hourly, into incomprehensible
dialect that filled my already full brain. My cluttered mind led me down
paths that were not free of debris; there always seemed to be an obstacle in
my way. It was more than obvious that my playing field was not level, for
my unclear thoughts rolled back and forth inside my head. As my intellect
grew, I became aware that many of the feelings that I possessed were not
necessarily my own personal outlooks upon life, but entirely someone else's.
Since not all of my contemplations were of my own creation, it became

apparent why variation was so consistent in my surroundings. Handling the bizarre information *that others were able to throw their thoughts into my head* was not an easy task. Not wanting to involve others with my lunacy, forced me to build barriers and, slowly but surely, I was losing touch with reality.

Another blotch of memories that hung high above my head, were those of my childhood. They showed pictures and short movies about a scared, naïve boy who did not have a firm grip on the handle of life. Instead, his grasp was loose and weak. That led to drifters *from other realms* breaching into the reality of a young, lost soul. The unwanted and unknown visitors caused confusion and frustration which led the boy down a lonely, secret filled path. The child learned, at an early age, that his secrets were never to be told so he began building his wall of protection, an obstruction to protect the house of lies that he was soon to be constructing. To keep private information of such stature, it was imminent that the truth was to be stretched. Frank had a mission. That mission was to find a way of bleeding the stories out of the young lad's head and feed them to another human. I was the young lad; he was the other human.

The world was a difficult place. It was engorged with free thoughts and beliefs. Billions and billions of outrageous tales lay in the open, yet there didn't seem to be anyone around that could decipher the bullshit from the news-worthy material. Was my story earnest? Was God real? Was there a heaven and hell? Were all humans as delusional as myself? Those were all examples of inquiries that could not be answered honestly. What occurred throughout my life was more than a figment of my imagination, that I was well aware of. One regret was that when I spoke of my difficulties, people would judge me as a storyteller, *which always meant that someone was fibbing*. It became clear that hiding my irrationality was going to be the key to my lack of embarrassment. On the other hand, hiding was not my strong suit.

The visions that were shown to me while my brain was at rest were portraits of other people's lives. More than likely the people were no longer among the living. Or, I should say souls instead of people. My definition of a soul was: not possessing any vital organs of any kind and still existing. We all had one as we walked in the world of the living, however, after our demise our soul became our identity. Lost souls were coming to me in my weakest moments. When my guard was distracted, they would enter my mind and relay their message. The difficulties were enhanced, because they were just as confused as I was, and neither one of us knew how to communicate efficiently, therefore the messages were not received appropriately. To my dismay our so-called souls had the power of memory. For some reason, still unknown, they were attracted to me. So, who was I?

I was an insecure man; in reality… not a man at all, but a naïve boy waiting for the right moment to convert to a man. As a child, my dreams planned my emotions. Every day I would wake feeling as if I was a different person than the day before; in my youth most of my dreams were forgotten. My family filled my mind with stories of how I would wander while presumed sleeping. Most incidents occurred during stressed moments, for when my mind was flustered, dreams took on their own reality. As a young person with a mentality that was mostly cluttered with moods that made no sense at all, I found myself to be filled with rage.

The cover to my life story was a picture of an honest, easy to get along with, sincere, humble human being. However, once the pages became evident, the story had many twists. Honesty was important, but unfortunately, I was not always able to speak the truth. My disappointment in myself led to anger issues and a countless number of fights. It was a way to repress all the emotions that I despised running through my mind. My hatred towards my own actions turned my personality into one that was unrecognizable. My tough guy act was exactly that… an act.

After the dust settled, I would gaze at my bloody fists and morph into an infant as my hostility drove everyone around me away. I was not the life of the party; I was the dunce in the corner dreaming of someday being accepted by others. Over the years my hands became weapons. Nevertheless, there was no reason to be proud of such unneeded violence. Regret flowed through my veins for each and every skull that my fists dented. Brutality did not naturally occupy my brain, it was learned, and it became the only way to react to the madness that was my realm and my reality. Eventually my so-called "friends" became quite scarce, because my temper proved to be intolerable. I beat everyone away from me. I would surround myself with people who seemed to accept me for the idiot that I was, but then found that they only kept me around for the entertainment value. My different personalities always led to an interesting story to share with their "real" friends.

Childhood was a difficult period. The ones who called themselves family were distant from my emotional needs. Love was not shown or accepted by my parents. Hurtful tactics that belittled a person were used often. Apologies did not exist, and self-confidence was not a part of my young life. The fact that my life was a mess made it quite difficult to connect with my kin. Lashing out at my parents became the novelty act and fighting for attention became the norm. My siblings had different connections with the people that created us; they held onto stories and secrets of their very own.

Not having a loved one to openly express my deep, dark secrets forced me to open up to those that could not be trusted. I became desperate for someone to understand and through despair there were many unfortunate decisions made. Harm was not meant for anyone however, merely by knowing "of me," a person was put in harm's way. The important decision was to realize how to be strong on my own and not depend on the comfort of others. Deep soul-searching was a definite; I had to uncover the truth and find the "real", Terry.

Throughout the years of my existence, it became clear that the coward in me was desperately searching for a way to take power. It was obvious that insanity was not corrupting my intelligence merely because of people such as Frank. He was proof that what was deep inside my brain was reality, or at least… my reality. He saw and felt pieces of my life before we ever met face to face. If my thoughts and views of life were only figments of my imagination, there would be no possibility of another human knowing that information without it leaking from my lips.

There were certain moments that occurred where a reasonable solution was available however, I always interpreted a darker version, a more illogical answer. One day my sibling and I were walking around a pond that we spent most of our young days at. We would collect whatever we could catch. Then we would bring them home to store in our family boat that sat in the rear of our house. This often upset our father, but he was soon used to the idea that his craft was now our terrarium. As my brother and I were searching for anything that moved, we found ourselves headed in a direction of an underpass (a small tunnel under the road). It was a drainage tunnel. We spent many hours of our young lives there. As we entered, we saw a garter snake, and in all honesty, water snakes gave me the creeps; through my eyes they were pure evil. To look into their eyes brought fear throughout my entire body. We came closer to the snake when one of our unruly neighbors reached over and grabbed it behind its head. He held the hissing black formation, and an uneasy feeling devoured my brain.

He then wrapped his free hand around its tail, and with a massive force of strength, he whipped its head against the side of the underpass. The sound was as if glass was being broken in the distance. I looked at the puzzled, disturbed expression on my sibling's face. He did not speak a word. Our acquaintance dropped the reptile. It was obviously no longer among the living, but he was not finished. He again picked up the lifeless serpent and pummeled its already deformed head. This time we heard a noise somewhat like a tire leaking its lively hood. The head cracked open as he threw it to the side. We all gazed at each other silently. I then approached the victim of rage. At that very moment hundreds of little snakes poured out of the cracked head. With a quick turn to my brother, I noticed he had already fled. He had the right idea, and soon I was running past him.

We sprinted all the way back to our house as he made a logical comment: "the snake must have been pregnant." I agreed merely to keep his mind at ease. When those slithering little serpents exposed themselves, it was certain that it was an omen. What happened to the poor living creature was going to haunt me for the rest of my life.

Why did I do the things I did? It was a question that had no answer. I was aware that I was not the one who severely destroyed the slithering menace, but for some reason, it appeared that what happened was my mistake. When I performed an act that was considered abnormal, the conclusion always seemed to be that I was missing some kind of chemical inside my head. It was clear to me that people depended on drugs to keep themselves in reality. I was not of my original makings either.

Throughout the years there had been many drugs that passed through my veins. It was a way for me to feel normal. As odd as that sounded, it was the truth. When my mind was altered, it gave me the chance to appear in the same state that my peers were in. Those who joined the drug fest saw me in the same way they saw themselves… "F'd up." The hallucinations that appeared from the influence of LSD were not much different than the sights I saw daily. The fact that the illusions were supposed to happen gave me a few hours of relief from my everyday occurrences. Many of my friends had been permanently altered by our recluse days; that did not add guilt to my conscience. There was no force on my part, and their choice of dosage was completely their decision. I, on the other hand, always knew when enough was enough. The reason for my foresight was unidentified and I did not question it. It was not that the chemicals did not have an addictive hold, it was merely that my self- control and willpower was on a slightly higher level than most people. The power to say no and mean it was one of my stronger traits.

As the past made its way through my brain waves, I began to think about all the deaths that had occurred in my presence. Unfortunately, my young life was surrounded by the passing of souls into another realm. I may not have been the exact cause of their fleeting, however, that did not stop me from accusing myself. Each and every person that left the land of the living took a piece of me with them. I was approaching the brink of disaster and sinking into a deep depression. Most of the deaths had to be kept silent, which did not help my mental state. The purpose of the secrecy was to protect myself and others that were involved: however, the information was sure to erupt at some point. As a young, confused child I was known for stretching the truth. It was an impossibility to be honest when what was being dealt with was so hard to believe, therefore if I did happen to spill the beans about the people I lost, it was certain that no one would believe me anyhow; there was absolutely no point in sharing the information that was locked deep inside my thinking organ.

The first incident of someone losing their life in front of me took place many years ago when I was a young child. As an adolescent, my mannerisms were quite awkward and most of my time at school was spent alone. Interacting with other children did not come naturally, therefore my schoolyard moments involved hiding from everyone. There was a boy who took it upon himself to approach me and offer an invitation to his fish house. His first attempt was met with a large amount of hostility as I used profanity to express the point that being alone was the way I preferred things. He was not led astray and continued to pester. He obviously had no other friends and decided that he was going to be my buddy no matter what. After a couple weeks of his relentless pursuit, I accepted his invitation. As he began to explain where the shack was located, I interrupted to express that it would be much easier if we met at his house and went to the fish house together. He was dead set on that not happening. He insisted that it was easy enough to find and his directions would be more than adequate. In the moment it seemed strange, however, I didn't question him.

The walk to meet my new acquaintance was a slow, bitterly cold venture that kept my mind busy with thoughts of why I was chosen. He more than likely viewed me to be in the similar mind state that infested him. I would soon find out that we may have had some shared qualities, however, we certainly did not handle our troubles in a related fashion.

As I grew closer to the destination my stomach began to churn and moan. It was undetermined what caused the sudden burst of nerves, something was just not quite up to par. The abrupt sensation was clarified as anxiety. My social skills were not well-rehearsed, and I took a deep breath and shrugged the unnecessary outbreak away. Upon reaching the small shack the boy described, I slid off my glove and reached for the handle. A voice deep in the cellar of my brain was desperately trying to persuade me to turn around and head home. I ignore the voice of reason and slowly turned the handle. The kid sternly instructed me to not knock. He stated that I enter upon arrival. It became relevant why as soon as the door was pulled past my eyes. The second my vision focused upon the sight, my life was changed forever.

The boy sat on a small bench. His back leaned against the shed, and his feet were parallel, about a foot apart, on a cooler. In between his shaking thighs sat a double barrel shot gun with the barrels pointing at his head. Instantly the sweat dripped from my brow, despite the freezing cold. There was no moment to react because as soon as he saw the whites of my eyes, a boom sounded, sending blood, brain, and chunks of bone to repaint the inside of the shack. My eyes were sticking halfway out of my skull as I had to pound on my chest to continue breathing. As the door creaked closed, I stood motionless staring at the wooden form before me. My heart was trying to break free so it could run and hide; there was a pain inside my ribs. It was early afternoon. All houses were out of range, and the few other fish houses must have been empty. That was the thought that crossed my mind because no one came running.

Once my legs regained the ability to move, I hesitantly wandered away from the treacherous scene that took place and searched for sanctuary. The next move was unclear; a quick look at my attire made it obvious that water and soap was necessary to proceed. The next stop had to be somewhere secluded, because if I was spotted in that condition, there was sure to be trouble. My clothes were splattered with flesh and chunks of meat, and my ungloved hand was red from his blood. My body trembled uncontrollably as I waddled towards a place that would provide the supplies necessary to cleanse myself. There was a small gas station a few miles up the road, and the bathroom was outside. It was normally locked, but easy enough to pick. As I moseyed along, the thought of the boy's head exploding was played in a loop inside my skull. I was certain that keeping the young lad's secret was going to age me faster than normal, but there was no way the story could be shared without unwanted interrogations.

After breaking into the restroom, the mirror portrayed a face that was unrecognizable. The blood was not the only change; there were wrinkles and creases that were not there before, and my eyes did not look ordinary. As the cool water rinsed the horrifying scene from my face, I became certain that I was nothing like the boy. I had my share of problems, however, in no way would I involve an innocent person in my cowardly ways. *Also, suicide would never become a part of my life.*

No one mentioned him after my return to school; it was as if he never existed. I stared blankly at his open desk, wondering why there was no announcement of his passing or any enquiry. He was obviously more troubled than presumed, and his actions were more than likely expected. What a sad, miserable way to go. Ten long years lapsed before his death ever left my lips, and it happened during a weak, drunken moment that would cause regret in the pit of my stomach for eternity. Fortunately, the person I told did not believe and left it alone. *Sometimes it was good to not be taken seriously.* The lost soul did not appear in the afterlife. We were not connected in the same realm. At certain moments it would have made my life easier if he was able to explain why I was chosen, but then again, some things are better left in the dark.

As my reminiscing session came to an end, I gazed into the water and struggled to keep my eyelids from slamming together. The overwhelming rumble inside my belly was startling and remembering my last meal did not seem probable. The secret to staying thin was to create a world full of chaos, torture, and constant fear. Force your appetite down deep and hold it there by pure frustration of the unknown; the pounds will melt away.

Even during moments when I was truly hungry, it became difficult to get the food down my throat. The acid churned inside my stomach and an ache made its way through my intestines and into my mouth, which then leaked through my lips as a burp. Food was the last thing that was going to capture my attention. The commotion inside slowly dissipated as it was ignored.

"How are we doing on this lovely day," squeaked a voice from around the edge of the rock.

I jumped to my feet to get a look at an old acquaintance of mine. "Hey Jay, it's been a long time."

"I was thinking about you quite a bit today. Anything I can do for you?" "How on earth did you know where to find me?"

"I always know where you are, Terry." "That creeps me out."

"No matter how hard you try, you will not get rid of me."

"I'm fed up with everything that is happening. Nothing seems to have an answer. Everywhere I turn is a new situation. I can't solve anything when new circumstances keep arising. I tell you what: I am willing to go to the point of no return. I'm tired of running, because wherever I run, I am always found."

"Damn, are you ever going to lighten up?"

"You of all people, have the balls to ask me a question like that! Most of my anguish has been caused by you."

"Good to hear you blaming someone besides yourself."

"Between Tina and Frank, I have enough problems. I haven't seen you in almost two years. You're going to have to give me awhile to straighten my mind before you tell me whatever it is that you've come to freak me out about." I hopped into my vehicle and left him without any more questions.

A few years ago, Jay and I were friends. We shared a mutual respect for one another, and were attached at the hip. Unfortunately, our friendship was cut short and all memories of respect were burned and forgotten. His appearance was more news that was definitely unwanted. I may have left him at the rock, however, I was certain that he was not through with me. Until then, all that stuck in my head was a thought of a nice comfortable bed. Sleep was going to be unattainable, but even so, my body desired rest. My thinker would have to find other means of staying strong.

CHAPTER FOUR

eaving the river behind, my journey home began. My eyelids weighed hundreds of pounds and my body was lacking the strength needed to keep upright. It was still early, but the day had been more complicated than usual. The next step was to catch my breath and then fall into a coma. I opened the apartment door with unknown expectations of what was lurking on the other side. The wooden object whimpered as it slowly revealed a view of the living quarters. I was surprised to discover that the area was free of all menaces. I approached the bed and exhaustion participated in throwing my body face-first upon the mattress.

The phone rang; Frank left a vague message on the machine. He apologized for not ever speaking of Suzie, his daughter. At that very moment, caring was not present in my thoughts. Rest was the only activity that received attention. My body rotated, and the ceiling came into focus as my mind contemplated on the possibility of sleep. A groggy brain wave took charge, and the spackle on the ceiling moved around in a panic; my imagination was making a mockery of me. The sound of running water filled the air as my body refused the notion of exploring the racket. The ceiling began to show movies: tales of people scrambling. I turned my head to the side as fog started seeping into the room. A shadow in the mist crept closer and with every inch it ensued, the blood in my veins pumped faster and faster.

The figure in the mist approached as mumbled words flew from my mouth, demanding that it made itself absent. I tossed a pillow from my shaky hand as the form drew closer. The head cushion landed a few inches from the mysterious creature, and then it stopped suddenly. The image of a small person became identifiable as the mist dissipated, showing a clear view into the cranium of a young girl whose eyes were torn from her sockets; she remained still. Panic formed inside my cranium and my legs hurled themselves off the bed. The maneuver seemed to go on forever as my body floated across the air unable to make a landing. Once gravity was regained, I lost my balance and slammed into the edge of the bedroom door. My limbs did not fight to stay upright, and I plummeted to the carpet below.

The sense of non-reality consumed the air. Suzie's afterlife was becoming my reality, and nothing was going to interfere with her plans. Crawling towards the next room, the sound of running water grew louder and louder. My living room had turned into an extravagant garden that held familiarity but could not be pin pointed. My arms and legs were covered with a red liquid as I entered the new terrain. Leaping out of the pond of blood, my hands worked drastically to cleanse my skin, and after failing miserably they moved to block my mouth as the disgust tried to escape from my insides. As I searched for an exit, a figure hovering over the vegetation caught my attention. Once I identified the object as a body, a sucking noise entered the atmosphere. The plants drank the gooey substance, and streaks of red appeared throughout their exterior.

Suzie sprung out at me from behind the foliage, and I fell backwards into what remained of the liquid. My legs quickly sprang into action and brought me to an upright position. The floating form also rose to a vertical position as if to get a more prominent view. As the body rose, so did my adrenaline. A light mist interfered with my view, and it was impossible to identify the face. I took a moment to concentrate on slowing my heart rate, but it was a struggle to keep a clear head.

There was heavy breathing creeping in the background; every second the sound drew closer. A trivial breeze brushed upon the flesh on the back of my hand as I covered my eyes from the bloody scene. The wind grew thicker and stronger, and my refusal to view the strangeness was sturdy. *Pretend she is not there and she will disappear.* The small gust of wind began to rise in temperature to a point of becoming too hot to bear. A faint, unrecognizable voice shrieked out informing me to relax.

My concentration moved towards the mysterious words of reasoning when a sudden scream burst into the air stream. The yell of torture erupted, and the pure power of it launched me back into the brook of pity. Rotating face down, the depth deepened as I sank further and further into the thick red mess. My lungs continued to fill with air even though it should not have been possible. Eventually, my eyes adapted to the cloudy darkness as shadowed figures appeared in the tainted liquid. Up, up my arms struggled for safety. The unknown objects rubbed against my flesh as my ascent to the top was on its way. Breaking through the surface, a huge breath of real air filled my organs as I floated in the middle of nowhere. I drifted in an ocean of stained liquid surrounded by thousands of cadavers. The solution was slowly absorbed back into the soil and eventually only my feet were wading. There I stood, surrounded by dead bodies in a shallow lake of blood. Then Suzie calmly approached.

"I have information for you," she broke the silence. "When I was alive my world was quite similar to the terrifying life that you live. I did not handle the situation in a manner that would be considered proper. I made a mess of my life and the lives of the people around me. I brought harm upon myself and am now damned in the afterlife."

"You don't speak as a ten-year-old would," I commented as I knelt down before her.

"I lost my life when I was ten, but in the after realm my mind continued to grow and mature," she replied. She situated herself so she could be viewed in a more proper manner. Her head turned so the empty sockets could not be viewed.

"You do not have to be ashamed of your appearance when you are around me. Trust me, what you look like is the least of my worries. Besides, it is very comforting, in a strange way. In most creatures, the eyes tell all the horrific stories that we all hold, so when I look upon you, I can only feel what you want me to. I cannot see it through your source of vision."

"I thank you for just being you. You have to trust me, Terry. I know all that haunts your mind and for that reason and that reason only, you have my complete and utter respect as a human being."

"Speaking of human beings… am I one?"

"While you are alive, you are exactly that. On the other hand, once you pass on to another realm you will become something else. You will have to wait until that time approaches."

"Why were you chasing me?"

"Each realm is very confusing, and I did whatever it took to get to you." "With all honesty, I thought my time had come."

"No, you were hoping your time had come. That is what you do." "Where are we?"

"If you think hard enough you will be able to put two and two together. This was my refuge when I walked among the living," she responded as once again the blood and bodies vanished, reviving the garden from before. She suddenly turned her body from me and let out an awful scream.

"We have intruders, I hate intruders," she declared.

"Who are you referring to?" I asked, hearing the same unidentified voice from earlier. It was the vocal sound of a woman, and she was calling out to me.

The ghost girl hovered to the end of the garden where she cried out, "we don't have much time; your friend is going to get herself into trouble.

You must go to the man that lingers over us and explain to him that what happened to me was my own doing. Stress to him that there was nothing he could have done to help. I took my problems into my own hands, and I shut everyone else out, especially him. You must make him understand. He is a stubborn man just like yourself, and he blames everything on his own doings. You must make him understand. You are the only one who can do this for me. You are the only one who he will listen to. Please, leave now and as you depart, his identity will become known to you. You have to act fast because he does not have much time. Also, tell him I love him more than anything I've ever come across, and I'm sorry for all the torment I caused throughout his life."

I found myself to be moving closer and closer to the man who lingered. The voice of the woman was becoming more prominent by the second; she was shouting my name over and over. The man in the garden began to turn in my direction. Everything suddenly became clear, and an intense rush of blood from my over-excited heart, put my mind in blackout mode as the ground began to move closer to my face. The mystery woman shouted for my attention as her voice became recognizable.

The shock and soreness were overwhelming, and even though I desperately wanted to answer my friend, it was not possible at the moment. I slowly pushed soil from my mouth with my tongue; the taste was bitter and dry. The woman persisted on informing me to open my eyes. With the assistance of an agonizing groan, my head lifted a few inches from the dirt and a tiny crack between my lids showed a smiling Tina standing directly above my head. A wider and more focused picture revealed that I was sprawled out in my neighbors' garden.

"What the hell is going on?" I snapped at Tina as my body was forced to its feet. Every move felt as if a million nails were being pounded through my flesh and muscle and settling into the bones within. My confusion was coming off as anger as I made my way towards home.

"You were sleepwalking."

Her words brought an immediate halt to my movement, and I took a brief second to examine my appearance.

"If the whole obscene event that took place a short while ago was just some story my brain made up while I caught a few Z's, why is my skin stained red?" After the question entered the air, my journey towards the bathroom continued. After a few moments, *which seemed like hours,* of trying to remove the stain that covered my bruised and scarred exterior, I dropped the cloth and stood trembling.

"Terry, you need to calm down."

"The last thing that I need is someone telling me to calm down," the condescending words entered Tina's ears and she made a face that filled my insides with regret. I was scrambling for some sense and was coming up empty. My delusional state brought me into the kitchen where everything in my view was tossed onto the floor. "Where are my frickin' keys?"

"We dearly need to talk; you are quite scary right now."

"Scary is my new thing," I said as my eyes met hers. There was a sinister expression painted upon my face. "Now, if you cannot assist me with the whereabouts of my keys, then you must leave me to my business." The thought of how depressing my life was shot to the front of my brain and became the main attraction; another dear friend was about to transfer realms and there was zilch I could do to stop it. The reason for my searching was suddenly a mystery. I stopped and noticed the tears on Tina's cheek. "I'm sorry."

"You have to explain to me what is going on."

"We both just came from my neighbors' garden and I did not see any blood in or around it… did you?" She shook her head and I continued. "So, you say that I've been sleep walking, yet my skin is stained with blood and what I witnessed was not imaginary no matter how absurd it may sound."

"You have outrageous dreams all the time."

"Never have I brought something out of a dream and into reality, and never has a dream felt so real. My mind is lost," I quit speaking and looked around the room in a daze. "What am I looking for?"

"Your keys… driving is definitely not a good idea."

"I agree one-hundred percent, but the choice is not mine to make; the freaky no-eyed girl said I had to." She had no clue what I was talking about and there was no time to explain. Spotting the car keys, my shaky hand clutched them up and my journey had begun. "All my love to ya, babe," I said with a sweet smile.

"Can you tell me that everything is going to be all right?" "That… I can't do," I said as I left her behind.

Once in the vehicle, I used deep breaths to aid in the relaxing of my mental organ. As soon as I regained stability, the metal tool was inserted into the ignition. The purring engine was soothing until the radio sprung to life with extreme volume. The backlash was my foot slamming the gas pedal to the floor and as the motor roared my brain turned to mush as my undisciplined hand put the car in gear. The sudden forward motion slammed the car into an innocent tree a few feet ahead. I pushed the door open and rolled out onto the ground as blood dripped down my brow.

A sudden burst of energy allowed me to rise to my feet, and my movement turned into a fierce sprint as I hurdled everything that got in the way. My heart was pumping stronger than it ever had before, and the adrenaline made me feel as if I was unstoppable. My breathing seemed to not exist; I took a quick break to make sure that what was happening was reality and not another delusion spawned from insanity. Once I was certain that I was not dreaming, my speed returned and soon my aching body was standing in the middle of a garden.

The fact that the garden from my earlier visions was unrecognizable puzzled me. With a slow, agonizing pace, I left behind the weeds of life and the house became the next objective. Arriving at the porch, I jolted up the stairs, lost my balance, and rammed into the front door. The force of my clumsiness was enough to open the wooden structure and I tumbled to the hard floor. A quick glance up displayed Frank lying a few inches ahead.

"What a day," I commented as my hand gently touched his shoulder. "You look like shit," Frank coughed.

Turning my head away from his sight line, I tried to hide my anguish. "You've had better days yourself old man," I said with a chuckle.

"There is no need for you to hide your face from me. Tears are nothing to be ashamed of. They are merely proof that you are human," he responded with a serious tone to his weak voice. "Terry?"

"Yes, Frank."

"I believe I'm dying."

"I will get you to a hospital. I will need your vehicle."

"You know as well as I do that my time on this earth has come to an end." "So, we're not even going to try to save you? We're just going to sit here and do nothing?"

"We need to accept my fate," as he spoke, I gazed at the blood that was leaking from his mouth. After pulling my body off the floor, my hands forced Frank into an upright position as his back rested against the sofa of relief.

"Are you in pain?"

"I've had worse."

"Do you know what I've been through this evening?"

"My mind was being distracted by a lovely friend of yours. She is a remarkable woman. I am sorry that things with the two of you did not work out. She was the reason for you and I coming together; she believed that we could help each other. It was my idea to keep our friendship a secret from you. I hope there is no resentment on your end."

"I was aware of your friendship with Tina."

"Are you going to tell me a sad story?" he asked, quickly changing the subject, because we both knew that his time was fading fast.

"Why do all of our stories have to be sad and depressing?"

"Maybe it's because our lives are sad and depressing," he said as he began to laugh uncontrollably. "I'm only joking. It only seems that way because that is how you look at it. For the entire time I've known you, that is your biggest fault. No matter how you feel about it, what you possess is a gift. I know it causes you heartache and drives you absolutely crazy, nevertheless, you have what no other human I've ever come across has. You have stamina!"

"Let's not overdo it. I have not helped anyone in my life, I only make things complicated."

"That's your opinion, and I know you'll stick to it. You must be told that your opinion is wrong. You help people every day of your life. It may be in a small way or an extreme way, point being… you help people. Someday soon, you will discover this for yourself. When that day comes you will be free to live your own life."

"Did you recognize the garden from our visions?" I asked, returning the conversation to the present drama.

"No, I put two and two together and figured it was my own, just a distorted version of it."

"I think it's time that you tell me a sad story."

"She was my daughter and I loved her so much; all I wanted to do was protect her from all the insanity that took over my life. All I've ever wanted was for this poor little angel to have a normal life. Unfortunately, that was not what she had. From the minute she was born, she was tortured by unexplainable fantasies. When she escaped from her mother, the doctor wiped her off and laid her on her mother's chest. Then they allowed me to enter the room," Frank stopped as he clenched my hand as the pain conversed with his mind. "As I walked in, I saw happy faces in the room. They were congratulating me on a perfect little girl. I was ecstatic. However, I could not smile. I felt as if I lost something, not as if I gained anything. The doctor asked me if I was going to be all right, I nodded affirmatively. He then moved so I could view my family. That was when I began to notice what my feelings were all about. We heard the sound, the sound of horror, the sound that ripped through my body, bringing tears with only the thought of it, the sound of a flat line.

"I ran to the bed to see my wife draining blood and what seemed to be foam from her already blue lips. The nurse tried to take Suzie away and, to our astonishment, she was holding on for dear life. She was gazing directly into the eyes of her mother. I could see the sadness in this newborn's face. I then knew that she was a special little girl because she had feelings of terror from the very beginning. My wife was pronounced dead minutes after the episode took place. The cause was never declared. To this day I do not know why my wife left me and our Suzie."

Frank told an undesirable tale. He nodded his head to express that he also knew pain via death. "After that moment, I let myself believe that I didn't witness anything strange. I made myself believe that Suzie was a normal little child. That was the biggest mistake of my life!" Frank took a break from the disturbing words. He began to hurl phlegm from his lungs. He wheezed, and the sound ran directly up my spine, for it was the beginning of the end.

I rose to my feet and made a dash for the kitchen. Wasting no time, I found a glass and filled it with water from the gracious sink. A panic attack was forming deep in my bowels and slowly but surely, was creeping towards my brain. My body convulsed and the crystal cup slipped through my quivering fingers, smashing to the floor below. My eyes rolled back as I slipped away.

"Terry, look at me," whispered a voice from beneath the dead silence. With my eyes glued shut, I pulled myself off the floor using the cabinets as guides. "Open your eyes Terry, we need to talk," the voice persisted on catching my attention. Turning my back on the nuisance in the room, my eyes opened to assist with the gathering of more water. Once I filled the new container, I rushed back to Frank, ignoring the intruder. Frank had somehow managed to get himself onto the stoop, and that was where I accompanied him.

"What was all the commotion in the kitchen?" Frank asked as he licked the last drop from the rim of the glass.

"Just a bunch of nonsense," I retorted with obvious aggression in my voice. "You need to continue."

"As I was saying, I did not give her the attention that she deserved. I ignored all the signs that were shown. I believed that if I left it alone, it would disappear. I haven't discovered the way to redeem life for myself; there was no possible way for me to help her. Funny thing about the whole ordeal was she never mentioned her problems. I thought she was handling them her own way. That was how I thought, until the day I met you. Your stories of your childhood remind me of the days when Suzie walked the earth. She spent most of her time alone. The garden was a place of safety for both of us. As you speak of the terrible loneliness that was put upon you, while you walked as a child, it made me think of Suzie. For she acted in the same ways you did as a child. She was extremely hot headed, and when things did not go her way, she relied on force. When it was all over, she would run to safety and shed her misery, alone! I was not there for her, for she could not talk to me. She did not know that I was aware. There is no possible way she wouldn't think I'd label her insane!" Frank stopped to regain his stamina, or what was left of it.

I had no words to comfort Frank. He knew how alone I felt as a child and that I still dealt with the situation. I nodded to him, a sign of understanding. All I could do was try to recognize his point. I truly believed that he should have communicated with her; unfortunately, that was not the outcome.

"You think differently of me?" He asked with a humiliated tone.

"You were trying to protect her by not involving her. I do that every day of my life."

"Not once did I tell her about my life… not once. I was an idiot. As she aged, the terror only grew. She would spend hours and hours alone in our place of refuge. I would watch from the window, I only hoped she was strong enough to rise to the challenges that lay before her. Suzie entered second grade as a child with special needs. She had no friends because her communication skills were lacking the power to work. She did not care about life, instead of staring at a young child… it was as if she was an old woman who gave up on everything. The rarity of her smiles grew and grew; I remember her straight face to this day.

"I decided to pull her from public schools, they were going to hold her back otherwise. I struggled with home schooling for the next two years of her short life, however, her mind would not let the information in. What was going on in her life contradicted all subjects taught from a book. How could she make any sense out of anything? She was only a child. I know that what takes over my mind, and yours as well, was the main ingredient in her life. I believe that her powers resembled yours; unfortunately, she was not as strong as you," he stopped speaking and moved his body down a step. He then added his friendly hand to my leg.

"I saw Suzie tonight," I declared. "You dreamt her?"

"I guess so, it all seemed so real. Look I'm still covered in blood." I showed him my stained skin. "She was in the garden. You were the unfamiliar hovering over the vegetation. That is why you did not foresee a body. I should have recognized where I was; I did not."

"It would not have changed the outcome."

"Unfortunately, I know. In the vision there were bodies everywhere." "They must have been the souls that haunted her throughout her living days," he added as he shifted his body on the stairs. It was obvious that he was suffering.

"That makes sense, I guess. She wanted me to console you. She said that she does not blame you for what happened; she acted on her own whim. Suzie loved you more than life itself, but she felt that she was bringing you grief. She only wanted you to have a happy life. In her eyes, she was your problem," I spoke as I moved to be level with Frank as he sat unresponsive. "It was very important to her that those particular words reached your ears," I said as there was still no response from Frank. "Her entire afterlife has been filled with guilt and torment because the two of you did not communicate while she was alive. I can relate to what is going on because I am guilty of the same useless acts. There is so much that I wish I would have said to those who no longer live in my realm, and so far, there is no chance for me to change that. Your daughter is reaching out to you, and you need to listen."

"That is hard for me to hear," he said in a sad tone.

"Both of you kept silent and it is the right moment to end that silence." Frank began to sob uncontrollably. His forehead landed upon my shoulder as his pain and agony soaked into the fabric that covered my scarred flesh.

"I wish I was a better person," he said as he lifted his head. "She deserved a decent father."

"That is what she is trying to get you to understand," I commented. "She loved you, and to her, you were perfect. You feel guilty about the way you treated her, and she feels guilty for the way she treated you. When you love somebody, you do whatever it takes to protect them, and that is what both of you did."

"I get it," Frank said as a tiny smile formed upon his face. "It is hard for me to hear, yet I see it for what it truly is."

"That is all she wanted," I replied. "You should finish your story."
"When Suzie turned the age of ten, she became even more distant. I no longer recognized my own daughter. I decided that I would talk to her about my life. However, I was too late. I entered my home after playing in the dirt. I heard nothing, and that was a scary notion. I then noticed that the bathroom door was shut, which meant that it was occupied. I ran to the door and shouted for her attention; she did not answer. I reached to the doorknob to find that it would not turn. I backed up, and with all my fright, I brought the door down. What lay before me was the most vulgar display of sadness I've ever laid my eyes upon. Suzie was on the floor in front of me, soaking in a pool of her own blood. I fell to my knees screaming vulgarities aloud. She told me that she couldn't bear to see any more pain. As I searched the room, I found glass shards that used to show my reflection. She used the broken mirror to free her head from sight, and then she bled to death. I was too late; she faded in my arms," Frank declared as he fell from the stoop.

I helped him situate himself as he brought up a new conversation, "I have a friend that I've known my entire life, his name is Dean. I left his number on the counter. I wish that you would talk to him."

"Why?" I asked out of confusion. "I don't understand."

"I swear to you that he is the only man that I have ever discussed you with. I am sorry, but he understands," Frank involved me in his betrayal.

"This Dean, he is like us?"

"No… he is a normal human being and we have known each other since our diaper days. He is a good friend, and he keeps secrets."

"I still don't comprehend what he can do for me."

"He can listen; he also knows everything about me. You can ask him the questions that you feel I have not answered. Trust me, he is a man of his word."

"I can't guarantee anything, but I will keep him in mind," I tried to let him know that it was an option that I would consider. "I am sorry for all your heartache," I spoke waiting for a response. I gazed into Frank's eyes; they seemed dry. They didn't have the spark that used to make me feel at ease. Truthfully, they'd never come across so dull, almost as if they were lifeless.

"Frank!" Misery rang out with my scream; he did not answer. Shaking uncontrollably, I wiped the death from his lips and held him close to my heart. His lifeless body soaked into mine, filling me with emptiness.

Memories of our past together took domination of my awareness; the sadness was too much to bear, and tears poured from my eyes. After what seemed to be an eternity, I pulled Frank into his home, rested him upon the sofa and covered his frail body with an old quilt. It seemed impossible to take my eyes off my mentor until I heard a familiar voice shouting for my attention.

The shouting led me outside to the magnificent garden that had been disguising itself during my recent visions. I gradually approached the menace to society.

"Why don't you give me some time to heal? I told you at the river that I'm not ready to deal with you, and things are even more complicated." Grief took sudden control and my knees landed in the hardened dirt as streams ran down my cheeks.

"That's a boy. Release the demons that haunt you. Get it all out," Jay patronized me.

"Go back to hell!" I shouted as I rushed back towards the house to check on my friend.

"I am begging for your forgiveness," he replied as I left him. His ridiculous words stopped me in my tracks.

"Why now, after all these years? I was left to clean up the mess of innocent souls that you destroyed; those spirits haunt me. Even after all that, I still tried to protect you in your final moments. What is wrong with me?"

"You went on pure instinct. I know that you would have died for me if you didn't think things through," he recited as he stared at my hip. "Do you still bear the scar?"

"I cannot look at it. It reminds me of you and then I become disgusted with myself."

"I need your help, Terry."

"I will not do whatever it is you want me to do; I can't help you. What occurred that night was something I did not expect, especially from you. Do you have any idea how hard it is to trust people after all the sick, dirty deeds I've seen you commit? Why?" I shouted across the space that separated us. If I had the power, I would have destroyed him. I gave my entire life to him; he was nothing but a coward and a liar.

"I can't explain my actions to you. You will not understand. You need to believe me when I tell you that you weren't supposed to be there," he continuously begged me to listen. "If you remember, you left me to die. I realize that you tried to save me, but in the very end…you walked away." "It doesn't matter if I was there or not. You still would have done what you did. I don't hate you because I saw it. You're lost with an ideal that life was for you to take advantage of. I do not and will not forgive the stupidity that runs through your veins. And besides, there were many other displays of random, merciless acts that you committed, besides our last evening together." I glared into his eyes as my own flowed with memories of depression and confusion. To lose a friend in any situation was regretful, when a friend destroyed your whole way of thinking, it was mortifying. "During our last encounter, I walked away because there was nothing more I could do to save your pathetic ass! I have dealt with the guilt for what I did. You will not make me go back to that state of mind. If you remember, we did not speak for months before that final night. I hated you for all the insane things that I saw you do. Then I find myself at the same party with you. Even though I despised you, I did try to stop your demise. I bear the scar that proves that even after I interfered, I discovered that I was acting like an a-hole, so I left you be. What happened to you after I walked away was your own doing, and I will not be responsible for your outcome."

"I have to leave, Terry. I need you to forgive me or I can't leave in peace."

"Screw you! You know what? The man that lies in this house is a man that deserves respect. He has lived a life of horror, just as I have. If anyone in the world deserves forgiveness for what they did in life, it most definitely is him. How dare you come to me at a time like this for something you know I can't do? I don't care what happens to you, you cannot make me feel guilty for your sins. You cannot!" I swiped the anger from my eyes and entered the house.

"I will come back to you to resolve this!" Jay shouted. He knew damn well I was not going to grant his wish.

I forced Frank's lifeless body over to make room for myself and wrapped his arm around my shoulders. Sluggishly, my lids sealed and I finally slept.

A few hours later, my eye lids snapped open, and my mind struggled to perceive reality. There was no recollection of dreams while I rested; it had been years since that had occurred. The strangest feeling was that my body and mind actually felt rested. I sat up and looked down at the poor old man. It was time to live my life for him and use his advice to get me through the next deadly adventure. If we were connected in the same realm he would contact me soon. If not, I would find a way to communicate with him eventually. After I placed a kiss on his clammy forehead, I moved into the kitchen. After a few moments of staring at the phone number that was in my hand, I finally built up enough courage to dial the numbers. As the ringing protruded through my ear canal, the urge to hang up was tremendous. The fact that I was tired, scared, and in desperate need of help provided the strength to stay on the line.

A man's voice said hello and I spoke: "May I speak with Dean?" "Speaking," the voice replied.

"My name is Terry. You do not know me, but I have been informed that you know of me. I have a situation that is taking place and I was hoping that you may be able to provide some help. It involves Frank."

"I know of the situation. I've been waiting to hear from you. I can only hope that the news isn't dreadful."

"I'm sorry to have to say it, but that is exactly what it is…dreadful." "Are you going to be able to deal with this?" He asked in a soft tone. I had not had the chance of meeting Dean before. His voice brought a calming feeling to my panicking brain.

"I'm fine," I said.

"Frank talked to me earlier this evening. He told me that he was not feeling very well. You calling me must only mean that the circumstances were devastating." As he said his words, I felt an enormous amount of anxiety building from beneath my bowels.

"He has moved on to something much better than the life he lived on this earth. I can only dream, anyway. I have a problem, Dean. His body is here, and I need to take care of it but right now, I am stained with blood. It wouldn't look very good when help arrives. I need your advice."

"I am on my way. You do not need to worry, I will take care of everything. Will you wait for me to get there?" He asked out of eagerness to meet the myth that he had only heard about.

"I can't at this time, but I want to thank you in advance. I would be up the river without your help."

"No thanks are necessary. I hope that you contact me soon. I am more than willing to listen," he stated as I hung up the phone.

I resumed my position over the man that gave me hope on life, and reached for a rose that was perched along the window. A tear from my bruised ego fell upon his cheek and soaked into his pale skin as I laid the flower over his chest. I repositioned him and walked away from a part of my life that was not ready to be parted with. The only thing that traveled through my mind was how happy I was that the day had finally said its goodbyes. Then I hid in the bushes and waited for Frank's friend to arrive.

CHAPTER FIVE

Once Dean made an appearance, I headed home and strolled down the driveway without casting another glimpse upon the house. That chapter was to be left in the past; the page was meant to be turned, revealing a fresh storyline. It would definitely prove to be the moment that changed my life forever. The garden would not be perceived in the same light, for the haunting images of Suzie would stick for eternity. Gawking upon the tough, leathery material that covered my muscles and bones, I questioned if the original coloring would ever return or if it was forever disgraced by tragedy. Suzie's purpose was not to frighten me, but her initial greeting made my flesh crawl from the graphic nature. I continued down the lonely, abandoned road that would lead to another fear-provoking tale. The worst of the worst was that Frank would no longer serve as an outlet for my confused emotions. No one else would be able to calm my nerves in the way that he did.

As my bottom limbs relocated the rest of me homebound, the memory of another unfortunate soul that had crossed my path began to play on the television inside my skull. He was a man who possessed a great power: a power that made every individual that came upon him feel as if they were special. The man had more friends than I had ghosts. Believe me, that was an extremely high number. The day we were introduced was a day unlike any other: there was nothing unusual hiding around the corner waiting for the chance to jump into my brain and show people how insane I really was. The sun was shining, and the temperature was a perfect seventy degrees. Everyone and their mothers seemed to be sporting a smile. There were a few people gathered at Jay's house, preparing for a mighty fiesta that was slowly being organized by yours truly. As I waited to lose my scruples from the two hits of LSD taken a few moments earlier, I noticed a stranger. He proudly strutted to my side with his hand cocked out for a greeting.

"Well hello Terry, I am Greg; it is about time that we finally meet," the man politely introduced himself.

"Nice to meet you. I'm not familiar with a Greg. How do you know who I am?"

"That's just like Jay to not speak of me. I've known Jay for many years now; he has told me quite a few tales of the infamous Terry."

"To my ears that doesn't sound too good," I responded, chuckling lightly. It seemed odd that I'd never met or even heard of Greg; Jay had his reasons for what he did, and I did not question him.

"It's all good. So, I hear yourself and Jay seem to be hitting it off well. You'd better watch your back," Greg said with a little more seriousness to his voice.

"Why you say that?" I asked. Obviously, Jay and Greg didn't have the greatest friendship. That was more-than-likely the reason for the late meeting. "I'm just joking, keep on your toes and you should be just fine; you seem smart enough."

"I'm not sure what you're getting at. I think we should stop this conversation before blood begins to destroy this beautiful grass," I threatened him in an immature manner.

"Sorry, that is one thing I know about you." "You know what?"

"I know not to piss you off. I've actually seen some of the people who did not know that general rule, or should I say I visited them in the hospital after their meeting with you. You're smaller than I thought you would be." "Powerful elements can be smaller than sight. The size of a man means nothing when it comes to defending honor," I enlighten him with some cocky, ridiculous bullshit.

My young mind had not yet matured, and my remarks proved to be quite naïve. At that particular time in my youth, I was not equipped with a conscience. Jay brought many new traits to my personality; being aware of the damage I left behind was not one of them. One of the traits was how to not let fear control my actions, for I was taught to become fearless. Another was how to survive in the face of danger. As a child I was in many fights. However, I was not always the victor. Jay taught me how to become a monster.

Knowing how to take care of myself during a scuffle came in useful. Jay's teachings seemed immoral, which did not bother me at the time. His methods were far beyond brutal. He taught me to not have a care in the world, and that philosophy led to a temper that could not be organized. In layman's terms, I had become an asshole. If someone looked at me the wrong way, I would commence to pummel them. All my anger was kept hidden until an unsuspecting victim let me release it upon their face. I quickly built up a reputation for myself. One would think that would keep people at bay, but it actually created a target. Everyone wanted a chance to bring down the tough guy. I would not classify myself as being tough; I just knew what to do in a situation that involved force. Jay trained me to never lose my cool no matter what the circumstances were. He would recite the words: *a calm man walks away from a scuffle while a crazy man tastes dirt.*

"I agree, it's not how big you are, it's how smart you are," Greg approved my words. "I am sorry if I upset you; that was not my plan. Honestly, I was hoping we could become friends."

"I have enough friends in my life."

"I did not know there was such a thing. I think the more people on your side, the easier life becomes."

"I think the more friends you have, the more chances of betrayal are in the future."

"Everyone has their different ways of grasping life, I guess. Anyway, maybe you'll change your mind. I will be around," he said with a smile and a handshake.

After his departure, I returned to the tedious work of setting up. The chemical that was placed on my tongue was slowly reaching my brain. I had become an acidhead. Altering my reality seemed to blend nicely with the unexplainable events that occurred in my life. It provided me the odd sense of normality. As my reality began to spin out of control, I roamed around the party searching for others who were destroying their brain cells in a similar fashion. After a few rounds through the crowd, Greg appeared before me.

"Are you tripping?" he asked nonchalantly. "Yes I am, how about you?"

"Sure am. I know a great place to peak out. You should join me." "Why the hell not," I expressed my enthusiasm. We hopped into his car to escape the chaos for a while, and as he drove, he reached under his seat and pulled out a glass bowl freshly packed with some herb. The smell was breathtaking. The aroma took over my senses, and with a huge grin on my face, I grabbed the bowl from him and begin to smoke.

"Easy there, that isn't dirt weed."

"That is for sure," I commented. "So where are we heading?"

"We are going to a very secret spot, and you will be one of four who knows of the place of peace and comfort. I expect you to keep it that way," he quoted as we pulled off the highway onto a dirt road that led into the woods.

"If it's so secret, why are you letting me in on it?"

"I've heard all types of stories about this young, long haired, recluse boy. Stories of an anger filled child that would blow on any little account.

Tales of a boy who could destroy the biggest of the biggest, the strongest of the strongest, and the wisest of the wisest. I've been warned a countless amount of times to not mess with this Neanderthal," he rambled as if he was talking about a legend.

"Sounds like a jerk," I rudely interrupted, knowing that he was speaking of me.

"Not a jerk, but rude at times," he commented on my interfering. "As I was saying, the stories were all about him being an unstoppable force, a good person to have on your side. All of the tales spread about this youth were dramatic, but not one of the stories spoke of disloyalty. In all truthfulness, they declared the exact opposite, for if this individual befriends you, he would stick up for you until the very end. He would do anything in his power to help a friend have any easier time in life, even if it hurt him."

"Doesn't remind me of anyone I know."

"I think we will be great friends," he said as we reached our destination. He brought us to a lake that was surrounded by enormous wooden statues. A quaint opening between the trees supplied just enough room for a small sandy area. The trail that we took to reach the heavenly body of water was barely large enough to fit Greg's vehicle. It was more than obvious that the path was manmade, and the time that it took to create had to be lengthy. The acid was now governing my every thought, and it took all of my awareness to focus in on Greg as he hopped from the car and dashed to my side. The door creaked open with the help from his hand, and I chuckled for no apparent reason. I discovered a large rock that sat a few yards away, and as my eyes worked diligently to bring the object into focus, the stone structure began to turn until it was upside- down. It took some time until I figured out that it was me that moved and not the rock. My legs were not communicating with the rest of my body, and somehow how my upper half twisted around to the point that the top of my head was rested on the ground below, while my legs still remained inside the vehicle.

Greg had found himself a pleasant spot in the blue liquid. The sparkle from the lake was absolutely amazing. My head rotated to look all around the lagoon. It was a fantasyland; we had fallen into a fairy tale. The trees were in perfect formation as they ran around the body of water. There were no signs of human life, however, there were croaking noises in the distance. Birds were trying to get my attention with their harmonizing, and a creature of the water launched itself into the air to prove it existed.

The water was clear, and the bottom was visible as I crawled my way towards it. The lake was calling me to enter as my hand plunged into the cool body of heaven. The feeling pounced through my body, the most refreshing sensation I had felt in quite some time. Greg splashed, and my clothes dripped from the enormous wave that he had created. Laughter erupted from deep within as my body flew into the air. We played like children for the rest of the day. We hardly spoke a word to each other. We swam, climbed the wooden protectors of the lake, and rolled around in the sand. As the sun decided to part ways, I found myself back in Greg's car.

"That was the best trip I've been on in a while," I expressed my gratitude.

"I knew you would enjoy it. I brought you here 'cause I know you won't reveal the location."

"Why are you so sure about me?"

"I just know. I've met many people in my life thus far and have become a decent judge of character. When I spotted you at Jay's earlier today, I knew we would hit it off. I am not very different from you, for if you are my friend, I will die for you. Now it's time to go find some women," Greg revealed his horny side.

"Sounds like a great idea," I declared. After that particular day, Greg and I became quite close. For some reason, Greg believed we had a connection. He did not possess the curse that led my life to tragedy and I, under no circumstances, revealed it to him. We had a normal friendship, or what seemed to be normal. On the dreaded day that I found out who Jay really was, Greg became my savior; he and I took our friendship to a whole new level of trust. He stood by my side through all the absurdity that followed. I did not tell him about my uniqueness, and he did not ask. Anytime there was a problem he was there to show an ordinary side of life. He did not try to understand; he only did his best to bring my confidence to a new level. Greg was a true friend, up until the day that my life sucked him in.

As my home was descended upon, thoughts of rest danced around my cranium. I noticed that my car had gone missing; bits of the front end lay around the bruised tree, merely another drawback to deal with at a later moment. I nonchalantly made my way up some stairs and into my apartment, where a familiar scent rushed through my nostrils and settled in my brain. It was the smell of the beautiful Tina.

"Is everything alright?" she asked with a sad tone to her voice.

"You don't have to play anymore; I know you have a connection with Frank."

"Are you upset with me?"

"You were part of the reason I met Frank, for that I thank you. He was the best gift that anyone has ever given me. I hold no resentment for your secrecy."

"Is Frank?" she began to ask the dreaded question as I interrupted her. "Yes, he is no longer a part of my life," I said as I entered the room for bathing and the question to if my skin would regain its normal color was to be answered.

"Anything you would like to talk about?" Again, Tina tried to offer her help.

"Not that I'm aware of," I replied as I wiped soap and water over my arm. "Right now, my mind is a jumbled mess. I'm not sure what I'm supposed to do next. That is the scariest part of my being: the fact that I don't have a clue what is around the bend."

"If you don't mind me asking, what did you do about Frank?" She had always expressed that the most fascinating thing about me was how I responded to stressful situations.

"He left a number for one of his childhood friends. He asked me to contact him when I need to release my brain waves. I called this man and he decided it would be better if he dealt with the body, being I'm painted red and all," I sarcastically recalled the earlier event. "Can you recall the earlier days, the days when we first met?"

"Of course I can, what's on your mind?"

"Before there ever was a… you and I, when I was dating Sydney, we were all at a party and I was messed up beyond belief," I started to tell a story when Tina interrupted.

"The night that became the final night between you and Sydney," she replied.

"Exactly, I cheated on her that night. To this day I still cannot forgive myself for what I did. I have distorted dreams about the whole situation. I know I apologized for my doings nevertheless, an apology really doesn't make up for such a mistake," I brought up the past once again. I was through trying to clean myself, the stain seemed to be lifting slightly. I was too drained to continue scrubbing, so I left the bathroom to situate myself closer to Tina.

"You have been beating yourself up for that all these years?"

"Of course I have! To me that is the greatest form of betrayal that anyone can do unto another. It is absolutely deceitful."

"You boggle my mind sometimes. You were so wasted that night; I can't believe you even remember having sex with that girl."

"I don't, but I woke up naked next to an undressed woman on wet sheets. Something had obviously happened. Anyway, do you believe that my actions that night created bad karma for the rest of my life?" I asked as I moved closer to her.

"You're trying to tell me that all the incidents in your life that cause you pain and frustration are based on that one night of stupidity?"

"I've made many mistakes and trust me, after that one significant moment, my mind changed. It was my wake-up call. After that day I really understood the importance of respecting other people."

"You've always had genuine respect for people," she stated.

"That was an act, I hated people. I took advantage of whoever stepped in front of me. That evening showed what betrayal can do to a person and I want no part of that."

"Well, I don't believe because of what you did to Sydney, your life is all messed up. You have had the outstanding gift of communication with other realms your entire lifetime. It is something that grows in you, as you grow your strengths become more prominent. Tonight, you helped your friend to see things from his daughter's eyes and not his own. If you didn't have your uniqueness, he would have died in vain. She came to you because she relates with your life. Do you get what I'm saying?" She asked quite sternly. "What you need to do now is figure out how to channel your feelings. Make them work for you, don't let them control you."

"I can't control them; they come to me whenever they feel. I don't have the power to turn them off. Believe me…I've tried. I am over my head in problems that aren't supposed to exist. On my way back from Frank's, I was thinking about Greg," I expressed frustration as I moved from the living room to the kitchen. I was feeling my lips crack with every tiny movement. As I refreshed myself with some cool liquid from the faucet, I began to tremble as the water trickled down my throat. My body had not received any fluids or solids all day long. I must have been dehydrated, for my body tried to reject the solution. I hacked up what resembled brain matter into the sink and resumed my position next to the lovely Tina.

"That is a name I haven't heard in ages. What brings him to mind?" Tina inquired with a concerning voice. She knew Greg for a short while; she had heard me speak of him many times.

"The whole depression scene: I get depressed, then I claim that I have no reliable friends and I bitch about how alone I am."

"I think of your life as the exact opposite, you have people in your life that would give up everything in the world to help you. I don't know anyone who gets the respect that you do. Don't get me wrong, you definitely deserve it, but you need to open your mind and realize why these people think so highly of you. Then, and only then, will you be able to rise out of the normal way of thinking. Once this is accomplished you will have an easier time dealing with the realms that seem to haunt you," her voice drained through my ears. Everything she said was true; I was too stubborn to realize it myself.

"I'm beginning to open my mind to that way of thinking. Greg was a man who had no clue about what my problems were. It didn't matter to him. He saw a friend that was hurting and did whatever it took to try to ease his friends' pain; he was a true human. I wish I had warned him, because there are definitely not enough people on the earth like him. My selfishness erased him from reality."

"Greg was one of a kind however, if you think back, you almost gave your life for Jay. Even after you found out who he really was, your loyalty wouldn't let you walk away. That is what Greg did for you. He knew what happened with Jay; he knew what your scar was from. He did what he felt was right when it came to helping you. He did what he thought Terry would have done. Can you honestly tell me that if the shoe was on the other foot, you wouldn't have done the same?"

"I believe that you're onto something. Greg learned a great deal from me, as I learned from him. It does make sense to me now, for if I died, Greg would still be around and he would be blaming himself for my demise," I had reached an understanding to the word loyalty. Loyalty worked two ways: both sides had to partake for it to seize its presence in life.

"That is what everyone you know has been trying to drill into your concrete head. You give yourself to them, and they will give themselves to you. It is an unspoken oath between true friends," said the wise Tina.

As she spoke, Greg's memory rushed back into my head. There was an incident that took place a few years ago: I had the day off and plans to spend the day with Greg were made a week prior. Unfortunately, my dreams were too much to handle and I was in no shape to have fun. Cancelling was out of the question. My reputation was that of dependability, and ruining that reputation did not work for me. It was not going to be easy to put on a happy face; there was no choice in the matter, and at that very moment, a knock erupted upon the front door. Greg was early and my false façade was not yet attached to my face. He waited a moment and let himself in, as usual, and what he saw was unexpected.

"Well, I thought we were going to have an exciting afternoon, but you don't look so excited," Greg had a concerned tone to his happy voice.

"It's that obvious, huh?" The dream that tormented my mind was of a young girl. In the past week, her face had shown up more than a handful of times, but not ever in reality. It was one of my first experiences with a dream that was persistent. Soon I would discover that a night vision of that caliber was to become a regular affair. There was no willingness to let Greg in on my thoughts. My state of mind at the time had no reason to be bad because my life seemed to be in order. For some unknown reason, depression flowed through my veins as if someone close to me had passed away.

"Want to let me in on your secret?" he asked with anticipation. I had not once told Greg about my situation.

"I've been having a dream of a young girl. I know exactly where to find her. I don't have a clue what her ordeal is. I know she is in pain, but from what… I don't know," as I told bits and pieces of my story, I was about to make one of the biggest mistakes of my life: I revealed the location of the girl to Greg. My thoughts were not clear, and confusion distorted my views. My motive for speaking was to release some of the stress upon my brain, I was not asking for help. All I wanted was for Greg to understand why his friend was acting strange, that was all. After I unleashed the information, Greg became quiet, his face looked as if he had found his best friend lying in the road unable to move from being crushed by a Mack truck.

"I'm sorry; I just don't feel like myself today. Maybe we should continue our plans at a later date," I said.

"Sounds like a good idea," Greg said as he gently hugged me. "I will contact you soon and make sure everything is fine." He left my home, and it was the last time we saw each other.

His heart was so large that his life meant nothing, and the information he received was his death warrant. All he desired was for his friend to be at ease, so he took my problem into his own hands. There was respect for his way of thinking, however, there was also resentment towards the fact that he did not consult me before he took action. At first, I had no clue that his disappearing act was my fault. There was some contact with his family and neither of us had any inkling to what had happened to him; he just vanished. We searched endlessly for indications and told the authorities all we knew. The cops conveyed on numerous occasions that people turn up missing all the time and usually were not found. Anger and sadness sat in the pit of my stomach for over a year.

The girl that possessed my head the very night that led to Greg's departure showed herself again over a year and a half later. She had no trace of sadness the second time around, and her background held a terrifying image. The tension in the air was thick as my eyes sprung open, and I desperately tried to visualize the scene while my mind was awake, but the memory refused to exist. Over the years, I learned an ability that allowed my eyes to close and resume a dream from the last second my memory recalled.

The girl came back into view after I dozed off and my mind sunk deep into an image that was hanging behind her. After the illustration became one hundred percent clear, my eyes burst open, and my hands clumsily battled with holding the phone steady as my fingers dialed the number to Greg's parents. The girl kept repeating the words very high, and those were the words that I left upon the answering machine, plus the location of where she was thought to be.

The next evening, my messages were maxed out and the flashing light filled my soul with regret. Whoever was on the tape was definitely not going to have good news, but for some reason my finger hit the play button anyhow. The first voice was that of Greg's mother, and her tone was hysterical. It took all my concentration to hear the threats and blame through her violent sobbing. My knees fell onto the hardwood floor below, and my heart rolled into a corner. She spoke of having me locked away, and screamed "murderer" over and over and over.

My outcome was not important to me; my entire body was numb and no longer was my life important. The following messages had the same intensity; the word murderer echoed in the room. I could not bear to hear any more, so I ripped the phone and its accomplice from the wall. My weary legs brought the rest of my body outside to wait for the paddy wagon to arrive. It was pretty obvious that they were on their way. To my surprise, someone did appear. It was not men carrying a straitjacket, nor the men in blue. It was the man who gave life to the victim of desperation. He departed his means of travel and had a seat next to me. His arm wrapped around my shoulder and, for a brief second, I felt a slight bit of relief. He turned to make contact with the fluid draining organs that provided sight. I could not return the favor.

"You do not have to worry. My wife is in a panic and handled the situation poorly. We do not blame you, for you know that all of our love is with you. We understand that this is as hard for you as it is for us. Please accept my apologies for the messages of insanity," Greg's father spoke with a tremendous struggle to not let his tears take over the moment.

"Why are you so convinced that I had nothing to do with his demise? I am the one who told you where to look," I asked with no courage whatsoever, for I could not hold the tears back. I began to sob as an infant would.

"I know how much Greg thought of you, and I believe the feeling was mutual. It took much strength for you to inform us of your vision. I can't see that you would have done that if you had something to hide," he remarked as his strength weakened and he began to sob. We sat together and let our emotions run rampant. "Do you know what his outcome was?"

"Somewhat."

"Very high, that is what you said when you called. Do you know what that meant?"

"I saw an image in a tree, assumed it to be Greg. I didn't want it to be." "Somehow, he ended up over twenty five feet in the air; he was hanging. He had been there for over a year and a half, experts say. I believe it was the time that he disappeared. There was no rope used. His neck was bound by the tree itself." "How in the hell does that happen?"

"No one seems to have that answer. I was hoping you had another vision."

"I am sorry, I have no clue," I said as I stood to stretch my sleeping limbs.

"That is what I presumed. I am sorry to be the one to tell you. I want you to know that you have nothing to worry about from us or anyone else. You are in the clear. His death was ruled as a suicide. I know, as you do, that it was not self-inflicted. If you receive any details, I beg that you come to me immediately," he commented as he also stood to stretch.

"You have my word. No matter what I find, you will be the first to know."

"That is something I won't take for granted," he set his hand on my shoulder and nodded. He made his way back to his escape.

Greg's family and I would unquestionably see each other in the near future, however, first the right words would have to form in my brain.

There were many similarities between Greg and I; loyalty was strong in both of us, for my life would have easily been given for his if only the circumstances were reversed. It was difficult to accept the fact that he died in vain.

"What's going on in your head?" Tina asked as I sat staring at the wall with an empty gaze.

"Just reminiscing," I responded.

"Now what do we do?" Tina begged of me.

"I try and figure out what to do from here," my answer was an obvious one. "I need to rest my mind. I will see you at another time," I commented as I entered my room, closing the door behind me. Tina would let herself out.

CHAPTER SIX

The afternoon was early, and my mind was pondering on the reasoning of why reality was so boring. Normal lives seemed so easy, yet the people that lived them had no idea about how trivial their problems were. I had observed human nature closely and discovered that most dilemmas were caused by individuals themselves. Even simple conundrums were made worse by outlandish and unnecessary lies. Once the truth was stretched, the situation grew into tragedy. There was no controlling a fib once it was released into the atmosphere where the fabrication would grow and grow until everyone in its surroundings was left shocked and in dismay. Why the average human felt that miscommunicating the truth would be a just idea was not obvious to me; it definitely destroyed the possibility of my life to be taken seriously. The horrible images that passed by daily prompted me to want to scream their stories from the tallest building, express all the hate and grief that consumed my every thought and wave a banner that listed all my deep, dark secrets. The secrets were remnants of acid flowing through my body. The longer I kept them in, the closer they were coming to burning through my flesh. The only issue stopping me was that all the trivial lies made my truth seem completely fabricated. Two of the longest years of my life had passed since Frank's departure. The movies that usually drenched my brain while I slept had now begun to show themselves when my brain was fully awake and alert. The obscure visions had become frequent, and each day drove me closer to insanity. The only source to vent all the frustration that was building inside was six feet under, and the possibility of joining him was creeping up; it was demanding dealing with my difficulties on my own. There was no understanding to the apparitions that shared my brain waves and that merely led to more frustration. Neither Frank nor Suzie had popped up in my life since the death of my mentor, and that led me to believe that they found each other in the afterlife and were content, or so I hoped, and that thought was what kept me going through the dark times.

There was a piercing sound that invaded my ear drums. It was thrown off as the fault of my roommate, until the noise kept creeping closer and closer, to the point where it could not be ignored. Erratic behavior was still the norm for dealing with my emotions; everyday seemed to bring more destruction to the part of my mind that held sanity. Running from complicated situations was still my way of coping. As my body fell from the two story drop out of the window, a pile of leaves broke the fall.

As the dried leaves were brushed from my clothes a voice in the distance rang out:

"Most people use a door, dumbass!" A neighbor shouted from his open window.

Ignoring the aggravated gent, I ventured to a quieter place to gather my thoughts. There was a river close by and the gentle flow always played a part in calming my tensions. Since Frank's departure my general rule was to keep others out of my madness. However, there was an odd attraction for certain people. Their lives seemed rather dull, and they were searching for excitement. My display of living seemed dark, secretive, and filled with adventure. My feelings on the matter were that once an individual became involved with my drama, they were doomed. There was no escape from my horrors except the one-way trip into another realm.

It was difficult to grasp how outsiders could be so intrigued by what my life entailed. People did not understand that what seemed exciting and interesting was actually aggravating and horrifying. It was easy to relate to someone who was searching to spice up their life, however, my torment was not what they were looking for. When it became clear to an individual that ghosts haunted my world, they felt as if such a situation would be filled with excitement and would lead to great stories to voice later. What I learned is that regular people have too much free time on their hands.

It was awfully isolated without Frank, and it became a torture to not let someone replace him. It was a shame that the only people that deserved to be trusted had to be as messed up as I was. That was a certain sentiment that would linger with me until my demise. There was an understandable want to speak my problems, but then again, my stories sucked people in and changed their perception of reality, and that ability was not to be abused. Those who were merely curious had to be shunned, or forever bear the burdens of my moment of weakness. In the future there may be an ordinary person waiting for me to confide in them, but it did not seem probable.

The past frequently ran in and out of my cranium, usually showing Tina in some manner. Before Tina and I became a couple, there was a period that was eroded with pure desperation. My connection to the infamous babe was her best friend and my girlfriend, Sydney. It was clear that my relationship with Sydney was not based on love, however, there was definitely respect between us. We may have been together for all the wrong reasons, mine were to be closer to Tina and hers weren't all that clear; there were ulterior motives. We made the most of what we had together and for the most part, we shared quite a few good times. Tina had her boyfriend and the four of us seemed inseparable. Except during the moments of lust, there were no orgies. One way or the other Tina would be mine; the first obstacle was to get rid of the boyfriend, Jacob. While I patiently waited for him to make a fatal mistake, a strong bond with Sydney began to emerge. She was a woman who had no limits, anything desired she provided.

Sydney lived her life day by day, and she received a large amount of respect through my eyes. My days were lived in the past trying to figure out what went wrong. My stories were not of her knowledge. She was well aware that strange tendencies pushed me through the hours; she did not pry, she merely provided comfort. Hiding my secrets from her was trying. As the days moved on, our relationships began to fall apart. First was Sydney and I, the sad story of betrayal. She did not forgive me for my affair and there was no blame for her on my end. The sad part of the breakup was that it had to end on such a horrible note. It would forever burn in my heart. The tension in the air when we were together was thick, and the awkwardness kept me away. However, there was a day that was permanently fixed in my thoughts.

Spirits were low due to the lengthy time spent away from the girls; it was the moment to reconnect. After a knocking frenzy upon their door led to no answer, I declared it an emergency and surpassed the wooden soldier with the help of a spare key. The kitchen and living room held no trace of life however, there were interesting noises erupting from down the hall. After further investigation, it was from Sydney's room that the curious sounds burst forth. My trembling hand slowly turned the knob, and the barrier was forced inward just a wee bit. There was an extreme amount of giggling and heavy breathing as four women were discovered upon the bed. All the renters of the home, except Tina, were present and completely nude. One of the gorgeous bodies of nature gave me a smile and with a significant finger movement I launched towards the excitement.

While engaging in depths of passion the door whined ever so slightly. Gazing in the direction of the whimper, there was a body. Tina overlooked the sexual chaos; she held the expression of distress. Without hesitation I soared to my feet and dragged my hand across the floor to find anything that would cover my body. Tina was shaking, and there was a swollen mess around her eye. Immediately my insides were struck with a tremendous force that pulled my throat into the deep dark depths of sorrow.

"Who did this to you?" I questioned sternly. She did not answer; the streams of dread ran across her shivering domain. Someone she trusted made a mockery of their relationship. There was no need for her to explain who was responsible for the outrage: it was quite obvious that good ol' Jacob had fallen into rocky waters.

Like a moth flying to light, I made my way out of the apartment. Voices screamed words of damnation. No one was going to stop what was owed. Racing through the parking lot, two of Tina's neighbors and close friends tried to grab my attention, but I quickly waved them off and the mission commenced. What was about to go down was a scene that I was most comfortable in, for massacre was my forte. The only objective during a fight was to be the one who walked away, and there was no doubt that the winner was going to be me. Anger pumped the blood throughout my veins as my heart took a break. The emotions were high, and tranquility was in my brain; I would not go at him like a mad man. Instead, my moves would be discreet, precise, and to the point. Jacob was going to fall; he was going to fall hard and bloody.

He was holding residence at his father's house, which was a few blocks from Tina's apartment. As my body approached the domain of my new enemy, the hate surged through my veins. Usually my battles were brought on by pure boredom, but this time there was a damn good reason for fists to fly. There was no need to announce my presence; he was expecting company.

"Where's the rest of the cavalry?" he snickered as he nonchalantly leaned against the side of the garage. "Hard to believe that you were the only one sent."

The sound of his voice sent the volcano inside into full eruption. I said nothing, the only sound he heard was the haunting whisper of the wind my fist made as it crashed upon his left eye. He stood straight to cover his face as my free fist found its way to his abdomen. In agony, his body bent. His head came down straight onto my knee which, in full force, was coming to meet him halfway. I felt sudden warmth upon my leg as his blood soaked into my jeans. He dropped to the ground passively.

Hovering over him, there was no sense of serenity. I actually felt sorry for the pathetic hunk of meat that lay before my feet. Some saliva flew from my mouth and landed on the piece of shit that was named Jacob as I turned to vacate the premises. My walk back to Tina's was spent trying to come up with an explanation, for she did not condone violent behavior and was sure to be upset by my actions. Just before my invigorated limbs reached their destination, a loud honking noise disturbed the air behind me. A one-hundred-and-eighty-degree turn revealed a pick-up truck containing the two neighbor friends. As the automobile approached, it revealed a beaten body that was chained to the rear bumper. It took all of my might to keep the corners of my mouth from rising.

"We don't believe he learned his lesson quite yet, there Terry," cried out one of the bandits.

"Untie him," I said to the eager-to-torture gentleman.

"If you say so, but you're taking the fun out of it," the other numbskull spoke his mind.

Tina was observing the torture session and to my surprise, she waved, smiled, and blew me a kiss. I returned the gesture as we untied the victim and tossed his limp body into the back of the vehicle. One of the assistants hopped into the driver's seat and the other joined in the back as we made our way to the scene of the crime. Upon arrival, we noticed a man standing in the yard with an aluminum baseball bat that was held by one hand and was repeatedly hitting the other. We were quite positive that Jacob's father was not trying to start up a friendly game of baseball. We stopped in the driveway, and I leapt from the back of the vehicle.

"I don't want any more trouble sir, I'm here to give you something that belongs to you," I pronounced as I lifted the lifeless body of his son out of the means of transportation. Jacob plummeted to the ground with an agonizing groan. He observed his dad with the weapon and urged him to swing.

"You have a reason for what you done to my son?" The father demanded.

"Your son put a not-so-attractive bruise on the most beautiful woman I have ever had the pleasure of sharing this planet with."

"Are you talking about Tina?"

"I sure am," I said being as polite as possible.

The father then held the slugger high in the air and with all his strength he swung it down to smash into the ribs of the bloody pulp that lay before us. His own father. I was absolutely speechless. He added a short and powerful kick to the inner thigh and remarked that his son may sleep in the garage. No one who hit a lady was allowed beyond his front door, son or no son. I made eye contact with the disappointed father. He merely nodded and told me to give his sympathy to Tina. He then disappeared into his castle with his own offspring puking guts on his front sidewalk.

We found ourselves back in the truck on our way to the damsel in distress. My mind scrambled to figure out what her reaction would be. Her sending a metaphoric kiss was puzzling. It would be refreshing if she understood that no matter what crossed our paths, she would always have me to fight for her. I gawked at the handle and the door moaned as it swung within the room, standing abroad was a face bearing an unnecessary vision of humanity.

"I'm sorry," were the only words that escaped my mouth.

The right side of her face lifted ever so slightly to curve her lips just enough for a half smile that knocked me to the floor. I landed directly on my nose, adding even more blood to discolored garments that were sticking to my skin. There was a gentle hand caressing the back of my neck that produced tingles everywhere. She reached for my hand as I turned and pulled her petite body onto mine. The sound of her giggle was music to my ears. While drawing her body away from mine she repeated the words *follow me*. With a nod and turbo burst of energy, I did what she asked.

She led us to her bedroom. Twice had my feet touched the carpet that dwelled in her domain. There was nowhere else that I would have rather been. Tina leaned against her bed, and, reaching for a pillow, she made herself comfortable. Her restless hand patted on the empty space next to her gorgeous body. I sat myself next to her and held her hand between both of mine, squeezing ever so gently. Her lips softly brushing the side of my cheek; her breath was warm and smelled of peaches. I turned, hoping to catch her lips among mine, even for a moment. Our quivering doors to our souls met at last, for the moment was long awaited. My eyes opened and discovered a tear forming in the neither region of Tina's blue gifts from heaven. Gazing upon her eyes would take a person to worlds not seen by just anyone. Only a few have discovered the beauties, and I demanded to be the last. I would not let her go unless that was her intent.

"Are you sad?" I asked as I wiped the tear from her face. She grew closer as her forehead found room next to mine.

"The day that you supposedly destroyed your relationship with Sydney, I saw you in a whole different light. To me, you've always been this honest, loyal protector. I can trust you with anything. You were a recluse. I was not scared of you, however, I feared for other males that pissed you off. What I'm trying to say is that I never saw you in pain. As if you had no feelings whatsoever. That one day…I saw your pain. Your eyes could not hide it. I finally saw the man I was in love with," she spoke as she slowly rubbed her soft hands down my face. "I told Jacob how I felt about you. He obviously didn't take it too well. I'm glad he did what he did, it only proved that it would have happened at some point in time."

My life just seemed to open up; I was living my greatest fantasy. As we began to enjoy each other's bodies, a voice called to us from beyond the closed door. We ignored it.

The following morning, I awoke on Tina's bed and was ecstatic to discover that it was not a dream. In an effort to be clear, my hand reached over the small body and ever so slightly gripped a piece of her thigh between two fingers. She moved hastily while slapping me away; she then grabbed hold of my neck with her teeth. We tumbled to the ground that waited below, laughing the whole way down.

"Were you making sure you weren't dreaming?" she asked as she flipped our bodies over so she could look down upon me. My head nodded and our lips met.

"Do you have any regrets?" I returned a question. "No, what happened yesterday?"

"Well, I met Jacob outside of his house and proceeded to make my way towards him, when he turned into a complete fool. I was willing to talk."

"Willing to talk, I don't believe you for a second."

"Anyway, he pissed me off. So I did the only thing I seem to be able to do right these days: I put him down. On my short journey back to you, I heard your neighbors' vehicle. They had chained Jacob to the bumper and were dragging him. They felt I wasn't quite through."

"They chained him to their truck!"

"Hold on," I said to get her to calm down. "So, I untie him, and throw his draping body into the bed of the four-by-four. We bring him back to his home, where his dad meets us with his bat."

"You didn't beat up his dad?" Tina asked with concern spreading among her face. Ken, Jacob's father, was a great man. I've only met him a few times, but he always gave a good impression. Tina always spoke with true kindness of him.

"Hell no. I couldn't lay a hand on Ken. He came over to us and I told the drastic tale of your outcome. He hit his own son with the bat, twice! Then he kicked him and told him to sleep in the garage."

"Ken kicked Jacob's ass? That's insane!"

"I know," I quickly agreed with her way of thinking. "I found myself in awe the entire time, I couldn't frickin' believe it, pardon my French."

"That's okay, that shit is crazy," she kept the cursing flowing. "So, you're not upset with me?"

"Why would I be upset with you?"

"For what was happening when you entered Sydney's room yesterday afternoon," I recalled earlier events that I thought would be an uncomfortable topic.

"You're a single adult, or should I say you *were* a single adult, with urges. I apologize for interrupting. Under different circumstances I would have jumped right in, it looked like you were all enjoying yourselves," she spoke with absolute logic to her way of thinking. "You do realize that yesterday was your last chance for that to happen, don't you?"

"Why is that?"

"You are no longer single."

I stood up and reached for my clothes. My eyes stared at the floor with a puzzled look upon my face.

"Is anything wrong?"

"Where are my clothes? I had some on when I came in here… didn't I?" "When you left Sydney's room you were quite angry. You grabbed whatever was in your reach. I was going to say something, but I didn't really think that it mattered," she enlightened me with an embarrassing tale of myself.

"I wore a blouse and girls' pants and I didn't even know it?" "You must be in love," she fed me a splash of dry humor.

I shook the reminiscent scene away and noticed that Tina had emerged at the river's edge. "Good afternoon, Tina. I was just thinking of you."

"Are you alright?"

"No. I am going to talk to someone I should have talked to a long time ago. Thanks for caring as usual, Tina," I revealed my gratitude as I walked back to my home, leaving her to watch the river flow.

CHAPTER SEVEN

y life was a vicious circle that buzzed around my head, causing one complication after another. There were few moments of peace, and those moments were on no occasion utilized in a proper manner. It was difficult to speak of the situations that festered upon my brain. The need to erupt vocally was overwhelming and becoming impossible to regulate. I was a desperate soul searching for someone with an ear. The numbers on the phone were fuzzy. I began to doubt my idea, however, my fingers pushed the buttons anyhow. After a few rings an old voice coughed hello.

"Hello… could I speak with Dean?" I asked.

"I presume I am speaking with the myth himself. It's been a long time Terry, you had me worried."

"I'll let you in on a secret. Don't ever worry about me. It is hazardous to your health," I spurted out and snuck in a chuckle.

"So I have heard. I hope you're calling to meet with me?" Excitedly, the question erupted from his mouth.

"I think that may do me some good."

"That is fantastic. I have many questions for you if that is all right?" He spoke as if he was a father that had not spoken to his son in some time. "That is fine. I will drop by later this afternoon. Same address?" I asked.

"Yes, I will see you soon," he stated his farewells as the phone clicked. It had become quite necessary to release some weight from my chest, and Dean was going to be the one to catch it. Time was running short, and my reality was diminishing; something drastic had to be done, and talking to a complete stranger about very personal information was going to count as a drastic move. There were so many questions bouncing off the inside of my skull that they were sure to cause internal damage. Just being able to hear the words aloud would be enough to settle my mind, or at least enough to get rid of the thoughts of suicide. I did not take myself to be a coward, and my life would most definitely not be taken away by my own hands. However, that did not mean that the thought did not occur often. It was time to make a new friend.

I had met many people throughout my life: some honest and loyal, others dishonest and shifty. The not-so-trustworthy folks outweighed the faithful by a significant amount. That was a sad premise to accept. I was not sure what went wrong in the world to spawn so many selfish human beings; it made my stomach ache. There were people who would tell a lie, and while all the proof of their disloyalty was being waved in their face, would still deny the truth. Liars should all be stranded on a deserted island, not to be blown up, but to live in each other's worlds that were made up by their own delusions.

Obviously, there was some deep frustration I held for those types of people. I knew of no reason why they couldn't accept themselves for who they were. Why must they live in a world of fabrications? It only hurt those around them. Those particular individuals were full of stupidity. When confronted with a problem, they would throw fault towards anyone but themselves. I ran as far away from the raving jerks as possible, but some circumstances in life made my departure problematic. Every time I had to look at their faces, I wanted to vomit with disgust.

I lowered myself into stupidity with my actions towards Sydney. She forgave me only because she could see and feel the regret that sweated from my pours. The lesson learned was to respect people's feelings and life would be a little easier. I could not and would not forgive someone who continued to live their life through deceit. No matter how much they desired, forgiveness was not handed out; it had to be deserved. The problem with that philosophy was the fact that the truth had to be hidden when it came to my stories, and therefore, I was a hypocrite. My disloyalty was not because I couldn't grasp the fact of who I was as a person, it was for the sole purpose that no one would be able to handle or understand the complexities that controlled my world. No matter what reasons or excuses there were, the fact was that my deceit was no better than anyone else's, and the deserted island had enough room for one more.

As I followed the paved road to Dean's, Frank's home came into view and the urge to make a stop was tremendous, but my foot never left the gas pedal, and the house disappeared in the rearview mirror. A few miles down the road, there was a long dirt driveway. As my vehicle slowly traveled amongst its path, there was hope that the stranger would be able to calm my nerves. As I sat in the car too scared to depart, a man appeared from the humble home and started to approach. He was older than I remembered and there was a definite inviting nature to his presence.

"Everything is alright Terry. We are completely alone, it is safe," the man desperately tried to ease my mind. I cautiously moved away from the four-wheeled diversion as my eyes faced the road behind us. I was waiting for the paddy wagon to come ripping down the road. Most people were frightened of freaks, and the only way for them to feel safe was to lock the crazies up. The problem was that once a person like me was trapped, our minds caved in upon themselves and we lost all control. So, through anyone else's eyes we were insane because we no longer had influence over our minds: someone, or something, else was the captain. I was fearful that I would end up that way someday.

"I promise no one is coming for you. Would you rather we go somewhere else?" Dean asked, his only concern was to provide comfort. "What happened with Frank's old place? Is it occupied?" I asked out of curiosity.

"That is a wonderful idea, it is unoccupied. We can definitely talk there. Hop in my truck and we will head in that direction." As Dean spoke, I felt quite comfortable, but still a little hesitant.

"I will follow you," said my emotionless face. Dean entered his four-wheeled machine and drove to my old place of reckoning.

The drive was quick, and the anticipation was high. As we approached the driveway, my skin exploded with tiny bumps. Our vehicles slowly rolled down the narrow path, and my imagination got the better of me. Frank seemed to be in a thousand different places; everywhere I looked, my sight displayed an image of my dear old friend. Once the key turned and powered down my mode of transportation, I departed to find myself staring face to face with Frank. His smile was friendly, and his eyes were as kind as I remembered. Then Dean walked right through him, and he vanished.

"Where would you like to have our talk?" Dean asked as his frail body shook from the excitement. His recent days had been filled with loneliness and boredom, so any change was a good change. The words from his mouth entered my ears as I noticed the garden looked exactly as I remembered it.

"I see you noticed the garden. That is my doing, I kept it as is. I thought Frank would appreciate that," Dean explained as he firmly rested his hand upon my shoulder. My head moved up and down with acceptance. We began to venture towards the porch when an overwhelming sensation to vomit consumed me. Fighting back the sick feeling, a glimpse of the first step came into focus: the last place Frank spoke to me. My knees trembled and my walk appeared to be that of a drunkard. I barely noticed Dean enter the house.

"Are you positive this is where we should be?" Dean asked as he handed me a cup of water.

"I'll be fine." The water ran down my dry, corroded throat, easing it the whole way down to the pit of my stomach. I gave the empty mug back to Dean, and my body drifted for the sofa. As I sunk into the cushions, it felt as if the heat from Frank's lifeless body was forever trapped. My mind was drifting through pictures and pictures that cluttered my brain. They were all of Frank and his darling daughter Suzie. "How have things been?" Dean questioned, as he situated himself in Frank's old chair.

There was a strange, but familiar scent in the air. My nose forced my legs to stand, and they marched out the door, leaving Dean's question unanswered for the moment. The garden stood triumphantly before me as the thought of not laying eyes upon it for two years crossed my mind. Each and every plant consumed my existence as the leaves tore into flesh. There was the sound of breathing as my eyes were attracted to the porch. Dean had made himself comfortable on the steps, so it was definitely not his breath that was creeping into my ears. Then my company became visible.

"So, what the hell is your deal anyway? Can you only find me in places of tranquility?" I begged for an answer.

"You haven't figured out how I get to you?"

My mind was cloudy, and a positive answer was nowhere to be found. After a few moments of silence, I put two and two together. The last time Jay appeared was when Frank left his body here to rot.

"Did you know Frank?" I questioned.

"You are a bigger idiot now than you used to be. Think. When and where am I able to find you? There is no hiding from me," he laughed hysterically.

"Why haven't you bothered me all this time, but years later in the last spot I saw you? It doesn't make much sense."

"Your life in general doesn't make much sense. I'm tired of playing games with you. Give me what I want, or you will find your life too difficult to deal with," he threatened me as he took a few steps back.

"You're delusional; my life is already portrayed in that manner. I learned from our last visit that if I ignore you, you will go away. Goodbye, Jay!" I waved my hand as I turned and walked away.

"I learned a few new tricks also," he said as he seemed to leave me be. Dean felt a slight breeze as my body brushed by him to resume a position upon the sofa. The old man drifted back to the chair and groaned as his bones creaked. It was certain that he had been a part of the madness that Frank called his life. The behavior that I was using was erratic and positively irrational; he didn't even flinch. He merely went to where he thought he was most required and kept himself calm at every moment. "Is everything all right?" he asked, hoping he'd get a response.

"My life is a mess," I spurted out as I covered my eyes with my trembling hands.

"I know it is. I see the same reactions in you as I once did in Frank. Everything about you feels like Frank. The way you're hesitant about every little move you make. You are always thinking of the outcome of your actions way before you do anything. Running away without a word, standing in the garden, it is like you are his mirrored image. I am sorry that I am fascinated by the resemblance."

"I understand, you are familiar with my kind, and it is common to compare us. I am also aware of the remarkable similarities between us. That is why I felt so comfortable with him. I felt as if I've known him my entire life."

"I have to ask you a question," he replied, staring into my eyes, waiting for my response. I nodded showing acceptance. "The day Frank left this earth, I came to honor my word and take care of the mess. When I arrived, I was surprised to see Frank sitting in his chair. Honestly it was quite startling. Please tell me that was how you left him."

"I didn't put much thought to your outlook. Please accept my apologies, for my intentions were not to produce fear. I put him there because I felt that was where he should be. Every time I had a problem, he sat there. Every time *he* had a problem, he sat there. So, I thought in the hour of his biggest dilemma, he should be in his chair. It made perfect sense to me."

"It makes perfect sense to me, also. I just had to know if it was you or something else."

"Thanks so much for your kindness that day; I would not have been able to handle anything. I was truly a wreck."

"Not a problem. I knew you were having a rough time. I only wish we could have spoken a little longer that day, for I knew I wouldn't hear from you soon after," he said. He shifted his body to a more comfortable position. "Why so long?"

"Talking to others about the frustrations that linger inside is an utter nuisance. I didn't have to tell Frank the gory details; he had seen them for himself. We discussed the aftermath, every tiny detail. When I talk to anyone else, I have to explain certain circumstances that I would rather not disclose."

"How can you make it in life carrying such a burden?"

To ever understand a person such as the type of person that I was, you would have to see things differently. It was not absolutely necessary to have the curse that I bore, but having a mind that was open to everything and anything was definitely required.

"That is precisely why I am here." I answered.

"I am overwhelmed with curiosity. How could any individual walk away from their dead friend and never tell a soul?" He begged for an answer, for that very thought had been lodged inside his brain for years, slowly scraping its way to eventual freedom.

"I bring Frank to life every day. He is, and will always be, a part of my world. I had no need to talk about him to anyone, because he was a secret in life as he now is in death. I did not let anyone come between us. I spoke to one individual about the blessed man."

"Who would that be?" He leaned closer to the sofa, waiting for an answer. "A mutual friend," I responded.

"I am presuming it to be a young lady by the name of Tina," he stated. As he discovered the look of acceptance upon my face, he continued to speak: "I have heard of her ways. She seems very close to you."

"Once upon a golden moon I met a woman who showed me how amazing it feels to care for someone besides myself. She taught me how to respect me for who I was. We still communicate even though we have no attraction towards each other. So, we talk about all the mystery that portraits my world. She is also a secret that I keep to my own knowing. That is why she does not help as much as I need her to."

"I understand that you keep quite a large number of secrets. I am definitely convinced that you are the strongest human I have laid my eyes upon," he tried to show his respect.

I jumped from the couch and stood directly over the surprised man who was only trying to help. I coarsely spoke my reaction:

"Look at me! My closet is so full that I need to buy a house and tear all the walls out. I need to own a large empty space to hold the thousands of more secrets I will possess in the morning. I am weak every minute I'm awake. When I am sleeping, I am living someone else's life in their world.

That is not resting, trust me. I wake more tired and confused than when I closed my eyes. I am beginning to lose sight of reality altogether. I don't do the things I do because I want to. It is all done because of the fact that I have no other choice."

"You can give up," Dean gracefully slid his opinion into play. "Weak minds give up, strong minds find a way through no matter what the consequences may be. You experience tortures of human beings, yet you hold these memories inside. They are making you weak. Open your mind and speak your horrors. I am only here to listen, not to judge or betray. I hold secrets in my life also, and I will hold them till I depart this origin. I do not believe telling you is breaking any secrecy." I stared at his face, completely blown away. He had respect for crazy people. Who would have known? "If you don't relieve your mind by releasing your thoughts vocally, how do you ease your pain?"

"I reflect. Every circumstance in my life, I cherish in my own personal way. I respect the ones who have been taken from me by remembering them. Every year I take one day and pay my respects to the ones I miss the most. I respect each soul in a different form. I want them to feel me in their new realms. I want them to know I will not let their memories waste away. I will keep their importance alive inside my head forever, and by doing such acts, I ease the pain that burrows inside of me."

"What kind of acts do you actually do?"

I stared deep inside of the brown masses that lay upon Dean's face, hoping my judgment of him was the correct one. There was still a strong urge to run. There were many pent-up feelings that were desperate to be released and the old stranger was the last resort.

"I have one particular situation that happened to me years ago. A young boy who I only knew for a few weeks decided to take his life amongst my presence. Every year I return to the lake and pay my respects. I don't have a clue if my actions ever cross his path, or if he even gives a damn. I felt an immense burst of sorrow as I watched the contents of his head hurdle across a small fish house, and that is the reason I pay my respect."

"How exactly do you show your respect?"

"I would rather not disperse that information. It becomes quite morbid," I responded as I could hear the hamster wheel turning inside of his head.

"I understand that you don't want to reveal what you consider wrong actions however, you need to realize that I know your life is not normal. I understand that you must do things that most people would find wrong or even morbid, as you would say. I feel that it is highly important that if you want to walk from this experience feeling any emotions of gratitude towards myself, you need to share all your thoughts. If you do not, talking with me will do you absolutely no good whatsoever," he desperately tried to get me to reveal my dark obsessions.

"I throw animal brains that I purchase at a butcher shop. I throw them all around the spot that his house stood when he left this world. I know that it doesn't make much sense, nevertheless, that truly is all I know of the boy. All I remember is the chunks of brain matter that lay upon the ice slowly seeping in because of the freshness. I did not know him well, so I react to what I saw to show my remembrance. I believe most people hope that in death, they will be remembered, so I remember," I stopped talking to catch my sanity. It was hard to believe that those words came out of my mouth.

"That is quite deep. I can't imagine seeing something like that with my own eyes. I commend you for your actions. Remembering the young man is a loyal action. You respect the souls that you didn't even have the chance to know, you are one of a kind," once again he expressed his thoughts of praise for my actions through life.

"I am sorry for what I am about to say; I mean every word of it, so please listen carefully. I will not sit here and listen to you tell me how great of a person I am, because I don't feel that I am. I know your intentions are harmless, but you have to comprehend that my world is nothing but lies and betrayal. I do not feel good about myself. I have no reason to. I only try to make it to tomorrow, even though I haven't figured out why. I do what I can to make it through another day and not hate myself. I don't want anyone to feel how I do, so I protect and respect everyone that deserves it. Do you know what guilt feels like?" I asked waiting for a response. He nodded, showing understanding. "That feeling haunts me every waking moment. I reek of guilt. It controls my entire body. My actions in life produce the guilt that eats at my weary mind and forces my gag reflex to commence. So if we are going to continue our conversation, there will be no more talk of such nonsense. Are we clear?"

"I respect your wishes. Let's continue."

I stared at the man that was seated before me with anticipation: anticipation for what was to become of the meeting. I needed to vent, and he thrived to comprehend. To accomplish both of the goals, I had to start from the beginning of what he knew.

"Tell me what you know of my world, so I can let you in on the truth," I demanded that he spoke.

"I am led to believe that you see and feel spirits who have left the world of the living. I believe they cause torment, for you don't understand what they want with you," he said, and then paused. "This isn't how I want to go about this discussion. If I may, I would like to ask questions and then let you respond," as he spoke, he again paused for my approval. "What about the cuts?" He questioned as he readjusted himself to become comfortable. "I remember Frank speaking of scars on your body."

"The lacerations seem to worsen as my days progress, only time will let me understand the truth about them. They are mostly random, however, there is a symbol that appears from time to time." After speaking I rose from the sofa and drifted for a source of refreshing liquid. Dean seemed to be portraying a look of concern as my departure occurred, but he kept his mouth shut. Everything in Frank's house was exactly as it was since my last visit. I added liquid from the kitchen faucet to an empty glass, and as the water flowed throughout my innards, a cough from Dean returned me to his side.

"Could you explain the symbol that you referred to? That is information that is new to me, for Frank did not tell me of a symbol," he expressed his curiosity.

"We will get to that information in due time," I changed the direction of the conversation for selfish reasons. "What are your opinions on my life?"

"I believe the wiser you become with experience, the more your life tends to let you in on what it holds for you. I know that you don't expect me to have answers."

"What exactly don't you have answers for?"

"Well, I have not one clue how your mind works, or why the things that happen to you take place. I only hear stories: some may be true, some may be false. I will never know which is which. As I sit here and let you fill my imagination with these disturbing events, I can only try to make them my own. I try to live through your life. What I am saying is that I am trying to discover what I would do in your place. If I were you, I definitely wouldn't seem as strong as you seem to be. Don't get pissed off, I'm not complementing you. I am only letting you know that I can't see myself handling the situations in the same manner as you do," he chuckled lightly.

"I'm not sure how to take that," I stated the truth.

"Your problems don't show up on your exterior. I am led to believe that helps you in reality, because when you rummage through everyday life, people can't see your heartache. So, they treat you as they would anyone else. You have no other choice than to hide what happens to you. That is a fact that I completely understand. I am sorry about the things that transpire in your life, because you seem like a genuine human being. I wish I had answers, but we both know that would be an impossibility.

"Anyway, I am hoping that as you talk out loud you may realize new points that you may have overlooked before," he took a breath as he observed my expression. He was trying to relate to what I was thinking.

"That is pretty much how I feel," I responded to his newly found wisdom. The minutes raced by, and I was beginning to let my guard down. "You say people don't see my heartache, I'm not sure that is completely true. Throughout my life thus far, I have noticed that I have trouble dealing with society, for I have my good moments and I have my bad. There are times when I cannot deal with being around anyone. Moments that I need to be alone. Unfortunately, in those moments, it is not always possible to seek solitude.

"I become quiet and straight up dull—expressionless, so to speak. I want to be myself, but the problem is that I don't know who I am. I am under the suspicion that not all my feelings are my own. To sift through all the emotions that fluctuate inside my head and figure out exactly which ones are my own is almost impossible. The reason being that I truly do not know who I am or how I feel about certain situations that take place in my life. Over the years I slowly discover bits and pieces of who I am, and it is a slow process. I am damn sure that not knowing my own feelings is most definitely the hardest part of my life to overcome. I'm not sure if anyone really knows exactly who they are as a person. I struggle everyday trying to discover the inner me. Take my word for it, the frustration at times is absolutely unbearable."

"I see where that would be a tough thing to overcome. I agree with the fact that as humans we never completely understand ourselves. Having other forces sharing their emotions in your mind would be a difficult premise to comprehend," Dean agreed with my philosophy. As he stared into my eyes, I could see his sympathy. He gently reached out his hand and placed it upon my shoulder.

"Life itself is only a form of frustration. Problems are a major part of living. It doesn't matter how petty a problem may seem to someone, for it may mean the world for the next person it invades. One thought that crosses my mind periodically is how people have become difficult to trust. With all the chaos that surrounds our every waking moment, you would think that working together and trusting one another would be the ideal way to reach happiness. Instead, we destroy each other and the beliefs of one another. Even with the idea of heaven and hell, people do not act the way we would like. Who are we, you may be asking yourself? *We* stands for every living being on the earth. No one understands anyone. I find myself to be too trusting. The past few years, I have been trying to rid myself of this concern because I need to see people for who they are and not for whom I prefer them to be. Of course, this is a difficult process because I want to trust each and every human that crosses my path. Even you for example, I truly believe that you are trustworthy even though I don't know you," I wiped my brow after I released my thoughts on the old man.

Dean positioned himself directly in front of me as he spoke: "You can trust me. I know this is something that doesn't come easy for you. You need to understand that Frank let me in on his life, so you can also. You are the only person that I have ever spoken of Frank's troubles to. I promised him that I would keep his disasters a secret, and that is exactly what I have done. I promise you the same. I will never tell a living being of what we discuss here. It is extremely important to me that you take my words seriously."

"A promise in my life is the only source of trust that I have. I believe that there must be one word that is taken more seriously than others, and that word to me is promise. If you break a promise, you are a waste of space and I will never give you the time of day. I am going out on a limb to give you the respect that you may, or may not deserve," I explained my thoughts as I heard a faint voice coming from the outer premise of the house. "I apologize; I am going to have to leave you alone for a minute or two. There is something I must tend to."

"Take all the time you need. I will brew up some coffee," Dean said convincingly.

My attention was grasped by a whispering voice which led outdoors. My feet stepped out onto the porch as a breeze swept across my face, filling my head with strange suspicions that were not comprehended. Once the destination had been reached the faint whisper ceased. Tina immediately popped into my head. Not once have I seen or heard of her frolicking on Frank's property. My reaction would have been something like that of being betrayed. My horrible habit was to ban people from my life who have lied or kept secrets from me. She did not want to come face to face with my wrath, and kept her secret locked away. Now that the slate was clean, maybe she was there to provide comfort.

My eyes focused upon the oblivious greenery that had shown me so much in my messed-up world. I was not sure how the garden played such a significant part in my life. Maybe it was built over an old cemetery. Frank did not ever let me in on the use of the shrubbery, except for the fact that he shoveled and planted his harms away. Even though Frank never discussed the vegetation, it was apparent that he was keeping secrets. There was something special in the soil. It was sure to find its way to me sooner or later, and the moment of truth seemed to be closing in.

Suzie appeared in my dreams, and she brought the garden with her. It appeared as if she was a part of the blossoming flowers that were within. When she came to me for the first time, the vegetation had a whole new look; it was a blood bath. All the images that I witnessed that dreadful night had to have some significance. Frank floated over the garden, which might have been the image of him reuniting with his daughter. That may be the only reason why I had not seen or heard from either one of them since the dreadful night.

My head turned suddenly, for a commotion coming from the opposite end of the soil took jurisdiction. My body froze, for whatever or whoever was trying to get my attention seemed to be making its way closer and closer. The plants leaned to get out of the way of whatever was coming. A gigantic lump inside of my throat appeared as I waited. It was difficult to understand why there were no deeper thoughts about the garden; it was as if Frank put a spell on me to keep me from digging in the dirt so to speak.

The anticipation for what was coming was too much to handle, and my quivering limbs brought me back to where Dean was last seen.

He flinched as I stormed back into the house and instantly approached him. My knees slammed onto the hard wood floor, and Dean's closest hand was covered by both of mine. We locked gazes.

"I am going to ask you a question and I don't want any lies. It is time that someone is honest with me and that someone seems to be you." My speech was rushed, and my body was trembling. My mind was racing, and my thoughts were uncontrolled. Frank kept a major secret from me, and it was about to surface. The problem was that I wasn't sure if I wanted it to. The courage to ask the dreaded question was disappearing and Dean was noticing the obvious.

"What do you want to ask me?" His question startled me, and I let his hand loose and rushed for the bathroom, locking the door behind me.

The mirror seemed to be glowing and I could not look away. Suzie's face appeared, and her shame and guilt made its way to me. Suddenly, my fist smashed into the glass, shattering her face, and sending my reflection to the floor. The instant pain tried to rescue me from madness; it was not strong enough, and reality was fading. Blood was spurting from the cuts among my knuckles as I reached for a glass shard from the floor. Dean was screaming from the other side of the latched wooden obstruction as I ignored his pleas to be let in. A piece of the broken mirror was digging into my flesh as my hand clenched around it, and then a loud bang brought the world of the sane into the bathroom as Dean broke the door down with a kitchen chair.

With a psychotic expression painted upon my face, the piece of shattered mirror rushed toward my eye and Dean turned super-human as his left leg danced through the air, kicking the deadly object free from my grip. He then grabbed me with all the strength he had left and squeezed the demons from my soul until I went limp and fell to the ground. His next move was to wrap my damaged hand tightly with a cloth from the cabinet. The red liquid quickly soaked into the white cloth, turning it a rusty red color.

Moments later I woke to a throbbing pain in my hand and an old friend face down upon the floor next to me. We were just outside the bathroom, and the mess that lay before us was disturbing. My memory was fuzzy, and the broken door and shattered glass was quite frightening because I had no clue to how any of it came to be. I then realized that Dean was not unconscious, he was wheezing, and his entire body was quivering. We struggled against each other as our intentions were to stand. Once we became upright, I sensed the distress that was being released from Dean's body.

He clutched his chest as a gurgling sound was surfacing from his insides, and he fell backwards taking the coffee table along for the ride. As the hot coffee found its way to my bare skin, I sucked in as much air as possible and bit into my lip. Dean's breath slowly leaked from his dry, cracked lips. With all my strength, I pulled his somber body onto the cushions and rolled him onto his back. My voice shouted his name hoping for some kind of response; there was nothing. His pupils hid in his skull, and his body jerked as he coughed fluids onto my shaky arms. I held his head at an angle to prevent him from choking, and with one last gasp for air, his entire body became silent.

The panic ran rampant, and all that was left to do was scream his name over and over. Another human was dying in front of me and there wasn't an evident way to stop it. He was an innocent and I would never be able to forgive myself if he passed on. Once again, my irrational surroundings had brought harm to another unsuspecting life-form. The tears were launching off my face and making their new home upon the man who only wanted to help. I shook his body and continued screaming in agony, not because of the cuts on my hand or the burns from the steaming liquid of vitality, but from sorrow. What had I done?

The final breath left the old man's oral cavity as my entire body went numb. My heart was beating inside my skull and my throat was growing a tumor. Every action was slow and intensifying as if time itself was coming to a halt. A ringing in my ears began to ignite a woozy sensation and blackness started appearing out of the corner of my eyes. I had one more desperate act before I gave up, and with that notion in mind, my hands rose above my head, the left one clenched into a fist as the right hugged it for dear life. With a quick and powerful thrust, my limbs slammed down onto the dead man's chest. A few obscenities and two more stabs later, it was time to accept the death of a dear old man. Awkwardly straddling my newest victim, my anger erupted and I lashed out by slapping the face of the deceased man I sat upon. As his face turned to one side from the force of the blow he coughed and spat a milky substance on to the floor.

He caught his breath to speak: "Pills in the truck."

I darted out the door, tripping and tumbling down the porch stairs, pulling myself from the dirt, and running to the four by four. I opened the door to the vehicle, and immediately the contents of the glove box, including all sorts of bottles filled with different pills, poured from the compartment onto the floor. Sprinting back to the house with an armful of drugs, it became apparent that we did not have much time since Dean was lying face down on the cold, wood floor. After dropping the plastic containers onto the sofa, my attention went to turning Dean from his stomach to his back. His breath was unsteady, and his eyelids were continuously opening and closing. The outcome was not looking worthy. Fumbling through the bottles, there seemed to be a medication for everything except the heart.

My head rotated side to side vigorously as frustration began to build. I was most certainly not a doctor, and the responsibility of giving him the correct pill was becoming an ordeal. Sweat ran down my brow as I begged for the unresponsive man to give me a clue which tablet was required. Throwing my hands up into the air, it was becoming prominent that failure was approaching. With an awkward glance towards the front door, my heart began to beat once more as a lonely bottle of medication lay in the doorway. With the words, *please be for the heart* repeated over and over inside my head, I made my way to the lone vessel. I read the label as fast as possible, and "acute coronary syndrome" caught my attention. I ripped the top off, destroying the child proof lock as I rushed over to my dear friend.

With a few pills in my hand, I discovered that any liquid that was close had been spilled from earlier events, and there was no time to fetch a replacement. Opening his mouth proved that there was no way the drugs were going down his dry throat without liquid, so I grabbed a piece of broken glass from the floor and tossed it into my mouth to produce as much saliva as possible. I then leaned over Dean, opened his mouth wide, dropped in the pills and spat into his mouth, first removing the shard. Then I slammed his jaw shut and caressed his throat, forcing him to swallow. For a brief moment he fought, but to no avail: his body became limp, and he relaxed. I quickly sprung to my feet and made a mad dash to the kitchen, grabbing a teacup and filling it with water. Returning in an instant, I poured the liquid into his mouth and was thrilled by the choking sounds that he generated. Once the worst of the worst was over, I stared at his chest as it slowly rose and fell. He seemed to be unconscious, but as long as his chest was moving, I was relieved and I would not take my eyes off of him until he asked me to.

After what seemed like decades, Dean's pupils finally made an appearance. He stared at me for a few moments, and then his neck creaked as he observed the mess that was all around us. His vision came back to me, and he tried to produce a smile but failed miserably.

"Looks like a hurricane came through here," he said with a whisper. "Something like that." I returned the banter with a hideous facial expression.

"What's with the wild face?" "I thought you were a goner."

"My mind is a little fuzzy and I am not remembering much. Whatever you did, you did it well."

"That's your opinion," I recited with a sarcastic tone.

"If you don't mind, I would like to rest for a while before we continue our conversation," he told me as he winked to show me he was able.

"Are you serious? Shouldn't I take you to the hospital?"

"Let me rest and we will see what I feel like in a little while," he spoke as his lids shut from weariness.

With a blank daze written upon my face I remained standing over the amazing life. I killed him, then I brought him back. There was no possible way it could have been real. I rubbed my eyes until they burned, and then noticed that the towel that Dean wrapped around my wounded hand had completely changed color. My traumatized body brought me to the bathroom where all the madness began. The floor was covered with broken mirror and blood. It instantly occurred to me that cleaning my wounds there was an unhealthy idea. As I refused to step into the stained room, the shattered portrait of still life caught my attention. There was newspaper behind the reflecting glass, and the date on the paper was very interesting. It was the very next day after Suzie's demise. Frank wasted no time replacing the object that brought sorrow every time he had to look at himself. I didn't blame him one bit.

I decided that the kitchen would be a safer place to clean myself up. I removed the dirty mess of a cloth from my hand and a small pond instantly formed in my palm. Water from the faucet washed the lagoon away, but it only took a few seconds to reform. While glancing around my surroundings searching for a tool to assist with rewrapping the wound, a trivial smile embraced my face when I discovered a roll of duct tape. I quickly applied the adhesive tape to the cuts and waited a few seconds until the throbbing turned into a faint numbness. After taking care of my hand, the next deed was to figure out what to do about the coffee burns. It was not obvious if my brain was in shock or if my pain sensitivity quit working for the time being, nevertheless, I was confused to why the blistering rashes did not ache.

A glimpse of the gorgeous garden caught my eye, and my brain focused on recollections. I've had to view the greenery through that very window at least hundreds of times, but I did not recall the view. It was as if the window was a picture frame, and the garden was a beautiful portrait. Grabbing some cleaning supplies, I scrubbed the window thoroughly. The scene of vegetation did not change. It appeared to be a painting, as if someone or something was determined for me to see the overgrown flowerbed from a different light. The misperception was overbearing, and my head shook vigorously trying to get the image to change. There was a unique presence about the garden, and it was becoming evident that Frank had been holding more secrets. If Frank was hiding something, it must have been horrible for him to keep it to himself. I wanted to explore the outside world, however,

I was not ready to leave Dean by his lonesome, so I moseyed back into the living room to be at his side.

My body was sprawled out amongst the hardwood floor while Dean rested above on the sofa. His breath was music to my ears; it brought a strange sense of security. My brain waves brought me to a world of death. Everywhere I turned, it was knocking at my door. A person in their late twenties should not have to continue to their toes while counting the number of people they "used" to know. The belief that I was being tested was prominent and relentless. A higher power was desperate in their methods to understand exactly how much my feeble mind could handle. It was apparent that life did continue once the body was no longer useful, but to what extent? It didn't matter what became of me when my soul was forced to move on. What mattered was that I continued to fight for those that were important and not let the irrationality or demise of loved ones interfere with what was to be my destiny. Wherever I ended up, I was certain that all my strength would be required to survive, and that was what Frank had strained to teach. It was important that I stayed levelheaded for people such as Dean, an innocent bystander that did not deserve what was happening to him.

I sat up and let all the remembrances of the dead drift away as Dean become the sole proprietor of my attention. It was a fact that the old man on the couch knew more than he was letting on, but I did not have the heart to wake him.

The outside vegetation was pulling me toward it and I was no longer able to resist. The moment to find answers had approached, and even though my mind was filled with fear and hesitation, the next move was to explore the dreaded garden. The wooden steps from the porch screamed out with agony as my feet put pressure upon them. My movements were slow, for hurrying was not my intention. My body turned to face my new destination as my skin became overwhelmed with millions of tiny little bumps. As I gradually closed in on the gate to the orchard, my thoughts drifted, once again, into the past.

A few years prior, when Frank still walked the earth as a human, my mind was captivated by an unknown force. The obscure presence demanded that Frank be found. Once his territory was reached the coward in me made existence as the side of the house became a shelter. There were sounds of shoveling coming from the garden, and my eyes peeked around the rain gutter, discovering Frank hard at work.

"I feel your eyes upon me," said Frank as he continued to throw dirt from one place to another. He did not even glance in my direction. "Come help an old man out."

The gate that blocked the entrance into the realm of beauty and grace was not extravagant, yet it held a form of disgust and uniqueness all its own. In simple terms, it was a four-foot-by-three-foot rectangle frame that was built from old planks of wood. The wood was aged and showed cracks of frustration from the many years spent protecting what was on the other side. The coat of sealant that was applied many moons ago had become weak, and the tears from the sky had protruded, causing permanent damage.

Two large poles stood from the ground on either side of the rectangle box. They were the guardians and supplied support for the frame. The first pole had two hinges that were connected to the wooden box. The very top of the pole was the home of a small statue. The statue was once nothing more than a stone, until some kind stranger had an epiphany of what the dull, regular rock should look like.

The boulder was carefully carved into the image of a small child that held a bullfrog in her petite hands. She was the image of grace and beauty. The girl was leaning over so she could view her newly found friend more appropriately. A Sunday dress covered her petite body, raising itself above her knees as she bent over. Her hands were cupped to form a temporary prison for the amphibian. A petite hat that resembled the makings of straw sat on her head as her gorgeous hair draped down her back. A bow was on the brim of the bonnet, which helped protect her innocent face from the burning rays of the sky. The stone creation was satisfying to look at; whoever created it must have been proud.

Parallel to the pillar that held the beautiful girl stood a similar wooden obstruction. Its job was to hold the frame in place so the wind would not carry it away. A metal latch was screwed into the pillar so the rectangle gate could push its metal pin into it snugly. The two separate pieces came together and clanked loudly to let everyone in close range know that the garden was once again secure. The second wooden pillar was also the home for a stone object; it was not beautiful by any means. It was the spawn of evil; a creature that came straight from the bowels of hell: a miniature troll that filled my body with rage every time my eyes laid upon it.

On top of the beast's head there sat a hat that grew smaller and smaller as it came to an end. The tip of the hat arose to a dull point that overlapped itself from its own weight, causing it to slightly hang over the monster's forehead. The texture of the troll's face was precisely carved to show the effect of old age. His nose was larger than a normal human's nose, and quite frankly, seemed to be leaping from his face. The eyes were sunken into his brittle head to give an image of evil, or that was how I viewed them. A granite beard flowed from his chin, resting itself among the frail body of its owner. There was a shovel in the deviant's hands, it was longer than the troll himself. The spade rested in between his feet and was the tool that kept him standing, for his arms were bent to show the strain of holding himself up. His feet were bare and very detailed, every toe was present. The troll was very frail and should not have been intimidating whatsoever, who in their right mind would be scared of an old brittle man that could barely stand? I was!

The object that held the most mischief was the center of the entrance: the infamous web. It was made of thin, pliable steel that produced the image of a magnificent sight of nature, since any spider that built such a home must have been the size of a bowling ball. Most humans appear to suffer from arachnophobia, so the perfect guard would be a creature of terror. The glorious spider would keep the weak minded from approaching. I poked the web many times as I walked beyond the gate just to remind myself that it was not real. I was not frightened of arachnids but I damn sure would run from one capable of making such a large obstruction. I placed my hand upon the gate and opened my ears to the creaking of the metal soldiers as they warned Frank of my intrusion. Frank was working around the center piece as he lifted his head to observe.

"I was not expecting any visitors today, but I am always glad to see you," he said.

There was a bare patch of soil that lay just beyond the gate that was circular in shape and the diameter was about five feet across. On the left and right side of the circle, there were minor weeds that were known as grass. The grassland also was about five feet wide and sprung out in each direction, stretching around the garden uniting on the other side. It was another barrier that sat just inside the fence. The dirt circle was usually occupied by tools that were not in immediate use; the assumption was that it was a refuge for the extra equipment that Frank would require at some point. On that train of thought, there was a lonely spade placed on the dirt sphere; I reached down and grasped it.

I began my journey towards Frank. Three magnificent rows of vegetation stood in my way. Each row was different than the next, but each individual line consisted of the same plant. The identical pattern repeated itself on the far side of the domain. The center of the garden held a mischievous center piece that was surrounded by warriors made from prickly rose bushes. Thirteen plants were scattered between the mighty lines and around the majestic core of the fertile region.

The first row of vegetation appeared to be stolen from the mighty jungle. A thick root the size of a basketball protruded from the ground, thinning out as at reached for the sky above. The plant resembled a giant, mutant turnip. The strange creation stood at attention, waiting for the orders from their sergeant. Oversized warts surrounded the base of the turnip; each lump produced its own family of leaves. Each obstructed growth grew a leaf about a foot long and was as wide as an average adult hand. As the blade protruded from the root, a quarter-sized spot appeared with a dark, gloomy, red tint, and it continued down the leaf, spreading a trail such as a slug would. Every three to four inches, the dark red stream exploded, creating two shapes on either side that bore the shape of a dragonfly. The unique portraits were black with a pink outline, truly magnificent to the human eye. The bottom of the green archway was covered with a dark red color. Truly the plant was created by an artist. Each individual part of the plant was unique in its own dark demented way, it was a scene of beauty. The leaves stretched out as the wind blew underneath flaying them through the air resembling a hypnotic dance. I would have to say that I saw the leaves dance even when there was no breeze present. Whenever I would comment about it, Frank would immediately tell me to stop doing drugs.

Two feet behind the Amazon illusions stood the second rank of defense; they were the protectors. A tree like branch protruded from the ground revealing the proportions of a young boy. The root was an abnormal twig, which grew a few inches in diameter. The center of the shrub was a home for thousands of smaller branches that stretched from their home for the capability to create their own family. Petite, enticing leaves bloomed from the edges of the siblings. The ornaments grew in flocks surrounding the twigs that created them. The smaller leaves resembled a ladybug, while the larger ones made it to the size of a large beetle. A bright green color covered the bottom of the bush. The color faded as the rays from the sun turned the glorious green into an earthy tone of yellow. The fading gave off a tie-dye effect which was, in actuality, quite easy upon the eyes. The hedge plant may have appeared to be friendly, however, behind each and every glorious leaf there stood an irritated thorn. Each spike waited to devour itself into the flesh of an unsuspecting passerby. More than once I became that unlucky individual. A few steps beyond the ravenous bushes stood the slender, captivating Generals of the crusade, they were similar to a stalk of corn. The plants rose high into the air. A tree-like root, thick and sturdy, grew from the mystical soil, sprouting leaves as it made its way towards the heavens. The foliage spread far and wide, protecting their domain by shielding the sight of intruders. They were grown to intimidate. Through the stalks was the meat of the entree.

In the middle sat a brick well that bore no water, instead it was used as a gigantic flowerpot. It upheld the queen of the fenced in territory. An enormous bulb displayed its uniqueness for all the vegetation to admire.

The egg-shaped creation had three green neighbors that surrounded her space. The security guards cupped the majesty, keeping her safe and intact. The bulb was a sparkling white color that even shined after the great flaming ball in the sky died out. Though the flower did not seem to bloom, I gawked at it every time I visited, waiting for it to explode and show what it was truly made of.

The lady in white had more security than the three large leaves from her sides. Four wonderful spheres of rose bushes surrounded the almighty. Each bush was plucked and pruned, giving the image of splendor. The circle of budding roses that were closest to the woman of desire were splendid as the red from their petals bled into the air above them. A ranting pink tainted the atmosphere from the second row of prickly bushes. The third special unit set the evening on fire with its canary yellow glow. The row farthest from the center piece produced roses that were black: the night made them invisible, a prickly surprise.

Around the queen and her army there were thirteen mischievous characters that were spread all about in no specific pattern. Each was unique in its own way; not one was alike. The sizes all varied, and their shapes were completely incomparable to any other. I did not grasp the true inspiration of the plantation. The truth be told, the garden made me uneasy, and even the beauty could not calm my nerves.

I emerged through the guardians and found myself face to face with Frank. As I drew closer to him, I observed the sky darken as the days' keeper vanished beyond the horizon. As the glowing ball dissipated it produced an orange ray that the entire plot soaked in. I watched as the plantation basked in the disappearing light. It was my first time seeing the sunset from the garden view.

"My face was frozen with that exact expression displayed upon yours the first time I saw the portrait," Frank said, as he smiled at my reaction. "I'm enthused," I commented. "How come during the two years I have known you, not once have we shared this moment?"

Frank flung his tool for digging over the vegetation and onto the clear circle with precise targeting that led onto the fact that it wasn't the first time he attempted that trick. He then approached me, reaching his hand out; I placed my shovel into his empty appendage. He then tossed it in the same manner as the first. The two metal objects collided, introducing a loud clank to the freshly darkened surroundings. Frank retrieved his hand protectors from the bricks that surrounded the main attraction, and carefully made his way towards the gate. I followed closely.

"I've also never seen you replant anything after winter," I proclaimed. "Another observation would be that the precious bulb has not once bloomed."

"I have always known that there was something very special about you, even before I actually met you. Underneath all your immaturity lurks a kind and dangerous soul," Frank declared as he wiped his forehead. "I know there are great things to come from you in the future. I honestly do not believe that you are always naive; I believe that you put on an act to fool the gullible people to leave you be. You have not seen the sun set here because it wasn't ready for you to see. Your mind will let you understand when the time is right; you must have patience and let the answers come to you when your mind is ready to comprehend them."

"You're trying to tell me that my eyes only see what my mind lets them see?"

"Exactly!" he exclaimed. "Let's remove ourselves from the darkness." "What is my subconscious keeping from me?"

"This is why you need to freshen up on your listening skills," Frank demanded. "Don't let the unknown eat at your insides. Focus upon the ideals that you can relate too. The images that are persistent and constantly pounding clues into your head, soaking information into your brain, bringing their animated opera into your dreams, those are the issues you need to ponder on. Everything else will be answered when the time is right." Frank nodded as he soaked into the darkness.

My head shook vigorously, filtering the information from the memory to make room for another. Due to illness, the night was spent upon Frank's sofa. The morning ascended and Frank was found frolicking with the vegetation. His hands were full of dirt and so were his clothes.

"Feeling any better?" He asked.

"I guess," I replied. "I had treacherous dreams involving your garden last night."

With an aggravated tone Frank said, "I think your mind is playing games with you. The garden provides you with curiosity because you tend to think that there is some haunting power beneath the soil. The sanctuary is my domain and therefore my problem, nothing that lies in the dirt has anything to do with you. That is how you should leave it."

"All the sights and sounds that fill my head have no relative connection to me. You of all people should know that. All my problems are based on other people's problems. I apologize for my questions, but I am damn sure you are keeping something from me."

"I find peace and tranquility from the vegetation that I planted. The center piece is important to me, and I take pride in the fact that it casts its beauty across my land. The entire foundation is sentimental. I grow the plants as if they were my family, that way I don't become lost with illusions that I cannot consume. You know as well as I do that forgetting the past is not always the correct thing to do, even when the memories pick at the inside of your skull, desperately trying to escape. We must remember the past and not let the memories fade, for they may contain answers to the future. I do apologize for the fact that I have to keep things from you; I am damn sure that you tend to do the same.

"All I want from you is for you to deal with the situations that present themselves to you. Do not overexpose your mind to ordeals that you do not need to let trouble you," he paused and smiled to comfort my wandering thoughts. "Your mind is full enough with predicaments that you need to answer, once you figure out those particular problems you will be able to allow another insignificant, sad tale to clutter your mind. Until then relax and don't overload your brain."

I had always taken Frank's advice sincerely, even if I did not quite see it the way he had. The life that Frank lived caused him to protect the innocent, and I had the same hindrance because secrets were the only way to keep the irrationality away from others. Both of us were cursed with skeletons in the closet, which could cause harm among an innocent bystanders' life. Neither one of us wanted to cause grief where grief did not belong. There was something strange going on in Frank's playground and he made it perfectly clear that it was not the right time for me to receive answers. The memory dissipated and I found myself standing in front of the great web of mystery.

The old yet proud gate stood between me and the vegetation. A rage burst in my bowels once the menacing troll was caught scowling in my direction. For a second, the sudden anger was subdued, then it came back with full force and provoked me to grab the nearest rock and smash it against the evil little head. As the guardian plummeted to the ground, a hysterical laugh rushed from the pit of my stomach and flew free into the air through my open mouth; *it was not my laugh.* The stone structure tumbled to the soil that it once stood above. With a glance to the other post, I noticed that the girl with the frog had turned her attention towards me; her inanimate eyes stared directly into mine and her small stone head had clearly shifted upward to get a better assessment. I shook my head and chalked it up to hallucinations due to a stressful day and continued on my way.

The very moment that my feet stepped upon the dirt circle my temperament changed. All the rage and anger turned to bliss. There was a slight buzzing sound in my ears that brought a calming sensation to overthrow the fury from my veins. I wondered if the sudden sense of enlightenment was how "normal" people felt most of the time. The moment gave me the ability to view myself through a stranger's eye. Of course, I did not enjoy the results; my life was one of a monster. It was assured that the dirt circle had a greater purpose: it was the circle of tranquility, a place to observe actions and decide if the path chosen was to be prosperous, or proven as a wrong turn.

The great blue ball in the sky produced enough light to help guide the way as I ventured deep into the extravagant greenery. The first row of plants had no defensive tactics, and with a large step, my feet moved over them without any hesitation. The prickly bushes that were next grew larger as I enclosed on their territory. There was some blood, but I made it through in one piece sliding right by the stalks as if my body became invisible.

My limbs moved on their own beckoning call, it was as if my mind shut down and instincts acquired jurisdiction. There was no thought of where to go; directives came naturally. Approaching the centerpiece, it became difficult not to notice that the magnificent bulb was standing straight up as if it was saluting my presence. I glared at the marvel as all the confidence built up from the dirt sphere left in an instant, and my knees plunged into the soil as my frame began to shudder.

The calm, surreal night dramatically changed as clouds covered the circle of light in the sky and even though there was no rain the dirt turned into a muddy mess as my appendages were sucked in. The rose bushes came to life right before my eyes, and each and every bud that rested upon the prickly sticks began to bloom and then wither and fall to the ground. The scene seemed to be on a never-ending loop as the withered petals started to pile up on the moist dirt. The queen shifted so that the top of her fabulous structure faced my quivering innards. The moonlight became so prominent that it forced its rays through the clouds and seemed to burn my flesh. Dizziness presented itself and I lost my balance as gravity pulled me back into the soil. The newly formed quicksand started to swallow my entire figure as my eyelids shut tight. My brain was growing and pounded on the inside of my skull.

The constant struggling was only making the situation worse, and it was becoming apparent that the garden may not have been such a peaceful place after all. The soil was angry and was extracting my fear. The less I moved, the less my body entwined with the ground. It was obvious that the dirt was feeding off my emotions and it was necessary to keep pleasantries in my mind and not let the darkness of the evening complete its hunt. Then out of nowhere a voice rang out through the still air. Over and over again it disclosed that it was aware of my presence.

Refusing to acknowledge the strange vocal tone, the thought of peace was destroyed and panic reclaimed its prize as I jerked crazily, trying to bust free of the muddy trench. Of course, my convulsions only worsened the matter. I couldn't stop the terror from enticing me. The words *I know you are there* echoed inside my head, driving me to the brink of absurdity, and then it all ceased.

The voice was gone, the clouds disappeared, the ground let loose its grip, and I pulled myself up onto my feet. The stars were bright and marvelous. The silence inside my head was a pleasure to be had, and the painful pounding had vanished. The plantation looked normal, and immediately I wondered what was coming; it must have been the eye of the storm. The smartest move was to escape the garden, store my distress for later, and ponder on the events that just took place. I retreated to check on Dean.

The bare dirt circle was in my sight when a gentle breeze caressed my physique. The ground below softened, and once my feet were buried past the ankles, it turned to cement. It was different than before. Earlier, it was as if I was slowly being eaten by the tainted dirt, however, the second time was more like a restraint. Someone did not want me to leave.

"Help me," echoed throughout the greenery, and I recognized the tone from earlier. There was no anxiety, and my thoughts went out to the dear soul who was in trouble. It occurred to me that the woman's voice was most definitely the property of one who was no longer a part of society. Her vocal tone was not familiar, and that led me to believe that she more had likely walked the earth before my days of living. She was desperate and had to have some sort of connection to my realm. I decided that it was time to suck it up and be a man, so to speak.

Bending over, I clenched my right foot with both hands and I pulled with all my might. After a few moments of grunts and curses, the soil cracked as my foot shot out to safety. The left foot broke loose from the force of the rest of my body falling backwards and I immediately hopped to my feet and made a mad dash for the center piece. It seemed that the middle was where the most action occurred. I stretched my trembling hand to touch the enormous fixture of nature and waited for the massive bulb to open and tear my arm from its socket. It was like a Venus fly trap, and I was a gigantic fly to prey upon. The back of my hand gently rubbed across the petals, it was soft and silky, and a slight smile appeared on my face. The queen was a giant pillow for the outside world. I wanted to rest my head and dream all the pain away. Then from out of nowhere a warm, gentle breeze landed on the back of my neck. A million tiny bumps exploded on my skin, and I shivered, not because I was cold.

"Dean?" I questioned out loud.

"Are you here to help?" a voice replied, and it was not Dean's.

"I am uncertain to what you need help with," I told the dead woman who was standing directly behind me. My body did not move.

"Will you not face me because you are frightened?"

I swallowed the large frog that settled in my throat. "I'm not sure what I am." A few seconds succumbed and she did not comment.

"Did you leave me?" I asked when her breath was no longer felt upon my skin. My body turned to face her, and it was discovered that she was gone. Then out of nowhere a large gust of wind appeared, rotating me back towards the amazing bulb.

"No!" exclaimed the woman as she suddenly appeared in front of me. The incredible image was startling and sent my bare flesh on a journey through the aggravated rose bushes. As I lay in the dirt, bleeding, the thirteen random scattered plants came to life. They were drastically trying to grab my attention.

"Can you free me?" The woman beckoned as she appeared hovering directly overhead.

"Free you from what?" I screamed at her.

"I am trapped," she added. I made eye contact with the spiritual woman. "You are not welcome here. You must leave."

"First you beg for my assistance, now you demand that I leave. I am quite confused," I commented as I discovered that the thirteen individual plants were warning me, not the woman.

"You are not welcome," they chanted over and over and over. My tiny human brain could not take it any longer. My head was about to explode! Millions of voices screamed inside my skull telling me I was not welcome. The breath of many souls blowing over my body was felt. The radiant woman was the only visible spirit, nevertheless, it was certain that there were many more in the area and they were not friendly.

"Run!" The woman shouted.

I ran and dashed through the army of vegetation, diving onto the empty circle of salvation. Turning to face the chaos, I found utter mayhem. The woman was no longer in sight and the plant life was mad with rage, flaying and moving and almost pulling their roots from the ground. My eyes shut and my palms rubbed vigorously, hoping when they opened, the scene would be passive. My lids snapped open, and the view remained to be something from a nightmare. Then a realization made itself clear in my head.

Frank said that the centerpiece was special to him. He said he treated it like family; it was sentimental. Family was the word that was sure to be a clue. What could that have meant? Frank also told me that answers will come to me when the time was right; the time was pretty ripe. The realization was clear.

I sprang to my feet and bulldozed my way through the green to come, again, face to face with the most important flower. I ripped each and every rose bush from the ground with my bare hands. In a moment of irrationality, I spread my arms from my body and let the blood trickle to the dirt. The red disappeared into the soil, as if it never existed. My knees protruded into the ground and my wounded claws were used to throw the moist soil from underneath the brick well.

"Terry!" shouted someone in the distance. I ignored the sound and commenced shoveling.

"Terry," said Dean as I saw him approach. "What in the hell are you doing?" I stood and faced him.

"Tell me what is under the bricks."

"I think we should go back to the house," Dean suggested as he tried to grab hold of my shoulder.

With one frantic action, I shoved his body from mine and screamed, "Tell me what you know!"

"You're freaking me out," Dean said as I could see him tremble. I was covered with mud and blood; I was frantically throwing dirt from the ground like a crazed beast; my mind was lost. Dean grabbed me with both arms and dragged me to the circle of trust without a fight.

"What is going on?" he asked with a confused look portrayed upon his face.

I stood shaking and pointing at the garden, "That…I believe is a burial ground." I waved my pointing finger in the air and kept nodding my head like crazy. "Frank's wife," I paused for a moment. "She is in there. You know, I know you know!" I lashed out and stormed around Dean, heading towards the tool shed in a furry. There was a lock on the shed door, so I kicked the damn door down, grabbed a shovel and scrambled back to the scene of torment. The gate held another unexpected situation. Dean stood between me and the entrance to my insanity. There was a shotgun resting in his quivering palms as he raised the barrels to my forehead.

"You need to calm down," he commented.

"You gonna shoot me?" I asked. A silly question. My mind exploded with thoughts of betrayal; Dean was a stranger and could be the cause for what was taking place. The digging tool slid through my fingers and bounced off the ground below. "If you want me to calm down, you better pull that damn trigger."

The gun fell to the ground as Dean swung his arms around me. He was sobbing hysterically; he tried to speak, but he was far too upset to conjure up actual words.

"I can see you're scared, old man. I do not wish for you to die in my arms. We both need to relax; you have had a rough day thus far," I spoke and tried to comfort the confused man. "Something is terribly wrong with the garden. I feel as if I am someone's puppet, and they are completely screwing with me. There is a strange woman that keeps begging me for help, but who is going to help me… who is going to help me!?"

"I will help you," Dean responded.

"Who the hell are you?" I demanded. "I don't know anything about you; you could be the reason for all this nonsense."

"I hope you really don't feel that way," he commented. "I think we both need to relax and talk. I am not here to hurt you in any way. I am here for a friend of a friend, and I am also quite curious of your life. I only wanted to hear it from your lips and not actually see it, however, I will do whatever it takes to keep us both safe."

We ventured back to the porch to try and answer the questions that were racing inside both of our heads. I spent a great deal of time on the porch. It was an excellent place to talk and figure things out. It was the first time that Frank would not be a part of the equation, which brought sadness.

"Frank's wife is buried under the glorious flower," I thought out loud. "Yes," Dean said in return. "She obviously has found a way to reach out to you."

"My entire life is filled with this bullshit: the dead finding me to help them through some situation. I'm tired of not knowing anything until the time is right. I am a pawn, and I do not control my life, someone else does that for me, and apparently that person is dead. One thing that puzzles me is: why now? I have been here hundreds of times; how come I have never felt anything before? I was pulled to the garden, when I laid you on the couch, I had a strong desire to go outside, some force pulled me out here. Not once when Frank was alive did I feel anything like what I am feeling now."

"Could it be possible that Frank blocked the sensations from reaching you?"

"I don't know how he could have hidden such a strong sensation from me, but what do I know?"

"I think you know a lot more then you give yourself credit for."

"Are there other bodies buried out there?" I questioned, changing the subject to something more important.

"Frank lived a secret life, as you seem to do. Having to hide information makes one's life seem quite lonely. Loneliness can lead to friendships that may not be compatible however, they fill the void for the time being," Dean explained in his own awkward way.

"Do you have a point to your ranting?" I asked as my eyes rolled out of sight and then quickly returned.

"He found himself being loyal to a man that did not deserve that kind of friendship. He had discovered that his friend was not such a great person. In actuality, he was a son-of-a-bitch!" Dean exclaimed.

"I am following the situation one hundred percent and I do not like where the story is headed."

"Do I need to draw you a picture?" I knew exactly what he was getting at, I just didn't want to accept the fact that Frank could be so naïve. "Just answer me this, does any other unlucky mortal besides the wife and the so-called friend dwell underneath that soil?" I demanded as I pointed towards the garden.

The world of the undead was a festering cesspool of complications. It had been discovered that souls could be trapped in segments of space that were referred to as realms. The two obvious realms would be the living and the dead. I believed that there were a countless number of realms and very few ways to cross from one to another. Through my naive years, I had become certain that some areas provide more action from supernatural effects than others. The surroundings that fluctuated energy was usually a place of someone's death. That was not always so, but most often it was the case.

That was what gave me the idea that once a person died, they would still have a connection to their rotting corpse. It would not be in a physical way, it would be through the spirit or soul. Someone who stopped breathing may become disoriented and take the forbidden trail that leads them to an unknown realm. A spirit that enters the zone couldn't leave the same way that they came. It was the standard story of vengeance and pain. The soul must do whatever possible to escape no matter how long it may take. Also, a soul may be sent to a frozen realm, referring to any realm that contains a spirit against their will. If an individual was sent to a holding zone, they were more than likely to be ticked off, so they became the haunting, scary ghost of a house or unoccupied land. Everyone has heard a story or two. Even more have seen something out of the ordinary, but they always seem to have an explanation or bury the memory deep inside to haunt them for the rest of their lives.

The trapped spirit would be held forever within the range of their decaying body. If the corpse was properly bound, then the ghost would not be allowed to communicate with the living. Once a soul had been secured, it was trapped in the frozen world until their body was released from its jail. Most exits to a realm were placed among the living. It was a cruel joke formed in the mind of the great creator of the universe. That was precisely where I, and anyone that was similar to me, came into play. I found spirits wanting things, but what they wanted was beyond me.

Frank's mischievous friend was definitely a creature that was stranded in a frozen realm. When a corpse was the provider of a dirty spirit, it tainted all of its surroundings and made every realm in that atmosphere dirty. If Frank's wife, a wholesome spirit, was buried amongst the same quarters as a tainted soul, her realm would become worse than the thought of hell. The wife must be put to bed in a more pleasant environment if she was ever to find tranquility.

"Are you certain that you do not know the information that you're asking about?" Dean reacted to my earlier question.

As I felt Dean's piercing stare, I began to realize the obvious: "There would be thirteen other bodies buried among the dirt."

"How did you arrive at that conclusion?" Dean wondered out loud. "Thirteen plants surround the center piece, each unique and having a different personality. Once I rationalize the situation it seems to make perfect sense. What I do not understand is why Frank would surround his love with such evil! I hope you agree that it is of great importance that we remove the woman from the damned."

"There is something else that I must tell you," he commented as he stood and took a few steps away from me. "Frank and his daughter Suzie also reside in the garden."

"What!" I exclaimed as I leapt from the porch and pounced towards Dean. My sudden movement made Dean back even farther away from me; his terror poured from his organs of sight. He was thinking about where he left his gun. The old gentleman did not know me. He did not know what I was capable of. He had learned the hard way that I was a recluse. He had the displeasure of watching me lose my mind a few minutes earlier, then he drops the bombshell about Frank and Suzie, he must have thought I was going to kill him.

Dean was a man possessed with courage and honor. His heart was forced into taking an unwanted nap, he was pressured into holding a deadly weapon directed at my head, he witnessed all sorts of craziness, and he was just told that he was to be a part of digging up the dead. There was not one other human in the world I was aware of that would have put up with any of those scenarios. He was a true friend to Frank and that was why he stood before me: to honor his dead pal.

It was difficult to comprehend the reasoning that Frank had to bury his wife and daughter with the likes of beasts; another tale that I would be looking forward to. It was now obvious why the sweet Suzie showed herself to me in a bloody garden. The blood represented the horror that she faced while the garden was her very own prison.

"I have an extremely difficult job ahead of me; I can only hope that I may borrow your truck and your hands," I remarked to Dean.

He nodded his head with acceptance. He was fully aware of what had to be done, and we both recognized the difficulty that lay before us. For the moment, we stood in silence to let our temperaments cool from all the drama that we acquired from the last few hours. I wanted to shout at Dean for burying Frank in the decaying land of filth, but he did not know any better.

CHAPTER EIGHT

With complete and utter reluctance, Dean and I foraged for the tools needed to deploy the relentless task that crept onto our list of things to do. We stole some shovels from the shed and sauntered toward the gate. I was ridden with sadness, for I was, once again, going to be face to face with the man I adored. The only setback was the fact that he was no longer a part of his body.

When we arrived at the entrance, I noticed that the mischievous troll had returned to its perch on top of the pole. My head shook with disgust and I raised the spade in my hands over my shoulder. Dean quickly jumped out of the way as I swung with all my might using my confused emotions as a source of power. Dean followed my lead and swung in between each one of my turns. We used the shovels like a dull ax and slowly chipped away the wood from the pillar; we were consistent upon our task. We kept chopping until the wooden pillar began to sway. I motioned Dean to back away and hurled all my pain into the gigantic sliver; I shouted "timber" as the beast fell to the ground and then proceeded to smash the stone creature until my mind felt clear. The sound from metal banging on stone echoed throughout the night. The old man next to me decided that the troll did not receive enough torture. He leapt from the ground screeching out all of his frustrations. He landed on top of the designated punching bag and continued jumping up and down until his weak legs could no longer lift his body into the air.

After all the commotion, we moseyed through the gate and found ourselves standing on the circle of bare earth. I sat myself down, crossed my legs, and began an attempt to assess the situation. My new friend plopped down across from me, and we sat in silence for a few minutes. I was not sure what was running through his head, but whatever it may have been, it was making it difficult for him to control the rhythm of his breathing. I hoped that he would be able to finish the journey.

Once I felt at ease, I broke the silence: "do you know anything about the sphere that we're sitting in?"

"Not entirely," he answered, "I have seen Frank sit here many times. Every time he seemed lost and spacey, he appeared to be having a bad day and the circle seemed to comfort him. Kind of like the two of us right now."

"I find it flattering that Frank and I have some of the same characteristics. It helps me get through the day knowing that there is some of Frank with me at all times, or at least in my thoughts," I commented randomly. "We should continue."

"Do you want to know why Frank is here?" Dean asked as we gathered our belongings from the dirt.

"Later, we will have plenty of time to chat," I responded as we slowly marched through the vegetation, neither one of us were looking forward to the task at hand. "Is there anyone directly underneath the well?"

"I am not positive; I believe the woman and the girl are," he answered with information I did not want to hear. "At least we don't have to worry about the rose bushes," he laughed as he made a joke about my earlier tantrum. I chuckled as I made my way back to the shed to find a more appropriate tool to bring down the shrine. On my way back from the shed, I saw Dean had returned to the empty circle.

"It's creepy in there," he quoted as he slid himself behind me.

We arrived at the stone well, and I signaled Dean to stand clear. Unenthusiastically, I swung the sledgehammer that I retrieved from the shed against the brick molding, but it did not cause any damage. I took a deep breath and raised the oversized hammer over my shoulder and channeled every bit of rage and confusion that festered inside as the forbidden object was struck over and over again. I became relentless and ignored the blood and pain that radiated from my ungloved hands; there was very little of the duct tape left among my flesh. The brick fortress began to give, and small cracks appeared spreading among its foundation. Dean held out his hand to replace me after he saw the skin ripping from my palm.

As Dean swung away, I noticed that the rest of the shrubbery was springing to life. The gravestones for the misfortunate souls that were buried below swayed back and forth in a hypnotizing fashion. The sound of my name was being chanted from their eerie leaves. After a few moments of their mocking, my rage level exploded, and I pounced on each individual plant and uprooted the thirteen little bastards. Dean pounded on the bricks, ignoring my outburst; he was focused upon the duty, for the sooner he finished, the sooner he would be able to get the hell out of the unholy surroundings.

The air became quiet, and I noticed that Dean had finished with the cement bars, and seconds later, we were working together. I flung dirt erratically, and the soil screamed each time I drove the spade deep into it. Dean's sudden shrugs were acknowledgements that he also heard the intense screeches. My muscles were aching, and my movements slowed down as the garden tool found the treasure with a thump. My attention shifted towards Dean as the same noise rose out of his hole. He was a mere couple of feet away. We nodded at each other and then simultaneously dropped to our knees and moved the dirt from the boxes as if we were two excited dogs playing in the yard. Dean then jumped into my rut and together we brought the box onto high ground. We then did the same for his side. We stared at the wooden obstructions with amusement in our eyes.

"Where is the third?" I asked with urgency, for we had to go, the grounds were becoming less safe by the minute. He pointed to bare ground, and we rapidly started digging. With the strength of two men, we quickly revealed the third carton. We removed it from the hole and immediately ran it to the sacred circle. Then we grabbed another box, and brought it to the bare sphere. As we scurried for the third coffin, I found myself being sucked into the earth once again. By the grunting sounds coming from Dean, I presumed that he was facing the same difficulty. Seconds before I destroyed the brick pot, I carefully removed the white beauty and rested her safely upon the ground. My eyes embraced the queen herself as she began to wither and turn to a coal-like substance. The dirt then swallowed the remains; it then became evident that we had overstayed our welcome.

"We must break free!" I shouted as I struggled to loosen my feet, and left my sneakers for the soil to consume as sturdy ground was sought out.

"Go without me," Dean stated.

"Don't be a fool old man," I responded, "leave your shoes and come with me." We scampered to the last box, each of us grabbed an end and we headed to where the other two boxes sat when an awfully familiar voice rose to the sounds of us scampering. I was flushed with surprise when Dean asked if I was aware of a man standing behind me. We came to an instant halt and the wood dropped from my hands and slammed onto the dirt.

"Your timing is impeccable," I said to the man that stood behind me. "By the looks of things, I can see that I am not the only one that you've pissed off," Jay laughed. "You causing some problems around here?" "Why are you here?" I asked angrily.

"Oh, the mighty, mighty Terry does not know everything." I glanced over at Dean and realized that he was shaking uncontrollably.

"Dean you must get out of here."

"Where do I go? You're going to need me," he said.

"This is not your fight; you must go, see if you can find some shoes inside," I told the old gentleman. I was severely confused about Dean being able to see Jay and was concerned for his safety.

"I think you're in over your head," Jay taunted.

"Nobody cares about what you think. What is your business here?" I asked. I was now quite intrigued to hear the answer. For some odd reason, Jay had always been able to find me at the garden, and it was time to find out why.

"The infamous Frank sure kept a lot of secrets," he responded. "Frank and I go way back; I have spent most of my days trying to get my revenge. You will not stop me from getting what I deserve."

"And what exactly do you deserve?"

"I deserve recognition for my doings and to be set free from the hell that surrounds me!" he exclaimed. "You will not deny me the right for revenge. I will not let you walk from here."

"Recognition, you have to be kidding me," I reacted impolitely. "Why would you want anyone to know about your dirty deeds?"

"You do not grasp the concept of my so-called dirty deeds," he remarked. "There are two sides to every story."

"I have witnessed your feats personally and there are no sides that make you look good. I am leaving here with the three innocent bodies whether you like it or not. I know that you cannot physically harm me, or you would have years ago."

"I may be barred from you, but I have friends in this realm who are not," he enlightened me with new information.

"Who would that be?" I asked as my eyes gazed around the darkened area.

"My father," he answered calmly.

"Your what?" I questioned with complete surprise riding my voice. "Frank and my father were best friends until one day, my dad disappeared," he vanished and wound up behind me. I turned towards his direction. I completely blocked out my surroundings and all of my attention stood waiting for the climax of the story.

"I went to Frank for help and comfort; he shunned me and pretended as if I was a stranger," he paused for a brief moment. "My mother spoke of tension between Frank and her husband, which led me to do some research. I discovered that the last place my father was spotted was here."

"So? That really doesn't prove anything."

"He never left these grounds. As a living person, I dragged myself through each day, bearing the burden of not knowing what happened to my father. Each and every miserable hour pulled on my heart as it passed me by. I went to a friend for support and he shut me out. He was the one that caused my grief. He was the one who pained me!" Jay screamed out with torment. "The day I became a prisoner of the after world, I was taught the truth. Frank murdered my father and buried him here in this garden. He kept the proof close to him and his entire family. That was his biggest mistake."

"I do not understand why Frank would have buried his family next to yours; I do not know why he had to do away with your father. I do know that he must have had a good reason, or he wouldn't have done it."

"There is no good reason! He is now trapped in the very same prison that he created. His plan backfired, and now he is ours to toy with. You will not deprive me of that joy," Jay demanded with authority. "My father is the master here and he has twelve loyal inmates. So I would have to say that your chances of survival are slim."

I panicked, grabbed one end of the coffin, and ran dragging the box as if it was nothing more than a sack of potatoes. The plants I uprooted had come back to life, and their leaves sliced into my flesh. I was sick and tired of the magical garden. The lengthy generals crouched together to form a wall. The crate was again introduced to the ground and the sledgehammer was fetched; I swung with an almighty force behind me. The gigantic weeds grew closer to the ground as they screamed in agony. I chopped through the bushes and stomped on the Amazon children creating a path. Dean was observing from the circle and ran over to help with the final package. We maneuvered back to the other wooden crates and plunged into a fetal position. We were both desperately trying to calm our breathing patterns.

"At least we're safe here," Dean commented.

I pulled myself closer to him and with my hands openly cupped around my mouth I whispered, "I don't believe that to be entirely true."

"Why you say that?" Dean asked as he showed aggravation with his facial expression.

"This sacred circle," I spoke as I stood up, "is nothing more than an illusion. It is a place to seek false security."

"Explain," said Dean.

"You believe that the circle provides you safety, therefore, when you lay in the circle, your confidence level raises. Everything in life has to do with confidence. If a person believes that they can do a certain task, with practice they prove to themselves that they are able. If an individual believes that they cannot complete a task, they will never achieve victory." Dean stared at me with a puzzled expression and said, "I don't get it." "When you think you are safe, you do not act afraid, therefore the spirits can sense that in you and think that you know something they don't. In most situations they will leave you be, however, this situation is unlike others. Jay knows my weaknesses and he also knows that I am not untouchable when in the circle, so he will definitely spread that information on to the thirteen ghosts that are not bound from me. In simple terms we are not out of danger."

"So, you are telling me that they can sense my fear?"

"Yes, fear is our worst trait. We do not act normal or cautiously when we are afraid. Most cases we panic and do not act in a positive manner, therefore we become weak. Anyone or anything can tell when we are feeble."

"Intimidation," he said.

"Exactly," I replied. "Get to your truck and back it up here, we must leave quickly." There was plenty of worrying going on by my part. Was his heart strong enough to endure? Was his spirit up to the challenge? Would he betray me further down the road? They were all questions that ran through my cluttered mind.

"Can we come back in the morning?" Dean asked.

"We can never return to this place, it will never be safe for us. We have started a war with the dead. They will not forgive and forget," I told him news that he did not want to hear. "Go, now!" I listened to Deans footsteps disappear into the night and rested my body between two of the crates. Inside the wooden boxes were the remains of my best friend and his family. That thought alone was enough to make every hair on my skin stand at attention. It was an eerie experience; I would not recover completely.

As Dean fetched his vehicle, I waited patiently, ignoring all the sounds coming from the garden, when a loud popping noise refused to be overlooked. As I lifted my head to observe the sudden racket, a hard, wooden object smashed the top of my skull. A quick movement brought me to my feet, and a glance around showed that one of the crates was missing the top. My body bent over the open casket, and I stood face to face with a small skeleton. My thoughts ran rampant inside my head; I felt pity for the young soul. We were unable to know each other during her short period of walking the earth, and that saddened me. The grief brought tears to launch from my cheek onto Suzie's corpse.

"Certain tragedies cannot be avoided," a whisper spread through the night air. I looked up and discovered that Jay had returned.

"Now you're capable of reading my thoughts?" I asked.

"I have many abilities that you are not aware of," he answered. "You can't blame yourself for every tragedy that crosses your path."

"What concern could you possibly have for my well-being?"

"If you can remember correctly, you would recollect that it was you who had a drawback with me. I was not upset with you," he reminded me. "There was nothing you could have done to save the girl, yet you blame yourself. You must be a savior or something."

"I don't believe that I can save anyone, I just can't sit by and not try."

Jay drew closer to me and said, "You should give some thought about your own well-being."

"I don't care what you think." He leaned over the corpse of the young girl.

"You are not a savior; you are a boy destined to find himself," he said. I found the true wisdom of his words. I was desperately searching for who I was as a human being. It was difficult to understand myself when my brain rented out sections to the dearly departed. Jay was right: I was no savior.

Removing my attention from Jay, I shifted back to concentrate upon the poor remains of a helpless little angel. As my thoughts were scrambling to make sense of the moment, her bones began to rattle. With a quick glance to where Jay stood, I discovered that he had gone. There was a loud sound of wind gushing by. My lips quivered as shouts for Dean excelled amidst them.

"He can't hear you," suggested a voice from the darkness. My ears heard more commotion coming from the opened crate when Suzie's skeleton came to life with a crack, and the top half of her frame lifted out of the box. Without any thought, my fingers crunched into a fist and slammed into the little girl's skull; immediately my knuckles began to throb. Then I grabbed the missing lid, and slammed it into her ribs over and over until she fell back into the wooden crate. Once she was back in the box, I reattached the lid and held it in place with the weight of my body. Once again, my voice roared through the night air trying to reach Dean.

"I told you he can't hear you," the voice returned.

"What did you do?" I asked the darkness when the sound of an engine grew closer and closer. Two gorgeous headlights appeared, lighting a trail through the darkness. The means of transportation then turned violently, almost tipping over as the bright white lights were replaced by two slender, red ones. The metal savior proceeded in my direction, crashing through what remained of the gate. Dean leapt from the vehicle and ran to the coffins, screaming for my help. He grabbed one end of a crate as I lifted the other; we hurled it onto the bed of the truck. As we slid the package to the rear of the bed, an ear-piercing screech ambushed the night air; it was a miracle that my head did not smash against the topper.

"It's not going to be that easy," Jay snickered from deep inside the garden.

"I am uncertain to who you are, but you may shut the hell up!" Dean angrily answered as we managed to get the second wooden creation to freedom. We scrambled for the third and were astonished to find it missing. "You got to be kidding me," I said aloud. "Where is it?" Dean pointed towards the area that we dug them from. I could barely see the shape of the box. It had somehow returned to where it came from. I hurried into the motor vehicle; Dean quickly realized my objective and darted to the center of madness. Maneuvering the stick into reverse and revving the beast as the brake was released, brought the vehicle to the middle of the chaos in a quick fashion. I leapt from the four-wheeled beast and dashed over to Dean; we placed the coffin with the other two and sighed with relief, for we accomplished part of our goal, but nevertheless, the night would be long. Dean scurried for the driver's side as I quickly made my way towards the other door where Jay stood grinning suspiciously. He had an army with him; I assumed there to be thirteen.

"Come on Terry!" Dean expressed from inside the truck.

"You have to leave the garden, I will meet you by the house," I replied. He drove away and left me to battle with a group of dead murderers. I faced the army; Jay stood before me baring a cryptic smile. The rage was seeping from my ears; my heart was pumping anger directly to my brain. I held my arms out as if to fly away.

"I am here for the taking. Do what you must to me, but also understand that I am not the cause of your pain."

"Yes, you are!" Jay exploded, as his form engaged my private space. "You are the source of life that interferes with the dead; you are the menace that knows no boundaries, and you need to be stopped. Release the prisoners immediately, or I will stop playing with you."

"I will do no such thing," I retorted. I felt an unusual sense of stability, as if someone was with me.

"Your friend will do you no good. I will bring you into my world," he threatened.

I peered through the night air to discover that Jay was correct; there was a friend. Deep inside my heart, I yearned for it to be Frank, but instead, it was the mysterious garden queen. I smiled and nodded; she returned the gesture.

"I appreciate you coming to me, however, I must insist that you let me fight this battle alone. You have been tortured for far too long, and it is time to set you free," I preached to the wife of my mentor. She vanished as fast as she appeared. "Okay, I am alone," I taunted Jay. "Do what you will for I no longer care for my well-being."

"You are a threat because you don't ever think about your own well-being. That is the loyalty that I felt in you the first day we met. You would have done anything for me, up until the very day you destroyed me."

"I am trying to rescue three innocent souls from a realm that they do not belong. I am no threat to you."

"Innocent to the naive," he bantered.

"What your father and Frank had between them was not my fault. I don't know the story and truthfully, I don't care!" I raised my voice aggressively. "I knew Frank as a caring, decent man who would not harm another living being unless that is what was necessary. He did what had to be done to better the lives of the people your father surrounded, and more than likely tormented."

"You have much to learn," he laughed as his soldiers walked through him and drew closer and closer to me. I fell to my knees and let out a screeching howl that tore my throat as it flew to freedom. Pressure increased upon my body and began to crush my bones. My mind pondered on Dean's safety. I hoped that he had enough common sense to leave this forsaken land without one glance back. The dirt felt cold and hostile as my face plummeted into it. My skin grew tighter and tighter; the pain was overwhelming. Warm liquid ran down my cheek and nestled among the soil. I was more than confident that it was not saliva. My depressing life sauntered before my eyes as everything turned black.

My eye lids opened to a surreal scene. I was in the cab of Dean's truck, and a comforting smile sat upon his face.

"It's nice of you to rejoin the world of the living," he commented. "I heard your scream; I have heard that scream before. That bellow screeched from the depth of Frank's bowels a long time ago. That was most definitely the sound of a broken-hearted individual who had given up entirely. Just as I rescued Frank from his time of weakness, I am privileged to do the same for you."

"I guess I owe you one," I responded.

"Let's call it even," he commented. "Once I heard your agony, I rushed back and found you face first in the dirt; you were convulsing tremendously. I flipped you over and observed a river of blood running from each eye socket."

"Did you see anyone?"

"No," he answered, "I definitely felt the presence of something, so I quickly threw you into the passenger's side and climbed over you, for I was too afraid to run around my vehicle. Once in the driver's seat, I ripped out of there and here we are," he finished his story of bravery.

"I commend you on your performance and give you my gratitude. I hope that your heart will make it through the rest of our journey."

"I'm surprised that it's still beating. I think I will be fine," he said with a laugh to ease the tension. "If I know anything about you, I know that you are not a boring person to be around."

"We need to verify that we have the correct three bodies," I informed my new hero, "and then we get out of here!"

We released ourselves from the metal beast and moseyed to the coffins. As I began to walk, it became evident that my muscles were sore and weak from earlier events and I fell, again face first into the unforgiving ground. Dean asked if everything was all right, and I responded with an affirmative. I lifted myself and glared at the garden, which was about fifty yards away. The darkness made it hard to see, however, there was a picture of the horrifying vegetation forever burnt into my brain. I joined Dean on the bed of the four-wheeled savior and noticed that he had already removed the lids; he was wasting no time. We sat towering over three unfortunate bodies; the girl and the wife were easily identified by the disintegrating clothes. For Frank, we needed to be certain. Even though Dean was supposedly the one who buried him, we still had to make sure Jay didn't pull a switch.

"Any clue what to look for?" I inquired

"I left his watch on his wrist," Dean answered.

The first time Frank and I met, I noticed the watch; it was gold and had four diamonds that stood above the twelve, three, six, and nine. He was never seen without it; I presumed it to be a gift from his wife. With a twist of the skeleton's wrist, a sparkle filled the air as the watch showed how stunning it could be. I was relieved and let out a sigh; Dean followed my lead. We then covered the bones and returned to the cab.

"Get us out of here," I beckoned. "We have a long trip ahead of us, and when we finish, the family will be safe." Dean nodded, and we drove from the newly formed disaster site. I rested my head upon the window and let my eyelids touch each other. It was time to close out the entire world and drift into nothingness. The thought of the cargo we carried brought my mind into a delusional state. We had dug up the remains of my best friend and his family, and my emotions were riding an unstoppable roller coaster.

"Where do I turn?" Dean questioned.

"Take the next left and follow that road for a couple of hours," I responded, "I hope you have time for this."

"I don't have much of a life anymore," he said as he repositioned his creaking bones. "Since Frank left this world, I have been quite alone."

"That is hard on my ears," I said sympathetically.

"I guess for the past few years, I have felt the way you feel every day."
"Loneliness comes and goes."

He turned his head toward me and gave me a look like nothing I had ever seen. I could not judge it to be pity or intrigue; nevertheless it was a soothing expression.

"Where exactly are we headed?" the tired old man beckoned.

"To a patch of land that holds much of my life. It is a place of peace and serenity. I discovered it many years ago, and to this day, I have kept its secret. I trust in you to do the same."

"So far you have shown me things I never thought I would see, or more importantly, I never thought I would believe," he snickered. "I will never tell another soul, living or dead." He gave me his word, and that I would take to heart. Loyalty could make a human feel power, for when an act of faith was created, an incredible force would impeach the aura of the trustworthy person and pride would consume the human's mind. Pride was an excellent source of confidence and confidence led to a natural high.

It was apparent that Dean was swerving.

"You must drive straight, for if we were to get pulled over, we would be in a great deal of trouble." He straightened out and agreed with my way of thinking. It had been a few years since my last visit to my personal graveyard; I tried to pay my respects at least once a year, but unfortunately, sometimes my overloaded brain could not handle the pressure.

CHAPTER NINE

There were no certainties that my plan was going to provide the results that I desired. There were few options, and only time would reveal if the idea I chose would be successful. The mother and daughter had been trapped in the mess that the garden made for a long period of time, and my goal was to provide them with some sort of relief in their afterlife.

After a few moments of awkward silence, Dean addressed the situation. "Who was the man in the garden?"

"His name is Jay," I answered. "Who is he?"

"He is an enemy," I said.

"Is he…?" Dean began to ask a question that I was well aware he was going to ask.

"He is most certainly not alive." "Are you positive?"

"The fact that Jay is deceased is something that I am certain about," I said as my left hand landed upon the old man's arm. "One thing that does fluster me is that you were able to see him."

"It has been a stressful evening and I am not certain that my mind is not playing tricks on me."

"I am sorry, Dean, but that was not a hallucination; we both saw him at that moment."

"Was that the only time that he was present?" Dean asked as I let go of his trembling arm.

"No, it definitely was not. For some unknown reason you were able to see him at that particular moment. I wish I had more answers for you, but to be absolutely honest…I don't."

"Are we going to see him again?" Dean asked.

"I am hopeful that you will not have to bear to see him again, but I am certain that he will be paying me more visits."

"Why is that?"

"It's a long story; we have many unfinished issues."

"Does he have anything to do with Frank?" Dean kept the investigation rolling.

"You didn't recognize him at all? Even his name does not ring a bell?" I questioned the old man.

"I definitely did not recognize him; it was dark, and difficult to make out faces. I did know a Jay and there is a connection to him and the garden. However, it was not who I saw."

"Who do you know that has a connection with the garden?" I questioned.

"A man named Jay, who used to be one of our friends." "When you say 'our,' are you referring to Frank and yourself?"

"That is correct. The Jay we knew was much older than the ghost of the person we saw."

"Did Jay happen to have a son?" Dean gave me a quick glance as the wheel inside his head could be heard turning.

"Good grief, it's Junior."

"Jay is a junior?" I questioned with shock expressed on my face. "If he is Jay's son, then yes," Dean answered.

"He told me that his father was buried in the garden, so it seems that we are referring to the same guy."

"I would believe that we are. It sure is a small world," Dean commented. "So, what's the story with Jay Senior?" I asked.

"He was a friend that went bad." "How so?"

"He turned into a person that was unrecognizable. He became filled with hate and rage; his mental stability left him and what filled the space was pure evil. I believe that he was always that way, but somehow, he was able to keep it from us. Then there came a point in time where he just didn't feel the need to hide his insanity."

"What happened between him and Frank?" "That is a tale that I do not know."

"You know he was buried in Frank's backyard… how did he get there?" I questioned.

"I don't know. Frank did not tell me the truth. He said that something terrible happened to Jay and that he felt it was his responsibility to hide his body and keep it a secret. He made me promise to keep my mouth shut and he did not reveal any details on the matter."

"Whatever Frank did, he had to do."

"I so wish that to be true," Dean pronounced. "Me too," I sincerely added.

"So, what is your connection with Junior?"

"We met when I was still in high school and he was twenty-five," I vacantly stared out the window as I remembered why the ghost chased me. "I looked up to him, as if he was my own blood. I did not have a true connection with my own family, so I viewed him as a brother. He accepted me for the freak I was, and I felt comfortable and strong when in his presence." It was difficult to admit that I fell for such an act. The traits that were admired about him turned out to be false identities. It was not easy to acknowledge that I could be such a fool.

"How did you meet?"

"I was working at a local gym, and he came by to check it out," I wiped my brow. "He was a co-worker of a friend of mine and he recognized me. He invited me to a party, to which I went, and that was the beginning of a terrible chapter in my life." My days of youth were filled with embarrassing moments, therefore it did not please me to speak of the past. Jay had taught me how to protect myself; I admired him for that. The problem was that we did not fight to protect ourselves; we fought for the adrenaline rush.

"Why was it a terrible chapter for you?"

"Jay made me feel strong and full of life, but it was all a farce. The people who felt our wrath did not deserve what they received. I guess when I am speaking to you, he should be referred to as Junior."

"So, you would pick fights with weaker boys?" Dean inquired.

"Not necessarily, more like we would pick fights with those who were not expecting it. We would befriend them, then all of a sudden, we would turn on them. I am not fond of my past; I have learned right from wrong, and now I only use my gift to protect," I sighed with humiliation.

"I can definitely tell that you have turned your life around. Everyone makes mistakes in life; it is important that we learn from our mistakes."

"I changed because I was disgusted by Junior's behavior," I spoke personally. "I felt that I was no better than him. I did not want to be classified with him, so I moved on."

"I am more than glad that you found the right path."

"It was a dark and gloomy adventure, and I am the person I am today because of who I was back then," I chuckled at the awkward sounding words that seeped from my lips. "I learned from Junior that I am the type of person who needs another person to confide in. Fortunately, Frank was found," I paused to clear my throat and lick the dried blood from my cracked lips. "A large fault in my personality is that I trust before I know."

"So, you meet someone and automatically call them friend until they give you a reason not to?"

"Something to that sort," I replied cautiously. "I agree that a genuine person should learn from their mistakes, and those individuals who do not have the power to displace the feeling of guilt. Now imagine not feeling guilt. Without that poison running through your veins, a person would, or could, do any horrible task without a negative outcome."

"Such as Jay and Junior," Dean commented.

"Those people have no conscience, therefore they become quite dangerous. Those types of people are strong in life. When they die, that is when their hell begins."

"Did you know of the father before this evening?"

"No, I am quite surprised to find out that I was deceived by the son of the same man who betrayed my mentor. The coincidence is quite dramatic if you ask me. I am sure that the story holds more information. Frank once told me that forcing data was unhealthy for my mind. He said that I must let the news come naturally, that is what I must do in this precise incident."

Dean nodded, showing that he agreed with my words, "Frank was a wise man. Do you resent him for holding things from you?"

"There are definitely moments that tend to be bitter. I told Frank things that I will never be able to tell another human. He let me grieve without having to be scared. I owe him my life for letting me free my demons through conversation," I cocked my head towards the bed of the truck, since I could feel my dearly departed friend listening in. "Frank held certain facts from me, not because he was trying to protect me, but simply because it was none of my business at the time. I had the same tendencies when I spoke to a friend. I did it to Frank, therefore a grudge against him cannot be held. Frank was the man who gave me a reason to struggle through my annoying life. If I had not met the mysterious old fool, I am certain that I would not be walking in the world of the living. My secrets are my greatest weakness. Frank allowed me to vent my frustrations out loud before my mind blew up from the tension of holding in all my dark, dirty thoughts." I stretched my aching muscles, turned towards Dean, and asked. "Have you ever seen an actual ghost?"

"Being a friend to a man such as Frank, one would assume that I had seen everything. Frank kept the reality of his life hidden from me; he allowed me to hear the stories, however, he did not let me see the tragedy with my own two eyes," Dean explained. "I am guessing that I have witnessed a spirit before, however, I was not aware. They seem so real, so lifelike. How do you decipher the living from the dead?"

"That is not a question with an easy answer. They all seem to be different; some manifest in ways that makes it obvious to tell that they are manifestations, while others have the ability to look human. I am also positive that there has been a spirit in my presence and I was not aware."

"What would be an example of an obvious case?" Dean asked intriguingly.

"Well, I saw Suzie before Frank's death. It was a dream sequence, yet I believe it was much more than that," I answered. "What made her look dead?"

"She didn't have any eyes. I could see right inside her petite head."

"Well, that would sure be a clue to her not living," Dean commented. "What did you actually see tonight?"

"I thought I saw the plants moving in the wind, but at that time there was no wind," he paused and shifted his body. "That gave me the creeps. When I started to sink into the soil, I would have sworn that someone or something was pulling me under." What Dean was trying to explain was more difficult to speak of, then one would think. The situations that took place were not normal experiences, and speaking of them made a person feel straight up foolish. It was as if we were reduced back to childhood and our imaginations had run away with us. Dean couldn't describe it to me because it made him uneasy. I was no stranger to that concept, so he was allowed to relax and take his time in telling his tale.

"I then saw the man behind you. I did not know why anyone would be out there with us. I was under the assumption that there was more activity going on than what my eyes were letting me see."

"I do apologize for the sights and sounds that you experienced; I am thrilled that your heart still beats," I said with a subtle amount of humor behind my vocal tone.

"I am an adult and I make my own decisions, therefore you have absolutely no reason to feel remorse for the incidents that took place this dreadful evening. I am also very happy that I have not experienced any more problems, I think one attack a day is plenty."

"Don't you think that we should get you some medical assistance?" I asked with a concerned tone.

"I would have died if it wasn't for your help; I owe you my life," Dean quickly changed the subject. "You handled the situation like a true hero."

"How do you know?" I responded. "You were doing the floppy crappie on the floor. There is no way that you could have been conscious enough to know how I handled anything. As far as you know it could have been someone else and I could be stealing their victory."

"I am aware that I don't know you that well, however, I am certain that you could not allow yourself to take credit for something you did not do."

"Anyway, I was a frickin' basket case when you were losing grasp of life. I was forced to do some crude maneuvers, also I guessed about what pill to give you," I admitted my carelessness. "If you wouldn't have pulled me from the garden, I would most likely be a new resident there, so I believe that we are even."

"No matter what you think about yourself, you should understand that your instincts are one of your best qualities. Don't ever forget that. Frank also had that gift," he again enlightened me by comparing the two of us. "A person who can accomplish a task under extreme pressure is someone who possesses a wonderful trait. I have seen you in action and it was impressive. You certainly have done a lot in your short life. You should be proud. I realize that you are not, however, I am telling you that you definitely should be."

"Whatever," I said as I rolled my eyes. "The task we just completed would not have gone so smoothly without your help; I could not have done it alone." Dean gave me a shocked look.

"You call what we just did smooth?"

"We are both still alive, and we have the very items that we were searching for. That does not happen often in these so-called situations," I expressed the seriousness of our accomplishments. "I have lost many friends because of my problems and usually I do not achieve my goals. So, our expedition went smoothly."

"I guess you may be right," Dean admitted. "By the way, there is some information regarding Frank's house that I think you should know." "The only thing that was cherished about the house was the man who lived in it. Now that Frank is no longer among the living, the house means nothing," I said, well aware that the house was given to me.

"I see," Dean commented as he changed the subject. "You know, when you called me about Frank's demise, it was a very disturbing moment. Out of the blue this stranger calls and asks for support with a very serious situation," Dean paused as he wiped the tear that was escaping along his face. "I agreed to help because I didn't know what else to say."

"Did you blame me?" I interrupted.

"I am not sure exactly how I felt," he answered. "Frank used to speak of you in a manner that only a father would boast about his son. He loved you as if you were his own offspring. I knew that you did not mean any harm, so I rushed directly to Frank's, hoping that I would get to finally meet you. I thought you would have stuck around to help, even after the fact that I told you to leave."

"You want to know a secret?" "Sure."

"I hid until you arrived, then I left knowing that he would be taken care of properly. I did not try to put you in such a horrible spot; I acted selfishly. I am truly sorry."

"Walking into Frank's house that day permanently etched an image into my brain. In all honesty, I had never seen a dead body that was not prepared and setting in a casket, so I was afraid of what I was about to see.

Not to mention that I had known Frank since I was in diapers, so I was not looking forward to seeing his lifeless body."

"I only called you because of the way that Frank spoke of you. I had a feeling that you would help, no questions asked," I reached along the cab to grab a hold of a dear friends pulsating shoulder. "I had no answers for the questions that the authorities would have asked, so I selfishly left that behind for you to deal with."

"Believe me, Terry," he put his hand upon mine, "I felt the same way you did about answering questions. I knew that his wife and daughter were in the garden. I didn't know that they were trapped. I thought that reuniting them in death was a wise decision. I am obviously having second thoughts after tonight. I didn't know what to do."

"No one has any doubt that you were trying to do a good deed, trust me. Nobody blames you," I said sincerely.

We were about twenty minutes from our destination, and the side of my head rested upon the truck window as a question bounced around my skull. How could such a wonderful man like Frank be buried in his own backyard without anyone ever missing him? I guess the great people of the world are to be forever forgotten.

All of a sudden there was a deafening pop, and the vehicle jerked, smashing my forehead into the dashboard. Immediately a drum recital began torturing my organ that produced thought as a lump began to surface upon my forehead. I reached for the handle and released myself from the metal prison.

"Terry! Are you alright?" Dean cried out as he towered over me. I said I was fine and watched him disappear from my sight. It was interesting to hear foul language flow from the mouth of my old, fed-up comrade. My desire was to follow the sound of the obscenities, however, it was not possible to direct my limbs. I was incapable of movement. My demands to travel were being disobeyed. After a few moments of bizarre silence, I regained mobility and saw Dean taking out his anger upon the deflated rubber sphere.

"How in the hell does this happen?" He shrieked. "This is very bad, very bad!"

"Calm down, Dean. It is only a flat tire; it won't take long to fix if you have a spare," I commented.

"Are you kidding me?" he ranted as he walked away from me.

It became certain that Dean may have lost his mind. The stress must have been too much for him. I watched as he moseyed a few feet from the metal machine, sifting loose gravel around with his shoes. I gathered myself together and turned towards the wounded vehicle, and then became clear what Dean's commotion was all about. Not one, but all four tires were no longer air carriers.

"Oh shit!" I bellowed. Dean came storming back as he realized I was on the same page.

"See! What is this all about? This doesn't happen by coincidence. No, no, no, this was not an accident." Dean was vibrating and he held a crazed expression upon his face. I opened the tailgate and urged him to have a seat. To my surprise, he didn't hesitate.

"This is definitely not a normal event, however, nothing about tonight has been normal. We need to get the goods out of sight," I chuckled from my crude reference. Dean did the same. "Actually, I am familiar with our surroundings. About a half a mile up that dirt path resides an elderly couple that I am acquainted with. I am thinking that we might be able to borrow their old beast of a truck."

"No kidding, that would be helpful," Dean responded.

My attention rotated towards the darkness when I noticed headlights approaching from the distance.

"Oh no," I mumbled. We had three dead bodies in the back of our vehicle, of which all four tires had been blown. We were not exactly looking very innocent.

"What do we do?" Dean questioned.

"Try the best you can to relax and not look nervous," I ranted. "Do you think they will stop?"

"Most definitely," I answered. "This is a quiet, friendly township. The people who reside here take care of each other. Whoever it is will stop to see if we are suffering." As the car approached, I noticed that it was a police car.

"Shit!" I shouted with nervousness.

We stood pinned against the evidence that would for certain cause us some difficulties. I did not have any rational excuse for the cargo that we carried and was not sure what the charges would be. Nevertheless, it was definite that a romp through my past was in the near future. The last thing in the world that I desired was for the men in blue to investigate my life.

"Dean, you should run and hide. Save yourself, this is not your disaster," I preached for him to escape to safety.

"I am not leaving you alone," he sternly addressed as the officer pulled up behind our vehicle. We strolled closer to the patrol car. It felt as if acid was eating up all my organs and a faint sensation began to buzz in my head. No matter what the circumstances, acting ordinary was of great importance. We had an inconvenient accident, and the cop was only there to help. If we did not act suspicious, he would have no reason to browse through our personal items.

I was thrilled to see Officer Olson release himself from the car. He was an old friend of Frank's, a decent law provider who was fair and reasonable. He was not a cop that provided panic. We had met a few times and he was thought to be a good human-being but then again, that did not mean I was in the clear. If he discovered that I had Frank's dead body rotting in the back of the vehicle, he would certainly take me to jail. He had a job to do and the fact that he identified with me would not stop him from doing his duty. The policeman approached us and recognized me immediately.

"Terry, what in the world are you doing out here at such an odd hour?" "I was hoping to see your magnificent face," I chuckled as my hand was held out, waiting for some respect.

"It is wonderful to see you again, how is Frank?" He asked. I stared. "I am sorry to have to tell you this, Frank left us a couple of years ago." "You have to be kidding me. I cannot believe that I was not informed about such a thing," he commented. "Where was the funeral?"

"I am not sure there was one, it was an unexpected dilemma and since he had no family, I believe that he was cremated without a ceremony," I lied.

"Well, that is sure some heartbreaking news, I am sorry to hear it," he pronounced his sympathy. "Who is this?"

Dean drew closer to Officer Olson, "I am Dean, an old childhood friend of Frank, and I must agree with you that the incident was awful." "You will definitely have to give me a call so we can catch up, Terry,"

Officer Olson spoke, "but you seem to have other things on your mind tonight. What exactly seems to be the trouble?"

"We have a flat, or should I say flats," I informed the man in blue. "Four blown tires," the officer said as he walked around the vehicle.

"Now that is something you do not see every day. I guess luck was not on your side this glorious evening." He walked around our broken-down vehicle as my mind struggled to come up with a story. Dean was standing in front of me, and his appearance gave me an uneasy, nervous feeling. I forgot about how we looked, for we were covered head to toe with dirt and the blood that had dried to our skin and was crumbling off onto the ground below.

"So where are you guys headed?" He asked with concern in his voice as he lit us both up with his metal stick of light.

"We had a late job and are now heading towards Dean's cabin to clean ourselves up and relax a little," I bent the truth.

"Exactly what kind of job are you referring to?" Officer Olson asked with an alarming look on his face as he studied our messy clothes.

"I am a landscaper now days," I spoke as I wiped the sweat from my brow. "I work for Dean. Frank got me the job. I thought with all the gossips around here you would have already known that."

"I guess I am out of the loop, for I didn't even know about Frank's demise," he answered bitterly.

I loathed the fact that it was necessary to lie, especially to a policeman that held my respect. There was no other choice, so the landscaping story was played for all its worth.

"We had a job that was supposed to be done a week ago, however, we have been really busy. We promised the customer that we would finish it by today, so we had to put in a long, treacherous day to get the job done," I continued to stretch the truth.

"It sounds like you haven't changed much, still good about doing what you say," the cop flattered me. "It seems you two are having a pretty rough night."

"You can say that again," Dean quoted from the background as a sudden clanking noise from the back of the truck interrupted the conversation. The officer began to walk towards the commotion; my eyes locked with Dean's as I pinched the inside of my thigh, hoping the pain would subdue the panic. I followed directly behind Mr. Olson, peeking through the topper window as we strolled by. The cover of the crate in the back had come off. I ran past the policeman and hopped onto the tailgate to fix the problem before his light could show the truth as a hand grabbed hold of my leg.

"What is the hurry?" Mr. Olson asked sternly.

"As we were walking back here, I looked through the window and noticed that the cover to our fertilizer box had come off. It is fine when it is covered properly, but once released into the air, it can be a quite disturbing smell," I continued shoveling the shit.

"Yeah, we're going to want that to be closed," Dean agreed.

"Oh, I get your point. Hurry now," Officer Olson gave me a shove. "So, what is in the other boxes?" Dean jumped to attention.

"Our tools." Dean handled the pressure with honors.

Reaching the last sarcophagus, I discovered that Junior was behind the fiasco. He sat crouched in between the last crate and the front of the means of transportation with an enormously hideous smile painted upon his deceptive face. I pounded the cover back onto the box with my fist as I whispered to Junior: "Don't mess with the innocent."

"What was that?" Mr. Olson asked. "I got it," I answered loudly.

"How do you suppose that cover fell like that?" the confused officer inquired.

"It must have loosened when the tires blew and slowly made its way to the ground," Dean quickly and intelligently answered.

"So, was there an object in the road that you guys ran over?" The cop continued to interrogate the situation. Dean began to feel more comfortable with the state of affairs. Being the wise man that he was, he stretched his arm around the shoulder of the officer and led him towards the front of the truck. I presumed that the old bat was aware that we had an unwanted visitor and was causing a distraction for me to deal with the disturbance.

I began to search for the menace, but he had gone missing. As my eyes peered deep into the bed of the truck, the sound of someone's breath gently entered my ears. Turning around showed a delightful view of the garden goddess. She was beautiful and quite glorious.

"We are close, you can save us," she declared with a quiet voice.

"You and your family will never be safe, and you will never find peace," said a mystery voice from behind Frank's wife.

Struggling to see the person with the interrupting vocal cords, I moved towards the sound, determined to stop the madness from spreading towards Dean and Mr. Olson. A few feet behind the cop car stood a complete stranger.

"You…I presume to be Jay Sr.," I muttered.

"You are the sad, young fool who is confused about the meaning of loyalty," he returned fire.

"And that would mean?" I said sarcastically.

"You remind me of a boy I used to know," he let out with a horrendous laugh. "He too was confused about loyalty, and in the end, he made a fool out of me."

"I am not aware of the entire story regarding Frank and yourself, and I don't need the details. The moral of this particular story is that you and your non-living friends are holding the souls of innocent people. The daughter had nothing to do with the grievances you have with her father. The mother also deserves to be freed, and your battle is with Frank," I turned away from the ghost and spit what I anticipated to be blood. "I will stop at nothing to make sure that Frank and his family are taken care of properly. You and your son will fail in death, just as you did in life!" There was a rumble in the air and my body shook as if the earth was cracking underneath me. The ground did not sway; only my body trembled fiercely.

"You have a voice!" Junior screamed from the beyond. "Too bad no one is listening."

"I sense your ears are bleeding," I expressed my reaction. "Come to me! Let's end this now!" He appeared through the darkness, walking directly through his evaporating father. I had no more tolerance; my hate for Junior took over and would be the key to defeat him.

"Your friends die!" Junior screeched as he waved his hand before my eyes. I cocked my head to look for Dean and Officer Olson when a gust of wind tossed me through the air. Once again, I found myself laying down on the job; it was a scenario that occurred frequently that evening. My fingers dug into the ground to provide an anchor for the rest of my body to pull towards. I hurled my aching bones upright and made a mad dash to find my two friends. Dean was laying on the ground; he rolled onto his back and revealed blood flowing down his wrinkled face.

"That was weird," he gasped as he tried to regain reality.

I kneeled down and grabbed his hand, "Mr. O!" I shouted over Dean. We saw a dark image a few feet ahead of us. We both scurried to the formation, and found it was the missing being. Dean lifted the body from the ground and checked him for a pulse.

"What in the hell was that?" Mr. Olson asked surprisingly. "A freak of nature," Dean answered the question.

My bloody palm rested upon the body of the wounded policeman. It was satisfying that both men still took breaths of the night air.

"Mr. Olson," I said as I released my hand from him, "what would you say about Dean driving your patrol car and taking you to the hospital?"

"I can comply with that request," he agreed as I stood and walked away from the scene of the accident as I motioned Dean to follow. Dean grunted as he raised himself from the ground. As he awkwardly approached, I had a feeling that he would be happier to get away from the depressing scene for an hour or two.

"What are you going to do?" He questioned as he leaned on me for balance.

"I'm going to see if another vehicle can be obtained. Once that is accomplished, I will retrieve you from the hospital."

"Be safe, and I will be seeing you soon," Dean gave me a quick hug and hobbled back towards Mr. Olson.

After ten minutes of extreme pain, I approached an old farmhouse. Next to the barn sat on old Chevy pickup that people referred to as "Old Rusty." A glance at the house showed a dark habitat and made me wonder if my idea was going to be salvageable. As my feet were placed upon the old wood of the porch, a loud creaking noise spread through the night air and shortly a light appeared through the window. There was commotion taking place on the other side of the entrance as I gradually moved closer. "Herb," I said posing my face close to the door, "it's Terry, I have a favor to ask of you." The door slowly creaked open to show an old frail man holding a shot gun in his hands. It was the second time a gun had been pointed at me during my so-called mission and honestly, I hoped it would be the last.

"Terry?" The old man questioned. "What are you doing here? It's been a long time since I've seen your face."

"I am so sorry to disturb you at such a late hour, but I am having a major crisis."

"Do you need a place to stay?"

"Not exactly, I am having vehicle issues. Officer O. came to the rescue and there was an unfortunate accident. My friend took him to the hospital."

"Oh my goodness, is he all right?" Herb asked, concerned. "I believe that he will be fine; he's in good hands."

"So what can I do for you?"

"I was wondering if it would be possible to borrow Old Rusty. I know it is kind of sudden. I will return it soon and pay you whatever you think is fair."

"I don't see that as a burden at all. I will find the keys, come inside," he said.

Herb disappeared down the hall. About five years ago, there was another tragic event that left me bloody and weary. I dragged my damaged body to an isolated field and lost consciousness. Hours later, I awoke to a strange man lurking over me. The man was a saint because he asked no questions as he picked my injured mass from the vegetation and brought me to his place of housing. His wife cleaned my wounds and they let me borrow Old Rusty. I was a complete stranger, and they treated me as one of their own. There are very few people in the world like Mr. and Mrs. Sanders. Herb reappeared and handed me the keys, he then shook my hand.

As our shake came to an end, I pierced his eyes with mine and shared my gratitude. He nodded and whispered words of encouragement. I loaded myself into the cab of Old Rusty and engaged the key into the ignition. The rust bucket purred as I turned the key. It was remarkable that something finally went as planned.

After a few moments of pondering, it occurred to me that it would be easier on Dean if the cargo was transferred without him. I backed Old Rusty up to Dean's motor vehicle and dropped both the tail gates; first the Sanders' truck then Dean's, creating a bridge for me to push the caskets across. As I transferred the crates, my attention was elsewhere. It was strange that my dead nemesis had not shown his ghostly face. I was certain that Junior was not through with interrupting my task. As soon as I completed the job, Old Rusty and I fled to retrieve my helper.

Once I arrived at the hospital, Dean was spotted resting his frail body against the outside of the care facility.

"I am glad that you made it back, and with transportation," he expressed.

"Were you worried about me?" I asked sarcastically.

"No, I was worried about how I was going to get home," he chuckled. "How is Mr. O.?"

"A few minor cuts and scratches. I am pretty sure he will pull through," Dean answered with a wink. "Do you want to go see him?"

"I would love to, however, I think we should hit the road. We will check up on him later, but right now, we must get your automobile towed." "I will run inside and take care of that. I will be back in a jiffy," he said as he headed towards the building.

After a few minutes Dean was spotted exiting the hospital and quickly I pulled the vehicle closer so he wouldn't have to walk far. He graciously nodded and hurled his creaking bones into the passenger side of the cab. Dean rested his heavy head as he grunted and groaned until he found the exact spot of relief. I longed for the night to come to an end and was sure that the man next to me felt the same.

"I have a question to ask you," he stated.

"I imagine that you probably have a few more than just one," I responded.

"That is definitely true. However, I only have one at this present moment," he turned his head towards me. "What happened between you and Junior?"

There were millions of secrets that dwelled deep inside my head; the one concerning Junior was certainly not leaked, not even to Frank. What happened between me and the twisted demon was something that did not fill me with pride.

"I am not ready to speak of that certain event," I said sternly.

"I watched a dear friend drown in his own reality as I sat in the corner and hoped for the best. I was never, not once, assured that he was going to make it through. It was no secret when Frank was struggling with a problem, even though he thought it was," Dean changed the subject and began to tell a side of the story that was foreign to my ears. "I feel his demise was my fault because I did not pry. He would never let me help. I was his closest friend, and not being able to assist him destroyed my pride. There is nothing worse than being helpless when it comes to caring for someone closest to you. Not even being thrown through the air by some unforeseen force. At least I was right in the midst with you, not in the corner doing nothing."

He spoke his mind and it ripped through my soul, filling me with knowledge from the other side of the table. If Frank would have let Dean in upon the catastrophe that was destroying his life, the possibility that Dean would not have survived was more than just an idea. I would let a friend hate upon me if that would provide a safe life for them. Frank was the exact same way.

"I view my life as a gigantic jigsaw puzzle." It became my turn to change the subject.

"Explain that to me," Dean said.

"Every adventure I must complete becomes an individual piece of the puzzle. Prime example would be tonight. When this journey is fulfilled, I will gain a piece to add to the whole picture. As pieces become clear they reveal a new scene to figure out. A puzzle slowly tells a story as the pieces fit together. Most often an individual will start with the frame of the picture and slowly build into the middle to discover the true and entire beauty of the project. This philosophy is quite true to my life as well. My life thus far I have been constructing the outer frame, each piece that is revealed brings me closer to the conclusion and it also opens up a whole new part of the image. I then have to presume what is being manufactured, which confuses and irritates me," I paused to gulp some air as my head tried to float away.

"Your life is a puzzle that does not have a box," Dean began to understand. "You must find the missing objects throughout your life and piece them together as they become known to you; you do not have any idea what the portrait actually looks like. Your puzzle could have many small photographs or could be one large obstruction. The tricky part would be that you don't have a clue."

"I think you're catching on," I commented.

"Well, I'm obviously not getting an answer on my first question, so I will ask another," Dean spoke aloud. "How do you deal with intimate relationships?"

"Poorly," I chuckled as a slight trickle flowed down my arm.

"Holy crap," Dean expressed, "your wrist is split open! You must pull over."

"Don't overreact, it is only a scratch," I tried to calm him down. "There is a small stream forming from your forearm; do not tell me to calm down," he insisted that the matter was urgent. "I have a first aid kit in the back, pull over."

"Wrong truck," I reminded him that we were no longer in his vehicle. "We'll find something," he declared. I reluctantly agreed and did what he asked. We both released ourselves from the vehicle and wandered to the eyes of Old Rusty so we could observe the lesion. Once we observed the abrasion with some light, we found it to be much more than a scratch. Dean immediately ripped one of his sleeves from his shirt and wrapped it around the gash. My pupils began to hide as I felt my body deteriorating;

I shuffled my feet to sustain balance. "You okay?" Dean inquired as my weight fell upon him.

"I've been better," I remarked, shocking myself. No matter how obvious my pain was, I generally recited the words *I'm fine.*

"I don't remember the wound from when you picked me up in town," the confused old man commented as he witnessed the blood soak into his loose sleeve.

"After all we've been through thus far; you want to question a small cut."

"It is far from a small cut. Look, the blood is dripping from the cloth," he ripped the remaining sleeve from his shoulder and reached for my damaged flesh. There was extreme discomfort raging from underneath the soaked material. It was as if someone was stabbing my skin over and over again. My free hand swung over the fabric as Dean was trying to wrap it for the second time. He pushed my hand from the scene.

"What are you doing?" he questioned. I continued to cause difficulties as both of Dean's hands grabbed my chest.

"It's fine, relax. I feel better," I sputtered as I made an escape from his clutches and turned my back to him. I unwound the bandage as the pain came to a halt. I stared at the injury with disbelief.

"Let me see," Dean said as he desperately tried to assess the situation with his own two eyes.

"Back off!" I shouted.

"What is going on?" he screamed back at me. "Let me help you." "We must continue, everything is fine," I ranted.

"Let me see your arm," he demanded.

"I have an errand to finish. You can bow out or continue with me, it is your choice. I will think no less of you if you leave. Maybe you will find the power to forget everything that you have witnessed tonight. I advise you to forget."

"What happened to all the trust?"

"I lie!" I blurted out loudly. "I took you for a man of some intelligence, I guess I misjudged you."

"I know what you're trying to do; it most definitely is not going to work," Dean stated as he fought to catch his breath. "I will not let you push me away. Now, tell me what is going on."

"I came to you for relief. I showed myself to a stranger so I could release the horrors of my life. That is all I wanted. Now, several hours later, we have written another chapter in the so-called life of a freak! It was not supposed to go down this way."

"It's not your fault."

"A good, caring, innocent man finds himself in the hospital only because he had the misfortune of crossing my path. Another innocent man had a heart attack and should be in the hospital. Instead, he stands before me confused and scared."

"I may be scared and confused, however, it was my choice, not yours. You were not the one who put Officer Olson in the hospital, it was Junior."

"Without me, there is no Junior. I am the reason for his interference, without me, there is no him."

"Without you, Frank and his family would be forever trapped in a horrible afterlife."

I walked towards the side of the pickup, "I apologize, I am leaving you here where you will be safe."

I entered Old Rusty and nodded at Dean as I turned the key to the ignition and gradually pulled away from the great man. Then there was a thump that came from the bed of the truck. I knew immediately that a determined old man had not given up. I slammed on the brakes and leapt from the cab.

"Before you say anything, I beg of you to show me your wrist," Dean sternly advised.

I placed my arm in front of him, and peeled the fabric from the flesh. The cloth fell to the ground, leaving a chaotic look painted on Dean's face. "No questions," I quickly remarked. Dean shook his head vigorously as he paced back and forth in front of me. There was a pulsating vein in his neck, and it was about to burst.

"No questions! Screw you!" He screamed into the night air as he wrapped his hands around my arm. "Where is the cut?" he questioned as he rubbed the bare, smooth flesh that only minutes ago was split in two.

"Let's just finish what we started," I commented. Many times I'd witnessed scratches appear upon my skin however, it was the first time one vanished. There was no explanation that could be conjured up.

"No!" Dean expressed passionately, "I won't let this one go. I have seen many strange things today, but this is too much."

"A few moments ago, I tried to set you free from my nightmare and you insisted on staying. I will be the first one to admit that my life is complicated and the things that happen on and around me can be very hard to deal with. You can walk from it at any given moment. Do not make me explain something that cannot be explained."

"I am a psychiatrist, I aid people with their insecurities. You have shown me that not all people are insane, and they may be dealing with a problem that no one can relate to. How can I go on living such a lie? I can't help anyone; my life will never be the same."

"You are overreacting. You must relax and clear your mind."

"Clear my mind," he repeated with a haunting chuckle, "try your best to explain to me how the gash on your wrist magically healed itself."

"The same as it appeared." "I don't understand."

"You said earlier that you didn't remember the cut when I picked you up from the hospital. The reason why you don't remember it is because it wasn't there."

"Do you often have cuts appear on your body?"

"Look at my body," I said as I lifted my shirt. "I have thousands of scars all over me. I think we should be positive about the situation, for someone is helping us by giving me the power to heal myself. Otherwise, I would probably have already bled to death."

"So, you believe whatever caused the wound was not the reason for its disappearing?" he asked in a rather calm voice.

"I have seen Frank's wife a few times tonight, maybe it is her way of showing gratitude."

"Finally someone is making sense," Dean mumbled. "She was the kindest woman ever to walk this very earth. I have no problem believing she helped you."

"So, we can agree that is what happened?"

"Yes, now let's get back into Old Rusty and finish this damn job before my mind goes on a permanent vacation."

"I will drive."

"Are you sure you are capable of driving?" Dean questioned, knowing damn well what the answer was.

"Look in a mirror, old man. You will see that both of us are in piss- poor shape. I know the way, therefore that makes me the lucky winner."

We continued to our destination as Dean decided to restart our last conversation: "Can you explain your thoughts on relationships?"

"They are completely disastrous. It is impossible for me to satisfy a woman."

"What sense of 'satisfy' are you referring to?"

"In the sense of a stable relationship and not a sexual drawback. I change my opinions on life daily. Anyone who decides to give their heart to me must understand that I am not always going to be the person they fell in love with," I weakly explained my thoughts. "I must first discover who I am as a person before anyone will be able to love me back. Most of my relationships thus far have fallen apart, because it is impossible to let another individual into my life. How am I supposed to allow another human into my heart when deep down I am not confident that I am a person who deserves to be loved?"

"Do you think that you sabotage your relationships?"

"I believe that I do, but usually only if I already know that the woman is not for me. If I sense a certain connection with a lady, I try to make sure that I am open and honest enough to not drive her away. I am a difficult person to relate to, so I am sure that I have sabotaged a relationship even when I wasn't trying to."

"Confidence is a huge part of any relationship. I can understand your thoughts on that specific ordeal. The only fault I find in you is the lack of confidence."

My mouth was dry, and my tongue had to be ripped from the sticky roof of my mouth. I briefly glanced at Dean and heard the commotion that was raging in his head. I didn't hold the answers that he was so eager to hear and could only speak in riddles that he could not solve.

"I am most certainly insecure; I will not deny that." "What about Tina?" He rerouted the subject.

"She was different." "How so?" Dean inquired.

"That was as real as it gets," I spoke as I cracked my neck. "What I had with her was complete bliss. Nothing she ever did made me angry with her. I truly felt that every single one of her intentions was filled from her heart. She was something special."

"How was she so different from the other women you've met?"

"I felt so comfortable when it was me and her alone. I have never felt that feeling with anyone else. She allowed me to be confident," I began to realize my mistakes as the conversation progressed. "Having assurance with yourself is such a powerful feeling. I know that when I trust myself, I can accomplish almost any task, and I find that I usually give up and blame the problems in my life. Bearing the burden of speaking to the deceased can be quite a chore, and I most definitely use it as an excuse to clutter my own reality. I have so many mixed thoughts that I become confused and run to the nearest exit. That exit leads to lack of belief in myself."

"So, Tina inspired you," he commented. "She most certainly did just that."

"I also had one of those."

"What's the tragic ending to your lost love?" I asked with sorrow pouring from my breath.

"I dated Marilyn for two glorious years before I dropped to my knee," his eyes glistened as he reminisced out loud. "I truly loved her; however, twenty years of love and respect was not enough. I arrived home one evening to a letter that was taped to my door. It was a Dear John letter. A patient of mine was a better fit for her liking, not to mention that the guy was a drug addict." I felt the pain that was lashing out inside his old heart and sat in silence to respect the moment. "Two and a half years later, Marilyn came crawling back. Her appearance was a mess; she looked diseased."

"Was she sane?"

"Absolutely not, she was out of her frickin' mind," Dean laughed out loud with a wicked wail. "Her newfound love was a coke head. I guess being a drug addict is quite contagious," again he howled with laughter. "She ripped my heart from my chest and left it in a corner to rot, all by its lonesome. I was never able to connect with another woman. I was so down on myself. I felt I wasn't good enough for anybody. I still haven't forgiven her for what she did."

"Are you saying that you took her back?"

"Absolutely not, I helped her check into a rehab clinic, and I have never tried to contact her since," he finished his story of shame. I did not pity the lonesome man; instead, respect and understanding were the thoughts formed in the nether regions of my mind. A broken heart had no friends, no relatives, no one to give special treatment. I found the similarities between Dean and myself to be intriguing. He mentioned that he had not forgiven his ex-wife. I was also a person that found it difficult to forgive and did not consider it a bad habit. I firmly believed that certain deeds could not be taken back or locked in a closet, never to be spoken of again, and I was tired of people hiding behind silence. The word *truth* would soon be an ancient myth that our descendants would read about.

We drove onto a hidden path in the forest; I hopped from the pickup and removed a giant branch that acted as security. Once on the dirt lane, the fallen tree limb was repositioned once again to serve and protect. The night was clear, and millions of lanterns lit the sky high above. The moon had cast its glow upon the hood of Old Rusty and the sight drew my eyelids to touch. My head dropped, and the four wheeled beast darted towards the trees on the side of the thin path. The sudden shaking quickly brought me back to life and I managed to straighten out Old Rusty before it collided with the wooden soldiers of the forest. Dean cocked his head in my direction and produced a stern expression upon his face. My head nodded a few times and a creepy smile appeared upon my mug. My foot slammed down upon the brake and my shaking hand shut the vehicle down. There were vibrations running up and down my spine as a slow creaking sound entered my ears followed by a loud clunk. I plunged from the cab to view the destruction that was caused.

Dean dragged his aching bones around the vehicle to view the calamity. There was a tear glistening under the moon light; he wiped it from his cheek. I turned to gaze at the unreal sight that had captured Dean's emotions. My careless driving had knocked Frank's casket from the rusty truck bed, and his bones were scattered amongst the dirt. It was a tragic sight. To be aware that my best friend was dead in the back of my vehicle was one thing, seeing his remains scattered throughout the night was something entirely different.

"This is terrible," Dean blurted out.

"I saw the moon's reflection and dozed off," I explained as I dropped to one knee and turned the crate over. There was a nudge upon my side. I fought to regain my balance as my eyes squinted to behold the purpose of the shove, but there was nothing to be seen. Dean was leering in my direction.

"Did you see something?" I questioned.

"I'm not quite sure, I thought I did," he replied. "What did you see?"

"I noticed some movement among the darkness."

We stood silently, glaring into the night. We were not alone. It was difficult to imagine how Jay and his newly formed gang were able to shadow us. What were they capable of? What was I capable of? Dean stood close, and his body shuddered. I began picking up the pieces to my friend. My eyes were still adjusting to the night, and even though the sky was clear, it was difficult to view all the bones in the soil. The stench was overwhelming, and the decaying meat was flimsy and sticky to the touch. There wasn't much flesh left but there was enough to cause a gagging reaction.

My balance began to slip as my left hand grabbed ahold of the crate to provide stability. I suddenly focused my attention upon my wrist as the sensation of another hand squeezing it came into play. There was no one in sight as the hold became prominent enough to cause pins and needles throughout my fingers. I grasped my aching wrist with my free hand. Then there was a sudden jolt and my body was forced into the box on top of my dear friends remains.

"Start the truck, Dean!" I screamed into the air, but there was no reaction from my demand. Again, I pronounced the agenda out loud and once again, there were no results. Leaping from the box, I stood in a weary state. The eruption inside my skull was driving at full force. The air was still, and the sense of danger was thick. A rustle from the side of Old Rusty captured my attention and I made discreet movements towards the sound. Dean was leaning against the door; his hands were cupped to his side just a few inches lower than his heart. A dark liquid that I assumed to be blood, was streaming from the cracks of his fingers, and his body was pulsating. "I tripped on something," Dean mumbled as I drew closer to him.

"Let's see what the damage is."

"No need, it's not what it looks like," he said quietly. A closer view showed an entirely different picture. It was not blood that dripped from his palms; it was a denser fluid. I ripped a piece of my shirt to wipe the substance off when Dean coughed and continued to throw up into his cupped hands. I separated his limbs and wiped his mouth.

"My stomach doesn't feel right," Dean whispered.

"Mine either," I reached my arm around him, "are you up for this?" "It is good for me," he recited.

"I'm not sure that is true, but if you're good to go, we need to be moving."

"Is Frank safe?"

"Get in and start the engine. When you hear your name, haul ass down the road. The first right you see, turn on it. It is about a half-mile ahead. Do you understand?" I asked, and he confirmed by moving his head up and down. He was obviously in a state of shock, and describing the details of the situation was not going to help, so I attempted the next best thing: I kept his mind busy with a duty.

Dean opened the door and hopped into the driver's seat. A deep breath and the adrenaline that was building from the distress gave enough boost to dash to the remaining bones. Quickly and gently, I returned the remains of Frank to their correct place. Someone was staring a hole through the back of my head, yet I ignored them.

Frank was returned to his family, and I jumped up to join them screaming: "Dean!"

We raced down the dirt trail. Junior and his gang emerged out of the darkness and grew smaller and smaller as Dean accelerated. The entire circumstance was misunderstood. My mind was drowning with questions. Why was it possible to run from them? Why did they not kill me? Was it possible for them to eradicate me? A warm sensation began to grow among my flesh until it became hot. My stomach turned and whatever was inside was now hurling over the tailgate and falling to the ground below. The truck shook violently as it came to a sudden halt.

"I found a flashlight in the glove department. It will come in handy," Dean referenced as he shined the newly found light onto me. "What's going on?"

"I'm burning," I said deliriously. "What is on your skin?"

"I'm sweating."

"I don't believe that to be sweat," he commented as he reached out to touch it. "It's gooey and cold,"

I felt my eyes bury themselves deep inside of my head as I lost all consciousness.

I later awoke in the cab of Old Rusty. All the vents were pointed in my direction as the heat hammered upon my face. The door was released as the cool air drifted in, causing relief. Dean was inches from the open door.

"What's with the heat?" I beckoned.

"Your skin was covered with this strange, sticky film. When I touched it, I found that you were freezing cold, so I wiped it from your body and covered your wound," he pointed at my wrist as he spoke. A piece of cloth was wrapped around it. "You lost consciousness. It must have been from the loss of bodily fluids."

I removed the bandage to discover that a laceration appeared upon my wrist. The same place that I felt pressure earlier. My head shook with misperception as I placed the bandage back on the suffering flesh. My weariness brought me to the ground where my back pressed upon it.

"Isn't it beautiful?" I asked. Dean realized I was talking about the moon. "Yes, it is quite beautiful."

We took deep breaths and sighed with frustration. My wrist was throbbing as my finger poked it. Gazing upon Dean's shrinking shirt, it became clear where the bandage was obtained.

"Soon we both will be naked," I laughed.

"Nothing would surprise me tonight," he chuckled back. We admired the sky for a few moments and let the breeze calm our nerves.

"When I was putting Frank back on the truck bed, something happened," I stated.

"Does it have to do with the condition I found you in?"

"Perhaps," I commented. "Junior was upon the tailgate. We shared the same space, as I leapt to unite with the passengers of the wooden boxes."

"Has that ever happened before?" "Sort of," I responded.

"Maybe you threw up on yourself, I've heard that happens to some people during an experience such as the one we shared," he said trying to bring some light to a dark situation by bringing up his earlier accident. "Did you feel him?"

"No. I saw him as I plowed right through him. I turned around and he was standing with his posse," I paused as my thoughts were collected. "What I do not understand is how he could have left the truck and rejoined his group so quickly, but when we run, it seems as if he can't catch us. Then, he always finds us again when we're stopped. I don't get it."

"By that way of thinking, he can't get to us when we're moving," Dean commented on my theory.

"That's not true either, because all four of our tires were damaged as we were driving," I added another fact.

"So then he must just be toying with us."

"Yes, I think he is toying with us. I don't understand why he doesn't just end it."

"There has to be some kind of power on our side," Dean began to brainstorm. "I overheard you tell Junior that you knew he couldn't hurt you physically. Why is that?"

"I am aware that he has tried and failed. I don't know why."

"There has to be something to that. We need to continue, and as we do so, we need to act as if we are invincible." Dean cleared his forehead from unwanted debris.

"You walked away from a heart situation. We survived two accidents and a whole lot of crazy chaos. I already think we are invincible."

"Good, we are on the same page. Now tie down the cargo and let's go before we have to prove ourselves. I would be pleased with a little break from the dead folk," he giggled.

Dean seized the wheel as I took some time to analyze the situation. When Dean stumbled upon me, my flesh was on fire. If I had the strength, I would have ripped the skin from my muscles to gain relief. My mind was not stable, and the sensation of being boiled alive was overwhelming. The gel Dean mentioned had to have some kind of thermal power. He said I was cold, so the outer casing was cool. However, the inside seized the heat. There was one other time that I could remember when a spirit crossed my direct path. I was young and didn't realize what had occurred. The experience took me back to the dreaded day of my first site of death: the fish house. When that disturbed young lad robbed his life, his spirit left his body and soared through me. I became sick and vomit gushed from my mouth. I witnessed a child blowing his brains out the back of his head merely seconds earlier, so it was certainly the cause for my upset innards. As the mess was scrubbed from my flesh, I pondered on why the blood was so sticky and gel-like. That was my first blood bath, so there was no way of knowing what it was supposed to be like. After more experience, I had learned that blood dries quickly or runs down the skin. Dean described the same gel-like substance from the young suicide. It was becoming pretty obvious that the substance was something other than blood. It seemed that somehow a piece of the spirit was stolen as we collided.

Dean turned slightly towards me and said, "I wonder if we'll see Junior again."

"He will not give up. We can be grateful that he has no physical power over us."

"Wait," Dean interrupted, "your wrist has been sliced twice. How can you say he can't harm us?"

"I said physically, not mentally."

"Your skin split down your arm; that does not happen mentally." "Your job puts you face to face with wild theories every day. You are paid to deal with those who seem to be mentally deficient. With that being said, you have to be able to remember stories that may be a little tricky to explain."

"To a degree, however, what you are speaking of is irrationality."

"I do not want to bring rationality into this. All I am saying is that you must have studied literature about the human brain, therefore you must be aware of how mysterious the large organ can be."

"I do, but not to the point of lesions appearing and disappearing in the matter of seconds."

"Have you ever heard of cases where a person contracts a deadly disease, only to have it disappear a few years later? I have read a few articles and watched a few television programs that discussed this very topic. I learned that these patients had a strong will to live, and that will reprogrammed their brain," I shared my knowledge on the matter.

"I have read a few articles myself, and there is no factual documentation that proves the occurrence was drawn from their drive to survive," he corrected me.

"Are you planning on documenting the things that you have witnessed this glorious evening?"

"No," he declared, understanding that my point was that people tend not to document the crazy. "I get your point. However, I still do not follow your theory."

"I am not sure that I will make any sense to a doctor, especially a psychiatrist. Think back. there had to be a moment in your life where you spent every minute of your day stressing out about a certain situation, only to discover the aggravating case actually came true. It doesn't matter if it is a good or bad problem. Ever act out the flu to get out of a particular duty, only to become sick in the very near future?"

"You are speaking of coincidences," Dean made an observation.

"A coincidence is nothing to me. It is the act of a weaker mind trying to convince me to believe that I am insane. The word is absolutely worthless in the life that I live each day." I stretched, for my bones were aching.

"Are you trying to tell me that my subconscious can leap from my body and cause physical damage upon another person?"

"I am saying that studies have proved that we do not use our entire brain; not in our entire lifetime," I pleaded for him to see it from my stance. "So, what happens if someone did actually use that part of their mother organ? Could it possibly be the source for supernatural powers, or even open up the realm to the dead?" I gathered my thoughts, for I was beginning to wander from the initial topic. "If Junior found a way to get into my mind, I have no way of telling what he would be capable of doing. He could turn my flesh inside out; he could have my veins explode; he could separate my skin from anywhere on my body. He is not cutting me; he is mentally forcing my anatomy to follow his orders."

"Do you honestly believe what you are saying?"

"Look at what you have seen tonight. You have been thrown twenty feet through the air from a freak breeze. The so-called breeze came and went within seconds. No trail was left behind, no fallen trees, no loose branches, a clear sky...that sounds odd to me. You watched a gash on my arm close up and show no scar in its place. It just vanished, right before your eyes. I was covered with a foreign substance that tried to freeze and burn me at the same time. Just another normal day where everything that took place had a simple and logical explanation," the sarcasm flowed from my soul.

We stopped conversing and let the opinions try to sink into our minds. We were not necessarily arguing. We were displaying our deepest thoughts for each other to comprehend. Neither one of us knew what was taking place, so we reached out to one another for answers. I respected Dean for his outlook on life, and I was beginning to sense that he respected mine as well. I have shown him a new way of life; a way that he had only read or heard about before. He now was a witness, so he now had to choose how to react to it. He could pretend that it was nothing more than a bad dream, or he could accept the truth and realize that life carried many secrets along the way.

"So, if Junior can control your mind, why can he not control your movements?" Dean asked.

"Control me to harm myself or another person?" "Precisely," Dean answered.

"He has the same difficulties that I face. He learns of his abilities throughout time, just as I do. He is not aware of his true capabilities; he will gain that wisdom through experience. I have no doubt that he is trying to control me, and I am quite thrilled that he has not found the strength to do so."

"So, the two of you are battling wits to see who can learn more, quicker than the other," Dean came to a realization.

"That pretty much sums it all up," I agreed. "For some unknown reason, Junior wants me out of the picture entirely. I do not understand his motives; I am sure I will later."

"Do you have any theories?"

"Of course I do. I believe that I am a hurdle, and he must jump me to reach his destination. In other words, I must be disposed of for him to move on. His biggest difficulty is the fact that I am a stubborn individual, and I will not give up without a fight."

My attention transferred to the woods as we drove down the path. There were many times that I had run through those very trees in a complete and utter panic. All the dreaded memories were crashing into the inside of my skull. Each one was in full force; they were begging me to remember them. There was no distress of death in my head. I fought to live because I was not going to fade away before certain questions were answered.

"Another perspective would be that Junior is seeking revenge. Revenge can make people do unforgivable things," I continued the conversation.

"I can relate to that," Dean commented. "How can you relate?"

"I dated women that were way too young for me. I did this because I thought it would drive my ex-wife crazy. My actions were not fair to the lovely women that I dated. I was taking advantage of them and was in no position to give them a loving relationship." Dean experienced some self-realization about how revenge was used. "I had a pretty decent friendship with Jay; I believe that there are many similarities between the father and son combo. Jay was a man who lived his life for revenge. He would stop at nothing to get back at someone who he believed had harmed him. That was why Frank stepped in: Frank was fed up with his tactics. Some of the people that Jay went after were innocent, and that did not stop their future from being destroyed. Frank felt that what Jay was doing was immoral."

"Was Jay evil?"

"Depends what your definition of evil may be," he replied as he yawned. "He was filled with pent-up anger and hatred for all of mankind. I think the real problem was that he did not respect himself. In the beginning he was a loyal friend, and that all changed towards the end. He became a bitter, sad man." I couldn't help but think that Dean was describing me. I did not want to turn out like the Jays.

"What was the outcome of his wife?"

"You are going to have to wait for the appropriate time for that question to be answered. I cannot divulge that information."

"Yes, Frank," I responded sarcastically. Dean chuckled for he knew that I did not mean any harm by my rude remark. I was frustrated with everything and wanted the entire scene to be over with; as did Dean.

We were closing in upon our destination when the air seemed to thicken to the point that I gagged. Dean slapped the middle of my back, just as a father would do for his son. It was a shame that Dean did not reproduce; he would have made a wonderful father.

"You gonna make it?" He crudely asked.

"I feel strange," I answered, and then concentrated on a tingling sensation that drifted down my spine. I had felt the same feeling before; Junior was among us. Dean pulled the truck to the shoulder when he discovered the look in my eyes. Solely from my scowl, he identified that we were no longer alone.

"He's back, right?" Dean begged for an answer.

"I'm not positive; something is definitely out of whack." "How much farther do we need to travel?"

"Not far. We have to lose our tail before we get to the bridge." "What do we do?"

"I'm afraid we are going to have to separate." "That's not happening," he said out of panic.

"We don't have any other choice," I said, sounding frustrated. It was definitely not in my best interests to send Dean out on his lonesome, however, it became necessary that Junior was misled. If the demon seed was distracted, that would allow Dean and the cargo to arrive at the destination in a safe manner.

"I realize that it may be scary by yourself, but you need to do what I tell you." My fist pounded on my chest to keep my heart pounding; desperation was showing its true nature. Dean watched my strange behavior in complete silence. He had learned to be still when I acted like a lunatic, which was most of the time. "Follow that path up the ridge, it will bring you to a large tree. You will not miss the giant; it is by-far the largest chunk of wood in the forest. Turn directly in front of the oversized weed. There will be no road, only a small trail. I know for a fact that Old Rusty will fit, trust me. A few yards from the tree, you will come to a creek, and there will be a bridge. Cross it quickly and do not hesitate. I promise that the bridge will hold, but do not park on it. Once you are across you will be safe. Do not cross if you pick up any company along the way. A spirit can only cross with a living soul; they cannot cross over alone."

"It sounds awfully close; I think you should just come with me," Dean begged for me to not leave him.

"Do you feel Old Rusty trembling right now?" "Yes," he answered.

"If I don't distract him, he will rip us apart. If you go on alone, I can keep him occupied, otherwise he will follow us across the bridge and our whole plan will be foiled. Trust me, Dean, I will make it through this; I will not let him defeat me after we have come so far."

"I am aware that it is necessary for me to go on alone; I'm merely a little leery after all the events that have occurred," Dean said as I departed the vehicle.

Every tiny hair that grew from my flesh stood as my friend drove away. My brain was dancing with thoughts of what was about to take place. I felt a familiar breeze gaining strength as the seconds traveled through time. I had learned that Junior entered with the wind. The blood in my veins curdled as my heart struggled to move the thick liquid throughout my body. My feet stayed in one spot as my eyes investigated the surroundings. The forest creaked with warnings of danger. A thumping sound pierced my ears as twigs snapped repetitiously. My frozen stance thawed as a large wooden plant fell upon the very spot I stood seconds earlier. Another began to plummet. Squinting through the darkness, my terror led me through the forest in a haste. A large branch took my legs with it as it fell from the sky. My back landed on the unforgiving ground, and my sight focused on a tree that was tumbling directly towards me. I took large breaths and let out a few obscenities into the debris filled air. The branch that stole my footing was kind enough to hold the angry wood just long enough to roll out of the way.

I emerged from the foliage and ran into the forest as the woods imploded all around. The sound tore through my head as I was able to keep in front of the destruction; the moon lit a path that was shadowed. It showed awareness that someone was assisting in the venture. A fallen tree that laid upon a large rock was spotted as my body lunged underneath it. I used my hands to plug my ears, for there was a war going on and there was an intense ringing inside my cranium. I took a fetal position as fragments of the forest struck my bruised flesh. My arms and teeth were clenched, waiting for an end.

The commotion died down as I slowly began to make my way out of the rubble. There seemed to be no end to the branches that covered the rock and tree that were used for refuge. It was like being buried alive. A slight case of claustrophobia shared my brain, and it took all my will to not let panic set in. An agonizing scream echoed throughout the wooded area. The haunting pitch boosted my adrenaline and I quickly tore through the rest of the debris, gasping for a breath of fresh air as the moon came back into view.

"Show yourself," I said and waited for a response. After a few moments of silence, my anger began to boil over. I threw a tantrum: I tossed anything and everything within reach vigorously around the woods. After a few moments of losing mentality, I gathered my composure.

"This is absurd. Come out here and we will deal with the situation. I'm all alone; just for you." Again, there was no response and my dilemma was now growing. If Junior was not there, it was possible that he had gone after Dean. Junior had learned how to unleash an awesome power using nature, and it was uncertain what his purpose was. Was it to distract me? Or was he trying to get me into thinking mode? He was aware that one of my weaknesses was to process new information over and over until it drove me mad and once my mind was busy, it was easier to take advantage of. I did not over think the situation, leaving my mind open and clear. If he was not going to show himself, it was time that I made sure that my old partner was safe. As my feet clumsily made their way through the mess, a dark image formed ahead.

Cautiously approaching the object, I discovered it to be a torn t-shirt. Once the shirt was within reaching distance, a sudden gust of wind circled around, carrying the garment high into the night sky. The floating cloth disappeared, and in its absence, a dark image of what seemed to be a body hanging by the neck appeared. Without haste, I climbed a nearby tree to grasp a better view.

About fifteen feet into the air, my eyes were able to distinguish that the neck was wrapped merely by the branches of the wooden structure. My stomach turned and my blood thinned as the victim was revealed. It was certain that Junior was doing all he could to frustrate me into making a deadly mistake. He was slamming into my sanity with everything he could muster up. Even though the vision of my good friend Greg hanging in the night was traumatic, it was not going to let me stray from helping an unrelated friend in need.

"Looking for someone?" whispered a voice from within the darkness. "I want to see you," I demanded.

"You want much more than that."

"What do you need from me?" I inquired as a stick slashed my face. "This is your master plan? You are going to beat me with twigs?"

"Whatever it takes," he hissed from directly behind me. "Are you enjoying yourself? I am having a wonderful time. Watching you lose your mind is quite entertaining; so much drama."

"Did you kill Greg?"

"Greg had a problem putting his nose where it did not belong. I merely showed him how helpless he really was."

"He did not take his own life!"

"I helped," he responded with a condescending tone. "Why would you do such a thing?"

"You know why," he said as he blew me into a tree.

"What's with the frickin' wind?" I said aloud as I picked myself up. "If you cannot kill me, how is it possible that you could take his life?"

"I told him he was a God. He was much weaker than you; most people are. Greg was easy to control. I pointed up and he climbed until a branch broke and he died the way he was meant to."

"What does that mean?"

"There is much you do not know. Greg's family had a history of hangings in the past."

"Bullshit! I know his family; no one spoke of such things."

"The people you know are not of the same blood. His biological parents participated in a mass suicide. They hung themselves in the same room as Greg. He was lying in his crib; he was an infant," Jay laughed as he told the astonishing story.

"The night Greg disappeared, how did he know how to find you?" I changed the subject. I did not want any more information on the tragic end of his parents.

"I cannot be found by just anybody," he spoke, "I found him." A loud, harsh scream ripped out of my lungs and filled the air. My heart pounded and with each beat it felt as if I was being stabbed.

"You deliberately went after him?"

"Your vision that day was of a young girl trapped in a certain familiar house. She desperately needed you and you sent someone else."

"I did not send him; he went without my consent," I interrupted. "Tell yourself whatever keeps the guilt at bay," he advised. "Screw you!" I yelled in his ghostly face.

"Profanity does not solve problems," he chuckled. "If you weren't such a coward you would have gone yourself. Instead, you revealed the location to your friend."

"I don't go to where the visions show me to go because they could be traps. I made a dire mistake for telling him the whereabouts. I will never forgive myself for that mistake," I was forcing the tears to subside. "Why did you hate him so much?"

"Greg was much like you; he did not agree with the way I lived my life. Once I let him see certain things, he fled and ignored me," he paused and gave me a hauntingly wicked smile.

"Greg was an intelligent man," I commented.

"If he was so smart, why did he fall from a tree?" Junior asked a rhetorical question.

"Because his heart was bigger than his brain," I replied anyhow.

"He does not matter anymore, you are my problem," he pointed his finger in my direction.

"He does matter! You took an innocent life to get even with me." "Greg was not innocent. What happened between me and him had nothing to do with you." "What did he do to you?"

"He abandoned me," Junior responded. "He was my only true friend and he deserted me."

"Greg was a great man and he never proved to be anything else."

"I was your friend at one time, remember!" He screamed into the darkness.

"Until I saw the real you," I replied. "And who is the real me?"

"A selfish soul," I responded.

"I took you in! I gave you the knowledge to protect yourself. I treated you as family."

"You should have taught me how to protect myself from you. You didn't have a clue of how to be a friend. It has nothing to do with bringing someone into a sick tormented life because that is how you lived. A true friend helps an individual when they are facing hard times. You brought on unnecessary moments that no one ever needed to deal with."

"You know nothing about me," he commented.

"I know that you are weak," I harshly pronounced. "Believe whatever you wish."

"So, what is your next move?"

"To rid the world of the likes of you!" He shouted as he vanished.

He was upset and more importantly, he was ruthless. There was no doubt that he had a plan, and it called out for suffering. While I was contemplating my next move, my wandering eyes discovered a pile of dirt sitting in the middle of a clearing. My intrigue pressured me to explore the open land. There was a sudden rustling sound, and my body prepared itself for the upcoming wind that never came. The noise dissipated and the surroundings made it very difficult to relax. After a few moments of standing completely still, the mystery rustling again entered my ear-canal. My feet took off in a rush, racing each other to the very spot where the sound was heard. No more being a coward; it was time to face my terrors. A tree stump took me by surprise and my face smacked into the ground. Trying to regain an upright position was much harder than it should have been, and I stumbled around like a drunk. Losing my balance from the pile of dirt, my body tumbled into a hole. The crevice seemed to fit my form perfectly and that was not comforting. Immediately I leapt from the crevice and noticed a small rabbit a few feet away. After convincing myself that the bunny was the cause of the noises that I heard, the next problem was to figure out what, or who, dug such a rectangular pit. I was certain that the cavity was meant to be my grave.

The distress that I endured was beginning to bleed into my mind. The grave no longer existed; instead, a very comfortable and much-needed bed lay in its place. My tired bones jumped at the chance to rest, and my back hit the illusionary mattress with a hard thud. The back of my eyelids began to show mini-movies of peace and happiness, until they changed to misery. A child stood surrounded by giant stalks of corn. There was a sadness that grew stronger and stronger until it squeezed the fluid from my eyes. Outlandish, uncontrollable emotions took precedence as my eyelids popped open and my top half snapped upright. I was overwhelmed by moving pictures; they were everywhere. There were thousands of tiny films scattered throughout the forest. Each showed a different outlook of the child's' life. He was always alone, even when the room was crowded. He looked as a stranger would, however, that did not mean he necessarily was. Soon all the pictures turned into one, and in the boy's hand there was a knife that glistened from blood. The young lad was smiling; it was not a comforting gesture. My sight pierced through the night to barely glimpse the figure of a woman. With every second that occurred, the woman lost her blur. She was clutching her throat, and blood oozed through the cracks between her fingers. A helpless man deliriously moved from behind her and held his intestines in his arms; his stomach was slashed horizontally across the skin of his belly.

I crept from the sunken dirt and proceeded to push the mound of soil back from which it came. If I was to die in that crevice, he was to dig it again. My attention was then refocused on the devil child and what seemed to be his family. The people were not real, just images that someone had somehow placed in my head. The man fell on top of the dying woman and they both flopped like fish out of water. The boy increased his grin as he watched the ridiculous act occur. The young butcher's neck creaked as his head turned towards me. He licked the blade of the knife and vanished from sight.

The small furry creature that I had seen earlier appeared in the boy's absence. I made the space between us smaller. The fur upon its body seemed wet as it glistened in the moonlight. My knees plunged into the foliage a few paces from the forest creature. There seemed to be a tear in the poor animal's eye. The rabbit seemed scared and tried to run, but its body jumped into the thicket as its head fell to the ground in front of me. I rolled my eyes and looked straight into the sky.

"You are sick!" I shouted. The horrifying scene made me wonder if Junior was able to harm me. Maybe he was keeping me alive for a reason. What about Dean, was he in danger? I returned the two halves of the small forest creature to each other, and made a hole in the dirt for its comfort. After replacing the last of the dirt, I paid my respects to the furry critter and returned to the mission of protecting Dean.

My mind was muddled as I became disoriented and lost. It was not my first time in that particular forest, yet nothing looked familiar. It was undenounced if Junior had put some kind of spell on me or if stress was the cause of my lapse in memory. Either way, it was important that I found my way to Dean soon. The location that I sent Dean to was near a small river, therefore, small bursts of running took place while sudden stops to listen for the sound of flowing water were intermitted. After a few minutes of the ridiculous behavior, it became a relief that there was no one around to witness the lunacy. The only souls around were Junior and his army of the dead, and their thoughts of me did not matter.

Soon it became evident that I was definitely out of my element, and I wiped my face with the blistering, bloody palm of my hand. My attention was then attracted upwards into the night sky, where I noticed a certain star. It was a hundred times brighter than the others, and seemed to be moving across the air. The celestial body was definitely in motion, and it did not leave my sight until it came to a halt. Immediately, I changed course and darted through the rampaged woods hurdling the falling branches towards the direction of the mystery light, until it became necessary to stop and catch my breath. Then the miraculous sound of flowing water caressed my ears ever so gently. The lighted salvation was no mistake; it was definitely sent to assist with finding my way. Everything came together and the location of the bridge was fresh in my mind. All I had to do next was get there in one piece and hope that my partner in crime had arrived safe. The only problem, for the moment, was that Junior had not played any of his tricks recently, and that meant he was up to something.

Dean's location was just around the bend, yet my next move was undecided. There was confidence in the thought that Junior was unable to cross the wooden path on his own, however, I was not certain that he did not find a way to connect his spirit with my living body. If he had, there was no stopping him. The risk of bringing him to the zone of tranquility was one that could not be taken. He would most definitely destroy everything in his path if he was given the chance. I desired to draw him out into the open so he could be physically seen as I crossed the bridge.

Just then the Satanist boy from earlier had returned; it was the clearest vision yet. The mortally wounded woman lay still, as the innards of the man were sprawled over her corpse. A desperate plea was revealed as he reached his hand towards the boy. I heard the name Stanley seep from the dying man's mouth, followed by the words, "how could you?" The man's head then fell upon the poor woman that he laid upon. My cheek was wet from a stream of tears. It was a hard scene to watch without showing emotion. It was then noticed that another man was hiding in the corn stalks. He seemed to be enjoying the disastrous scene before him. The boy looked at the stranger and put one thumb into the air. The mystery man returned the hand motion, and I ran into the vision, screaming at the two demented figures; my interference forced them to evaporate.

Why would anybody want me to see such a horrible story? My mind was overflowing with questions, and concentrating became impossible. The bridge had disappeared, and my knees plopped into the ground below to give my weary legs a rest. I was not sure if the wooden obstruction really vanished or if my thinker was not in working order. My vision was blurred, and nothing seemed real; I was exhausted, physically and mentally. After a few moments of silence, I decided to look for the bridge once again. While rubbing my eye bulbs and doing everything possible to relax, the bridge suddenly reappeared, and the second my foot stepped forward, it was gone. My eyes rolled into the back of my skull and I screamed Dean's name through my mouth; there was no response. Then an unfamiliar voice was thrown into the silence. The voice was that of a woman; she told me to pay attention, and once again, Stanley and his victims were standing before me. The movie was meant to be played out in its entirety, so I fought the urge to interfere. The boy's name was Stanley, which I remembered from the last time the senseless vision was present. The man from the thicket removed himself from the plants and joined Stanley as they stood over their victims. Stanley seemed to be quite pleased with the outcome that had arrived. The mystery man was also gleaming with delight. I, on the other hand, was horrified and disgusted. The Man placed one of his large hands upon the small boy's shoulder. He then leaned down to face him. Stanley dropped the bloody blade and swung his arms around the stranger's waist. "You did well my young protégé," said the man.

"I only did what you asked," Stanley responded. "Now what do we do?" "We start our life together just like we were meant to."

"I think I'm going to miss them," the boy said.

"I will take their place. You will see that everything is as it was meant to be. It is now time to give you the name that has been waiting for you."

"Am I officially your son?" Stanley asked.

"Yes, and no longer will you bear the name Stanley," the man commented as he began to walk with the boy. "You are now a junior."

"Jay, just like my new daddy," the boy said excitedly.

The scene made my blood boil and I launched through the fantasy as it vanished right before my eyes. I spun myself around and around, looking for anything that would show itself to me while panting like a tired animal. My heart was beating against my chest; it was erratic and out of sync. Junior was once named Stanley, but more importantly, he killed his parents under the command of Jay. What was going on? Why would Junior show me such a horrible secret? It could not have been him.

It must have been whoever told me to pay attention. There was someone else among us and she wanted me to know the truth.

The bridge had returned in one piece but, before I had the chance to cross it, the wind began to pick up which was a sure sign that someone else was present.

"What do you desire of me?" I asked while my face stared at the bridge. "Your demise," said Junior.

I rotated to face him. He appeared to be alone; that did not mean he was. After learning about what he had done to his parents as a young child, he was now even more treacherous. He was a coward. That was the reason he behaved the way he did; cowards were unpredictable. He was a scared little boy that was easily manipulated. Jay was an evil soul that found lust in obscure brutal acts. It was becoming easy to understand what went wrong with Junior.

"Again I ask: how my death will improve your well-being?" I made direct eye contact with the danger.

"The pleasure of bringing your soul to my realm will be enough to keep me amused," he retorted.

"I just want to finish what I started. I am begging you to leave me be," I cracked my neck, "Stanley."

With his real name spoken out loud, he ceased to appear. The gust of wind began to swirl in front of me. I used my forearms as a shield from all the roughage that was tossed. The wind died down, and my arms rested along my side. Junior then appeared; he didn't look amused.

"Who do you think you're talking to?" he asked forcefully. "Something you would like to tell me?"

"It seems that you already know the story," he began to circle my body. "Don't play dumb with me."

"I know one of your secrets; it does clear the air as to why you are helping a mad man."

"Jay is a scholar and a gentleman," Junior stuck up for his fake father. "He is the reason for my power today. Without his teachings I would be a weak, pathetic soul such as yourself. He made me into a man and showed me how to live large. I tried to teach you and you were not cooperative."

"You honestly believe that you lived large? You're dead! No one alive even remembers you. You may have powers, but what good are they? They are not going to bring your life back."

"You don't know!" he screamed as he walked away from me.

"I know that your games aren't working!" I yelled back at him as he moseyed away. "Look, I still control my mind. I won't let you drive me insane!" I was instantly granted a throbbing pain inside of my skull, and heard many voices that I could not decipher. I clutched my ears and clenched my teeth. I had to concentrate. Somebody was trying to get a message through.

"Leave here!" Junior shouted from the distance.

I screened a picture in the darkness that was caused from my shut lids. It was an older woman whose face I could not identify. She was quite persistent on getting my attention. I strained to block out all the other insignificant souls that were trying to reach me.

"Talk to me," I pleaded.

"The garden was a cage for everyone in it," the woman pronounced. "Stanley was the keeper."

"Why would Junior trap his self-proclaimed father?" I asked.

"You have broken through the gate with your dear friends, thus you have set the others free as well," the woman explained. "They are not a threat to you." The gracious woman disappeared from sight. I whispered a thank you and stood to face Junior.

"What do you know?" He demanded.

"I know that you are weaker than you wish to be," I followed my comment with a smirk and a wink.

"That's funny," he commented. "You are crazy. Look at yourself! You are in the middle of the woods carrying dead bodies. You are talking to the deceased; you've gone mad."

From what the old lady said, I was led to believe that Junior's army had no power towards me. All that had to be done was cross the bridge with him still in sight and his mob was of no relevance. I stepped backwards slowly and was only a few feet from the destination. Junior glared at me; he seemed to be confused. He was still waiting for me to respond to his candor. There was no plan on debating; it was time to flee. I felt the wooden angel under my feet and an overwhelming feeling of relief flowed through my veins. Junior threw a tantrum that suggested my thoughts on the matter were correct; he was not able to follow. I expressed my gratitude verbally into the still night for whoever deserved it.

"I will see you soon," Junior mumbled as I pushed him from my mind. I turned around and discovered a familiar face; Dean was more than happy to see me. I greeted the blessed creature with a full body hug and enough laughter to become contagious.

"Old Rusty here?" I asked. "Yes," Dean answered.

"The kind owner of the beast snuck a paper sack behind the seat." "You saw him?" Dean inquired.

"It was her, and I didn't have to see. I just know," I winked. "Go find it and we will replenish our appetites as we watch the sunrise." I laid on the dirt and rested the muscles that were screaming out for attention. My head rested against a rock and my lungs were filled to their capacity with the beautiful morning air.

I greatly appreciated the splendid gift of nourishment supplied by the lovely Mrs. Sanders. The sounds bursting from the mouth of the old man next to me proved that he was also enjoying her kindness. I washed the sandwich down with some water, which was also in the truck, and closed my eyes to fully enjoy the feeling of liquid running down my throat.

"So, what happened between you and Junior when he was still alive?" Dean broke the silence with a direct and personal question.

"We've been apart for hours and that is the question that rolls off your tongue," I said as the sarcasm plunged from my mouth and into the cool, calm atmosphere.

"I think that it may have significance to our ordeal."

"So, enlighten me with your wise and noble idea of what drove Junior to be banned from my life."

"I can only imagine that you witnessed something unbearable, and the cause of the act was certainly his doing." I was proud of the old fool, for my behavior was out of line and my tone was that of a jerk. I was rude and livid. The old soul did not break one bit: he was solid. My eyes locked with his.

"I respect you as an honorable friend. I know the only reason you sit on my side is because Frank asked you to."

"How do you know that?"

"Frank and I think alike, remember?" I nudged the inside information to him. He nodded his head and curved a tiny start of a smile until his expression turned serious.

"Stop evading the question and tell me what I want to hear!" He demanded.

"What you want to hear is a story that I may not be willing to part with."

"I have been more than patient with you. I have followed you through the brink of hell and all I want is an answer to a question that I know you have the answer to. I will not judge you or think any different of you. It is a known fact that your life brings you to do certain acts that most people would not be able to comprehend. I was best friends with a person who had the same characteristics as you and I never judged him." "Did you know that Junior did not have the same blood flowing through his veins as Jay?"

"Are you saying that they are not father and son?" "Yes, that is what I am saying."

"You have acquired information that has to be false," Dean set the water jug down and wiped his brow.

"I was told the news by a mysterious voice; it was an old woman's voice."

"You must be imagining."

"Don't tell me that I am imagining," I said angrily. "I know my life is filled with nonsense. I have to learn to deal with what is dished out to me. I know what I was told, and I saw a vision. A vision was what led me to Frank on his day of reckoning, so I have learned that what I see in my head are stories that should not be taken for granted."

"I am not saying that. All I am saying is that you may have received a clue that is false. I knew Jay for quite a few years; it is hard for me to understand how and why he would keep such a secret from me."

"He is an evil, twisted man! Why would you think that he would not deceive you? Trust me; you do not want to be that guy."

"What guy is that?"

"The type of guy who believes that no one will take advantage of you," I scolded. "I used to be that person and there is no more room in this world for another naive misfit."

"What are you trying to say?"

"Jay corrupted little Stanley and brainwashed him into doing very bad things."

"Who is Stanley?"

"Junior," I simply answered. I laid myself back onto the dirt and stared at the enormous sun that hung above. It was a sensual feeling to be amongst its glorious rays. The night was tough, yet we survived to venture another day.

"I'm not sure I even want to know the answer to my next question, but I have to ask," Dean took a drink of water and wiped his mouth with his forearm. "What did Stanley do?"

"Stanley made it possible for Jay to take care of him, Stanley made himself an orphan."

"You have to be kidding me," Dean commented after the astonishing news reached his delicate ears. "I knew his mother. Jay had a wife."

"His wife was not Stanley's mother." "How do you know this?"

"I told you that I was given the information from a strange woman."
"Who is this woman and what does she look like?"

"I did not see her; I only heard her voice. I did not recognize the voice, so I don't have a clue on to who she could be. If I had to guess, I would say someone that has a problem with Junior; possibly his mother."

"Do you mean his real mother or the fake one?" "Did his fake one die?"

"I assume so. She vanished." "That sounds just about right."

"How so?" Dean pumped my brain for information.

I leaned close to Dean and whispered in his ear, "The family is a little nuts if you know what I mean."

Dean let out a loud laugh that echoed throughout our surroundings. It was a masterful break from the intense moments that cluttered our moods. I enjoyed the time of silence that followed my rude remark and thought of nothing. It felt fantastic to not carry the burden of having to make an immediate decision. My eyes closed and sleep would have been a helpful act to commit, but then again, my conversation with the old man next to me was not going to end so suddenly. He would not quit pestering until I coughed up the words he so desperately needed to hear.

"Could it be possible that the voice you heard was once again, the voice of Frank's wife?" Dean again started with the questioning.

"No," I answered. "How are you sure?"

"It wasn't the same voice. I may be insane, but I can tell voices apart." "What exactly did she say?"

"She told me to pay attention. I then saw Stanley standing over his murdered parents with a bloody knife in his grip. Jay was hiding in the distance."

"He stood back and watched?"

"The sick bastard stood back and watched," I repeated the horrible words.

Dean laid back; he had a blank look portrayed on his wrinkled face. It was easy for me to understand his mindset. It was embarrassing to realize that someone played you for a fool, especially if that someone was close to you at one point in time. The biggest problem that I had with liars was the fact that they did not ponder on the everlasting torture that they added to their victims' lives. They just went on with their deceitful days like nothing ever happened however, the poor individual that was the pawn in their little game, would forever be burdened with the memory of being a sucker. "If what you say is the truth, then I am a fool," Dean had a self- realization.

"Not necessarily," I said.

"All the disturbing words I've been told about Jay are true," he hung his head with shame. "I can't believe how someone could be so two-faced."

"The world has gone down a long road since you've been born. The path has taken an ugly turn and is now dead center in the bad part of town. Honesty faded away just as disco and whatever else thrived during your day of bliss," I leaned towards Dean's ear. "Something in the air sucked away everybody's conscience. The voice of reasoning has been drowned out by the screams of chaos."

"I don't believe a word of it," Dean reacted to what I said. "There is still good that roams the earth. You're honest and you're young."

"That is what I've been trying to get you to understand," I paused for dramatic intentions. "I am just like everybody else. I bring pain to other living beings. I can be nice and charming if I have to be, however, most often I am rude and annoying. I can be trusted if I want or need something, otherwise I don't care. I lie, exactly like the people I despise. I am far from being a good person."

"You're loyal," he commented.

"Only to the people I need something from." "I don't believe that."

"Seconds ago, you became angry when you discovered that an old friend was not what he seemed to be. You felt like a chump. That man played you. Played you for a weak-minded person. That makes you feel sick. He was searching for the right sucker to fulfill his dementia," I took a deep breath and sighed loudly. "That is who I am. I make you trust me… then I change."

"You do the things you do for far different reasons than a typical low-life person."

"It doesn't matter what my intentions are. Honestly, I don't try to hurt people and I always put others before me however, the outcome is the same as a typical low-life person. I may not mean any harm with the actions that I perform, but I am two-faced."

He shook his head with disappointment, "I think we should roll over and take a cat nap, Frank."

Dean turned his body from me and closed his eyes. He was not happy with the way I felt about myself and him calling me Frank was not a slip of the tongue. He was sharing the resentment that he held for his dear, deceased friend.

I awoke and brushed my palm across my face as I glared upon the ball of flames that hung high over my head. My sidekick was no longer sprawled out next to me. I leapt to my feet and searched the area as it was discovered that the old man had found comfort in the shade that Old Rusty provided. After creeping close enough to see that his lungs were receiving the fresh air, I left him be. He certainly could use the down time.

My limbs took me on a short walk that ended on top of the remains of one of my best friends. Kneeling down and brushing the grass and weeds that had grown over the bare soil, I knew that the person six feet under was watching me at that very moment. If there were any tears left in my ducts, they would have been shed. However, the past twenty-four hours had bled me dry. I sprawled out over the grave and began to reminisce about the strange island.

The land was quite extraordinary, sitting four hundred feet long and sixty feet wide, the oasis was a quaint surprise in an otherwise normal river. The waterway was nothing special and many, many hours of my youth were spent walking up and down its banks. Nowhere did the small brook seem to stretch over twenty feet wide. One day my anxiety got the better of me and I found myself lost in the woods. The sound of flowing water caught my attention and soon the bank of the brook was where I stood. I was certain that the river was familiar, however, my eyes had never seen that particular region before. It was miles from my usual dwellings. If I would have followed the flow of the water, it would definitely had taken me home; I decided to mosey in the other direction and see where it led.

About a mile up, the canal expanded its width. Sitting in the middle of the water was a small island. There were no trees, only dirt and weeds. I swam over to the mound of dirt and strolled up and down the terrain looking for any signs of life. It was deserted, and seemed as if no one had ever set a foot upon it. There were a few animal tracks in the soil, but nothing living was found. Once the island came to an end, the banks resumed their twenty-foot width. The river was like a snake, and the mound of dirt was its lunch. I decided to keep it a secret.

As the years progressed, I visited the wild obstruction when isolation became necessary. There was no road that led to the sanctuary; I leisurely made my own trail and did my best to keep it hidden so no one would follow the path. The area was so peaceful and tranquil that it became a safe zone. It was declared that nothing could hurt me while on the island. Sometimes, believing in something was all it took to make things possible.

Soon the land mass was turned into my very own secret graveyard. A small bush was planted in the ground to serve as a head stone.

The shrub that sat next to me while Dean caught some Zs belonged to a dear friend of mine who I met through Junior. He was the first to be buried on the sacred land. Getting his lifeless corpse across the rapid water was quite difficult and incredibly strenuous. It became evident that a bridge was required. It took over a year to build the modest passage. It wasn't much, but it did the job that it was intended to do. The wood used was from the trees that surrounded the river. The task at hand proved to be quite difficult, but somehow, I persevered and finished the structure on my own. It was difficult to not tell anyone of my accomplishment since I was quite proud of my feat, but it was important to keep the island undisclosed.

It had become time to add three more victims to the island. Silently, I retrieved the tools I needed from Old Rusty; my motive was to not wake the sleeping gent. After taking a few moments to find the perfect spot for the new arrivals, it became time for manual labor. The sun was in full force and the air was still, so the heat was high. I removed my shirt from my skin. I plunged the shovel into the dry, flaky crust of the earth. My muscles cried every time they were forced to work. It was far from an easy task after all the digging that was done during the night. About an hour lapsed, and the first hole was finally complete.

"Starting the fun without me?" Dean inquired as he approached. "Well I'll be damned, the dead walks," I chuckled. "You are definitely a good ghost."

"I am not a ghost," Dean rebutted with extreme seriousness.

"I was only joking," I said as I wobbled backwards, falling into the freshly dug crevice.

"You don't look so well."

"What?" I asked as I awkwardly pulled my bones from the crater. I had the damnedest time keeping my balance and my speech was slurred. Everything in sight started circling at great speeds. "I am fine. You're being weird."

Dean's head moved side to side as he left my presence. I couldn't decide if he was upset. My mind was wishy-washy and for the life of me, I wasn't able to recall what was said to him. Staring dumbfounded in the direction Dean headed, my train of thought dissipated, and my surroundings were unrecognizable. After a few moments of studying the terrain, there seemed to be some familiarity but then again, not enough to fully reveal my location. Then a sound of an engine broke the silence and soon an old truck moved into view. The vehicle came to a halt and an old, dirty man moved from the cab. With each step he took forwards, I took one backwards. His clothes were torn and bloody, and after further observation it became clear that my condition was the same. There was dried blood all over my skin and there was no remembrance of what occurred.

"Terry," the man said with a quiet whisper.

"What?" I whispered back sarcastically. I was rolling my eyes inside my head.

"Do you know who I am?"

I tried to focus upon his aged face; my mind was cloudy, and I ran. The sound of running water was all around as the end of the dirt came into view. The strange man kept approaching as I dove into cool blue liquid. The old man jumped in after me and his speed and agility were overwhelming. My arms and legs moved as fast as they could, yet the aged soul was able to grab hold of my ankle. With a quick kick, his grasp was lost, and my direction quickly changed. A few seconds later, he regained his clutch. He then was able to pull me back to shore. I struggled lightly; my goal was to break free of his grasp, not to break his arm. Once back on shore, his hand let loose as we crawled out of the water. I was first on my feet and, hovering over the old gent, who was still on all fours, my foot raised over his head as if it was going to smash down upon him. He began to tremble, and my plan changed to fleeing. My mad dash brought me back to the truck and I discovered three crates. My curiosity got the best of me as I heard the stranger's footsteps approaching. Ripping the lid off the closest box, my eyes stared at the rotting corpse inside and my innards immediately flew out of my mouth and on to the ground below.

"You are a sick one," I yelled to the stranger. He did not respond; he was nowhere to be found. Reluctantly, I made my way towards the other two crates. I was certain that opening the boxes was not in my best interest, nevertheless, I had to know what the old man was up to.

"Terry, stop," screeched the geezer.

"I am not sure how you know me, but you'd better keep your distance if you want to continue living," I threatened and continued to reach for the second lid.

Before I opened the box, I listened for the man. The only sound that pierced my ears was the sound of my heart beating. Wooziness took over and a faint feeling occurred. I consumed a deep breath as I spotted the aged gent running up to me with an object in one of his hands. It was high in the air and as he approached, it was lowered quickly. There was a ferocious stinging sensation that surrounded my face as I fell to the ground. Another sharp pain attacked the back of my head as my eyelids slammed together. I awoke to find myself lying in the dirt and immediately jumped to become vertical. A few moments ticked by before I was able to view my surroundings clearly. I shook my head as Dean approached. "What happened?" I asked.

"I am so sorry," he ranted as his knees plunged into the dirt and weeds. "I did not mean to harm you. I had no choice."

While Dean seemed to be having a freak-out moment, I rubbed the wound that sat on the back of my head. There was an enormous abrasion that the tip of my fingers discovered. It was presumed that my newfound agony was caused by the weeping old sack in front of me.

"Say something; tell me you know who I am," Dean spouted out with urgency as he pulled upon my pant leg.

"I know who you are." My mind was feeble, and the throbbing pain did not allow me to comprehend what Dean wanted, so I walked back to the last place I remembered being. Preparing to bury my three dead friends was the last memory that remained alive. Reaching the area that I chose, I discovered that the holes were completed and the three coffins were sitting next to them.

"I wasn't sure what order you wanted them in, so I left the decision for you to make," Dean recited as he narrowed the space between us. "I have some aspirin for you," he held out his hand, "and some water."

I swallowed the bitter pills and washed them away with warm water. Every emotion that was ever discovered clouded my brain. Sadness, confusion, frustration, and most of all: shame. Shame of my actions that persuaded Dean to use force to keep me under control. On the ground next to my feet, there was a shovel that had blood on its spade. I assumed that the red paint came from the back of my head, and that Dean had used it to stop my demented behavior.

I did not recall what went on. Often in my life there were experiences where my mind slept, but my body continued to thrive. Usually the outbreak lasted only a few minutes; some had been famous for lasting hours. The blackouts where not so common, but as the days progressed, they appeared more frequently. I did not understand my actions during an episode, and feared for the unlikely folks who were around when they occurred.

"Did I try to hurt you?" I sat my tired, sore figure upon the dirt and let my legs hang into one of the apertures in the ground.

"Do you know what went on?"

"I regret that I did not warn you about my blackouts. I really didn't even think about them with all the stressful situations that were happening. Also, I am not known to have an episode very often."

"So, it is not a new trait?"

"Not exactly, but like I said, it doesn't happen often," I continued rubbing the stump underneath my hair. "I should have warned you."

"You did not attack me. You were scared and tried to run." "Did I cross the bridge?"

"No… you tried a water getaway," he responded. "I had to swim after you and pull you back to shore. Once we arrived back on land you became defensive. It looked as if you were going to kick me, yet for some reason you did not. Instead, you ran to Old Rusty and discovered the crates. Once you saw what was in the boxes you became crazed."

"Crazed?" I asked.

"Yes, you were delirious and scared out of your mind. You did not recognize me or your surroundings, however, you did respond to your name."

"I knew who I was, yet I was confused about everything else?"

"You responded to your name. That didn't mean that you knew who you were," he reached for the jug of water that sat next to me. "It could have been a trigger of familiarity. However, it did not pull you from your trance."

"Why did I make you hit me?"

"After you discovered Frank, you started calling me vicious names. You thought that I did something horrible. What I have learned about you is that when you believe that someone has done wrong, you correct the matter. I did not want you to hurt me, so I knocked you out."

"You did the right thing," I laid my hand upon his quivering shoulder. "I wish I wouldn't have done that."

"I also wish I didn't do what I did. I do not blame you. I know it was out of your hands," he said as he leaned closer to me. "I didn't really think that you were going to hurt me. Nevertheless, I had to keep you under control. I did not wish to harm you."

"It is alright, I understand that you did whatever it took to protect yourself and the cargo. Again, you did the right thing."

More than once, I have witnessed a man lose his mind. Each showcase was committed by a different hindrance. Some were from too many drugs pumping through the blood. Some were forced into insanity by a reckless thump to the head. Some were caused by a chemical imbalance inside the brain. There were even incidents that were brought on by mind altering diseases. The reason for a man to lose his mind was irrelevant. The important part of the information was that a man had gone mad, and he became a complete stranger. No matter how close I was to the particular person, he would no longer see me as a friend, but as an enemy. That was how Dean viewed me a few hours earlier, and he was having a hard time processing what occurred.

"Listen to me," I moved closer to Dean and stared directly into his dilated eyes. "I have witnessed people become somebody else, just as you have today. I do not blame you for your actions, and you must believe me. It is very important that you trust what I am saying, for if it happens again, you need to respond the same exact way."

"I don't know if I can handle this anymore," Dean replied as a tear showed itself upon his cheek.

"I can relate to how you feel. I know how scary I can become," I started to speak as he interrupted my words.

"It's not you I am scared of," he commented. "It is the ghosts or spirits or whatever they are that keep chasing us and manipulating you."

"We are safe here."

"I don't believe that for one second," he stood and moved away from me. "You told me that the circle of bare dirt in the garden was safe, and then you changed your mind. You have told me yourself that you do not know what these things are capable of. You told me that Junior's powers grow every day, so why can he not find a way to cross the bridge and destroy us both? Why?"

I honestly did not have an answer for the old man and was completely absorbed with the intense look that appeared upon his face. He was turning into me.

"You must get into Old Rusty and go home," I demanded.

"You do not order me around!" He shouted back as his arms flew into the air. "I have come too far to leave you stranded. That would definitely not make me a good man."

"I am astonished by the fact that you still stand before me," I stressed my opinion. "You have survived a heart attack, a twenty-five- foot throw through the air, and you have seen more blood last night than you have in your entire life. A man that no longer walks the world of the living appeared to you. I assure you that Junior is dead, and you saw him," I paused as I circled Dean's confused manner. "My life makes me want to run from myself. I do not expect anyone to handle the pressure that I face. I begged you to leave and you insisted on staying. I appreciate all that you have done for me and so does Frank and his family, but it is time for you to exit the stage. You are one of the greatest men I have ever had the pleasure of freaking out in front of. Return to your home and rest."

"It's not that easy. I can't get it out of my head. I thought I would be able to handle it, but my mind is spinning out of control," he frantically walked in small circles. "If I leave, it will continue to haunt me. I can't even imagine talking to another normal human being. I will look at every individual that I meet as if they are a ghost lost in my realm."

I looked upon Dean with pity and was overcome with sadness and anger. The anger was aimed at my stupidity for each and every time I brought another living soul into my world. Even though I did not force the gentle man to follow me, the guilt still ate at my innards.

"You need to not feel at fault, for what is happening is my own doing," he tried to ease my aching organs.

"I destroyed yet another innocent bystander, I will never be able to look at it any other way."

"I finally understand why Frank was so secretive. It is clear to me now," he dropped to his knees and held his head with a disappointing posture. "I damned myself and now I must learn to live with the irrationality that I deserve."

"If you blame yourself, you will only be mimicking the ways of Frank and myself," I knelt down next to him. "The thing that made you angry with your best friend will destroy you if you let it. You can walk away, and I promise you that nothing will follow you."

"How can the tone of your voice sound so sincere?" he asked as he turned his ashamed head in my direction.

"There is nothing that you can offer Junior. He cannot benefit from you in any way. I will not let any of them harm you," I spoke what I believed was the truth.

"I think that you are toying with me," he gazed at me with crazy eyes. "You want me to leave because you have other plans?"

"I assure you that I do not have another agenda."

"I think that you are Junior," he observed me closely. He was quite skittish with his movements. "Is this the part where you attack me?" I lightly chuckled at his remark because he looked so intense. His eyes were glazed over, and his face bled for sympathy.

With my arm blocking the sun from my face I said, "I think the best move is for you to find some shade and sing some songs."

"What?" He expressed confusion.

"I'm telling you, it will keep your mind occupied and relieve your anxiety," I shared one of my secret methods for sanity.

"What type of song should I sing?" he indulged me.

"Any song that occupies your thoughts," I answered with a comforting smile placed on my face as I left him alone.

It was time to complete the job and bury the three bodies where they would be safe. Suzie was placed in the center hole so she would be surrounded by the love of her parents. As I flung dirt onto the crates, I heard Dean singing in the background.: *If you want my body and you think I'm sexy, come on baby let me know.* It was an odd choice for the old man; it was quite humorous and most definitely eased some unwanted tension. I patted the dry dirt and collected a few stones to build temporary gravestones; shrubs would be planted on a future day. I then spoke some words of grace. It was an emotional ordeal to see Frank in the form of a decaying corpse; I would not forget the picture.

Exhaustion was present, and the heat was causing my brain to spin in circles. The inside of my stomach was facing a deadly hurricane that was ripping into my innards. Dean was finished with his version of the Rod

Stewart song and shouted for my attention. I yelled back, revealing that everything was fine, even though it was far from it. My body had enough and was rearing for a seven-day nap.

As Dean approached, I was planted in the dirt. His boney hand was placed out in front of him. I accepted his gesture as our dirty skin came together. He pulled, lost his balance, and fell on top of me. He then gradually removed himself from my exhausted bones.

"I guess I'm as old and frail as I feel," he said.

"Maybe you're just weaker than you thought," I said kiddingly. "Oh, is it time for jokes? I'm insane, remember?"

"Good for you, welcome to the club," I said as I hopped to my feet and assisted my assistor. I then made my way towards shade. It was obvious that my walking was unsteady.

"So that's how it's going to be?" Dean questioned as he joined me, leaning against Old Rusty.

"How is what going to be?"

"I'm just a joke to you now," he looked at me with complete seriousness printed across his face.

"Are you kidding me?"

"I told you that I was insane, and you laughed and said welcome to the club."

"Humor is your only friend now," I said as I laid my dysfunctional body flat on the ground. "If you are not able to laugh at yourself, you might as well go drown in the river. Trust me, the only way to live with the thoughts that will now be terrorizing your mind is to laugh at them." "I'm sorry. I guess you're right," he followed my lead and stretched his bones on the ground. "I feel at ease and that kind of bothers me. The song idea was genius."

"An old, ancient secret," I stated. "Did Frank teach that to you?"

"Actually, that is something I taught to him. He used to sing 'When I Think about You I Touch Myself.' It was truly hilarious and comforting; your Rod Stewart was pretty impressive also," I said with a wink.

"Am I a bad person?" he asked.

"Not at all," I commented. "Grief and anxiety have a strange way of creeping up to you. You may feel at ease this moment, but that will change. You now have to learn to deal with fast-changing emotions. That is why I said welcome to the club. Everything will go on just like it did before we met. The difference will be that your mind will start to scare you without any notice whatsoever."

"I'm not following you."

"You will be doing a regular activity, such as brushing your teeth, or cooking breakfast when all of a sudden you will become scared and restless. You will ponder on all the events that took place yesterday. It will occur often, and it will frustrate you extremely."

"What do I do when that happens?"

"Sing," I laughed. "If you think I'm sexy and you want my body come on baby let me know." He sang with me, and we chuckled as we rolled around in the dirt and weeds. We threw dirt at each other and frolicked like two school children. It was fun to have some company. It was unfortunate that his life was forever changed, I hoped he was a strong enough person to make it through the tough times. He did witness many horrific scenarios, but it could have been much worse. No matter who you may be, it was not an easy task to deal with, viewing a person's death; Dean did not have to add that to his book of nuisances.

"When I was friends with Junior, he had an amazing beauty that called herself his girlfriend," I started to speak of a horrifying experience as Dean sat up so he would have an easier time paying attention; it was the story that he'd been waiting patiently for. "Her name was Nicole and she had amazing red hair that hung just above her belly button. The only problem I had with her was the fact that she was with him. Even though she declared them a couple, he would never admit that he was not single, unless Nicole was within hearing distance."

"So, he cheated on her?" the eager gentleman asked. He was finally receiving some answers and his anticipation was clouding the air around him.

"Everyone was well aware of his behavior except for Nicole. It made me pity her because I knew that she could do so much better. Junior was my friend and that was the reason I did not tell her about his affairs," I rolled to my side and stretched the kinks in my muscles. My stomach became infuriated, and I dry-heaved a couple of times.

"He impregnated a random cutie, and I was only clued in because he had no one else to tell. Then late one evening during one of our famous parties, I had far too much to drink, and it was all on its way back up. I struggled up the stairs to the bathroom when the sound of a girl whimpering found my ears from the laundry chute. I forgot about my angry insides and immediately ran down the hurdles to investigate." I stopped speaking, stood on my feet, and motioned my hands in front of me to let Dean understand that I was going to have to take a minute or two. He acknowledged my plea and fell onto his back as I ventured off to unload my bladder. It was not enjoyable spilling my guts to Dean, however, he paid his dues and I owed him the truth.

I rejoined Dean on the grassy plain that was shaded by our transportation as I continued.

"I stumbled to the basement. The closer I ventured, the louder the weeping became. My stomach churned as my hand slowly reached for the doorknob. I turned the knob quietly, and slowly pushed the door open enough to peer inside."

"What did you see?" the eager old man questioned.

"I saw a pool of blood on the concrete floor and noticed an unraveled coat hanger in the middle of the red puddle; it was dripping with a gooey substance. I instantly felt as if my heart had run away; I dropped to my knees."

"What was it?" Dean eagerly asked.

"The girl had her legs spread and her insides were seeping from her. Junior turned to me and said that he had to do what he had to do. He then laughed loudly. I was horrified and quite angry. The victim stared into my gushing eyes and held out her red stained hand to help her escape. Junior knocked her arm down and pushed her from the chair in which she sat. He then told me to mind my own business and forget what I saw. He called the scared girl a bitch, and kicked her in the ribs as he departed the room," I paused and wiped the sweat from my forehead. "I crawled to the helpless female and wrapped my arms around her shaking body. I squeezed tightly to smother all her fear. She begged me to believe her when she told me that none of it was her idea. She said that she passed out and awoke to a tremendous pain in her nether region. By the time she came to, the damage was already done." Dean gazed at me with pity protruding from his balls of sight.

"What became of the girl?" he asked.

"Not sure, she disappeared, and I never heard from her again," I looked at Dean with sadness in my eyes. "I can only hope that her fear led her far from Junior, for the more I learn about his younger days, the more afraid I become."

"Do you think he hurt her?"

"He drugged her, then with a coat hanger he ripped her innards out, what do you think?"

"I was referring to after all of that," Dean made himself clear.

"I want to believe that she escaped; no matter if she did or not, her life is a disaster."

"That was the reason why you and Junior became enemies?"
"Surprisingly, no," I said as a creepy grin appeared upon my face. "I never told another human what was witnessed. I avoided him for a couple months after the incident and he did not like the fact that I was no longer a part of

his life. When I gave up on him, he realized how alone he really was. In his eyes, he was a god, but what kind of god has no followers?"

"Did his girlfriend find out?"

"About two months passed before I showed my face in his vicinity. Throughout my absence, he pursued me a few times and I ignored his advances. My time spent on this earth has taught me that the best way to show someone that you're tired of them is to snub them."

"What was the reason for you to go back to his house?" Dean asked. "I wanted closure. I was searching for Nicole. It was as if I had control of her life, for the information in my head would presumably force her into changing her outcome."

"I bet that ate at you."

"I couldn't take it anymore; I wasn't a person. I became a mediocre painting on the wall, for everyone else on the planet, I was stationary. I played dead to the world," I rolled my eyes as the dread that possessed me so long ago resurfaced. "I found Nicole and told her the sad tale that haunted my every thought. Shortly after I leaked the news, I found myself face to face with the heartless soul who committed the dreadful act. He gave me a beating and I stood and took it until my body was too weak to stand. Once I fell to the ground, I immediately leapt back to my feet. Every second infuriated him; when his knuckles became sore from bashing them into my face, he abandoned the area."

"Where did he go?"

"I didn't know. I did not see him for another few months," I took a deep breath and sighed out my agony. "I searched for Nicole, however, I never heard from her again. It was funny how anyone that had a problem with Junior was disappearing. I anticipated that I was next on the list."

"Did he come back for you?" Dean asked.

"No," I simply answered. "Later that same year, I wound up at a bonfire party that was held out in the middle of nowhere. After the beating from Junior, I pretty much stayed to myself and avoided everyone. I was upset by the fact that my negligence allowed me to trust such a deviant creature, plus I had to hide my tortured face. I became a shut-in, so when the news of a large gathering approached, I decided to attend. I soon found out that showing up was a big mistake."

"Why was it a mistake?"

"Junior was there," I simply replied. Dean became more enthused every second.

"Did you confront him?"

"I completely ignored him. There were a few occasions when we ended up talking to the same group of people and I just pretended like he was a stranger. My reaction aggravated him, but he handled himself quite well. He let me continue with my act and not once did he shatter the invisible wall that I placed between us."

"Something must have happened," Dean questioned.

"The night went on for hours with no interruptions, until the Junior that I identified with resurfaced," I sat up and leaned my aching back against Old Rusty. "He began to make a scene. I heard the murmurs from the mouths of the other guests. They were talking about some jerk who kept trying to start fights; no one was complying with the invitations to rumble. For the most part, the people at the party were laid back. When he was unable to taunt anyone into punching him, he took the first move and knocked some sorry fool to the ground. Once he initiated force the rest of the partygoers became upset and protected their buddy, who was sprawled out on the dirt."

"He found what he was looking for," Dean commented.

"Yes. He had to fight. He had some kind of imbalance in his brain that made him violent," I paused and took a deep breath. I also had a tendency to battle. My temper was evil, and my fuse was quite short.

"So, what happened?" Dean asked.

"He was outnumbered, even for his skills; he held his own for a few minutes until the group took control of the situation," I said as I wiped the fountain on my forehead. "I had not seen Junior overpowered before; it was a strange sight to behold. Usually there was always someone on his side to lend a hand once he was helpless, but this time he was all alone. He had pushed everyone that once cared about him into submission. I watched as he curled into a fetal position and took the blows that were thrown amongst his bruised sides. All in all, it was hard to watch. I was conflicted with what to do, and the part of me that helped people sprang into action. I stepped in and explained that the sorry shit did not know any better, and I stated that he had learned his lesson the hard way."

"Did the group listen to you?"

"They took what I said to heart as long as he would leave the premises immediately," I stood and stretched, for my muscles were screaming for rest. Dean observed the stretching as he began to think I was preparing to leave.

"I hope you know that we are not leaving until you finish the story," he said with a serious look upon his face. I crouched down next to the curious old man and continued.

"He did not depart the battle grounds. He was forced into his vehicle and observed until his car was out of sight. Once he drove far enough away, he hid his four-wheeled transportation and snuck through the trees back to the festivities."

"He seems to be quite bull-headed, if you know what I mean," Dean commented as he followed up his words with a wink. I knew that Dean was trying to compare my stubbornness with the likes of Junior, however, I did not agree with his thoughts.

"I may be many things, but I am not like him. I know the difference between right and wrong."

"I am sorry, that was not what I meant," he replied sympathetically. "Whatever," I snickered back at him. "Anyway, he was bull-headed and did not give up on a fight. He hid for hours, waiting for the perfect time to strike. I watched a couple of guys who were involved in the confrontation with Junior; they walked into the woods, away from the rest of the group. I did not personally know the two boys, yet for some odd reason, I could not look away from the spot that the two lads disappeared. I knew something was not right, even though I was not aware that Junior stuck around."

"When you have a feeling that something is wrong, do you always act upon it?" Dean inquired.

"If I don't check into things, my mind drives me nuts. I do not always discover what my eerie feeling is caused by, and I must investigate every possibility, or I cannot rest."

"You definitely live a difficult life," the old gent commented. "I live a life that I brought upon myself."

"What do you mean?"

"It's not important," I remarked. "What is important, to you anyhow, is that I finish the story," I stopped speaking to read Dean's reaction. He nodded his head with acceptance, and I continued the disastrous tale.

"I snuck into the bushes and peered at the two gentlemen that I presumed to be in danger. They separated from the crowd so they could get high. I watched for a few minutes, and then decided that I was being foolish. As I started moving in an opposite direction of the two strangers, I heard some commotion. I quickly turned to face the noise when Junior jumped from the shrubbery; he held a large branch in his hands. He swung a mighty swing that connected to the head of one of the pot smokers. As the branch connected with his face, the man immediately dropped to the ground. The other guy started to run and was tripped up by the large stick." I felt a strange breeze across my dry, cracked lips. It was obvious that Junior did not enjoy his story being expressed, and I was certain he was listening. I gazed around my surroundings, even though I thought we were safe on the small island, there would always be doubts. Dean began to feel uncomfortable.

"Is he here?" The old man questioned as he quickly looked over his shoulder.

"No, it's going to be fine," I soothed the man's wandering mind and continued the tale. "I saw the handle of a gun that Junior had stuck in his pants. I became lightheaded and had to close my eyes to regain stability. When I opened my lids, I witnessed Junior's boot as he held his leg in the air. There was something dripping from the sole. I tried to make out if the pot smoker next to him was moving, however, I heard and saw nothing. I started to panic and was furious with myself for having a weak moment. I had to stay strong under every circumstance. My dwindling state had caused the life of an innocent human to be taken. I thought about my move, was I to attack or was I to wait things out? I noticed that the mad man was heading for the other victim, and I leapt from my hiding place. Junior turned towards me once he heard the rustling," I took a moment of silence as I wiped the horrible memory from my eyes,

"You can't stop now!" Dean demanded.

"I approached the body on the ground," I stared deep into the eyes of the old gent in front of me. "The head was bashed in, and his face was unidentifiable. I glared at Junior with my nostrils flaring. As he was occupied with me, the other young man turned from running and attacked the distracted maniac. As they scuffled Junior's shirt was torn, revealing the deadly weapon. The innocent partygoer saw the glare of the gun and immediately snagged it from Junior's belt. He held it against the temple of the crazed predator. The young man was shaking with fear, which made me well-aware that out of pure panic, he would most certainly pull the trigger." I cracked my neck and reached for what was left of the clean water.

"I had a few options to ponder over and not much time to do so. If I waited too long to react, Junior would most definitely be taking a dirt nap. I instinctually leapt from the ground and knocked the gun from the hand of the confused, high young man. The agitated bloke ran to the corpse on the ground and reached into its pocket. He then turned and attacked Junior again. I pushed Junior from the oncoming rampage and felt an instant sting upon my leg just a few inches down from my pelvic region. I stopped to view the blood spurt from the tear in my jeans. A faintness began to take over as it was fought," I rubbed my leg over the scar as the memory resurfaced. Dean moved from laying on the ground and crouched closer to me; he did not want to miss a single word.

"I stood in shock as Junior pulled himself from the ground. He approached me with a sick and twisted look upon his dirty face. He gave his gratitude and looked at me smugly. He told me that he knew I was forever loyal. I was disgusted by his words and looked to the other person with us as he was spotted picking up the firearm. Junior also saw the motion and laughed as he put his arm upon my shoulder. I instantly removed his arm and shoved the deviant to the dirt. I bent over him and told him that we were done." As I told the horrible story, it became difficult to look Dean in the eye.

"The young man had a knife?" Dean asked to clear up his confusion. "The knife was in the pocket of the dead stoner. He was trying to stab Junior as my instinct to protect took over and I jumped in front of the blade," I paused to make sure that Dean understood. He nodded, and I proceeded. "I did not have a clue what to do next. I knew that Junior was in serious trouble, but I no longer cared about his life. I stared at the dead body that was sprawled amongst the dirt and leaves. I was a witness to a murder, maybe two. As I turned to face the cowering demon, he began to grovel. He pleaded with the young man. He asked that he talk to me about his character. He was hoping that I would talk the scared boy out of his plight."

"Did you intervene?"

"I walked away. I went a few feet into the forest and plunged my knees into the dirt and let the sadness and frustration seep through my eyeballs as the panic eating at my insides took over. I ripped my shirt and tied a piece of it around my wounded leg and then there was a gunshot. Not one, but two."

"Didn't anyone else at the party hear the shots?" Dean interrupted. "The party was quite loud, there was music blaring from someone's Bronco, and we were quite far from the fire. So, surprisingly, no one came to the rescue," I took a deep breath and screamed into the air. Dean did not react to my outburst. He knew that I was struggling with the memory. "Anyway, after I noticed the second shot, I became curious, so I returned to the scene of the crime. I now saw three bodies lying on the ground instead of one."

"Were they all dead?"

"The lad with the gun was sprawled over the top of Junior with a hole through his head. Junior also had a hole between his eyes. There was no sign of life from any of the three," I spoke as liquid from my eyes ran down my cheek.

"Did the victim shoot himself?"

"I believed so. I pondered on my next move, but my mind was blank. I was faced with so many complications; I could not sort out the ramblings in my head. I kicked Junior's body merely to prove to myself that the son-of-a-bitch was no longer breathing."

"I think you did what you had to do," Dean stated to cover up the sound of silence. "I would have done the same thing. Junior was a bad person and needed to be put to rest. As far as the other two people, you couldn't have known their fate; it was not your fault." I angrily leapt to my feet and hovered over the small, shriveled soul.

"Don't antagonize me with your mumble, jumble bullshit!" I screamed in Dean's face. "I am a murderer, I did nothing to stop it!"

"Then what is the scar upon your leg?" Dean demanded as he pointed towards the spot that I was caressing earlier.

"A reminder of a half-hearted try to save another human's life," I sat myself back upon the grass, "I could have done something, instead I willingly walked away. I knew what was to come, that makes me guilty of something."

"What did you do with the bodies?"

"If I have learned anything about myself, it is that someone or something is watching over me," I paused as I looked towards the heavens. "It seems that every time I find myself in a great deal of trouble, someone shows up to pick up the pieces. Just as you did," I looked into Deans eyes. "I believe that I am who I am for a reason and until that reason is shown, I must continue to live freely."

"Such as a guardian angel," the old gent commented.

"Something in that general idea of things; there *was* someone who heard the gun shots. It was a guy I didn't know well, but we had met on a few occasions. When he saw who the victims were, he chuckled and jumped for joy. He then looked at me with a blissful expression painted upon his face. He said congratulations for ridding the world of a few more rodents. I stared back at him with a confused expression printed upon my face. I said that I was not responsible for the mess that was sprawled out before me. He punched my shoulder and winked as he recited the words *sure you didn't*."

"Was he serious?" Dean inquired.

"I asked him what he thought I should do and in a cocky manner he held his hand over his eyes and said, *about what?*"

"He just wanted you to leave?" Dean questioned.

"I felt as if I was in the middle of an intense practical joke. I kept drifting my sight towards the woods, waiting for someone to jump from them, revealing the gag. The witness then grew closer and, with the help of the full moon, I could see that his face had turned serious. He asked me if I knew the two smokers and I told him no. He then admitted that Junior was a stranger to him, and he had an intuition that he was probably not such a great guy. I admitted that I knew him and agreed with his intuition. He then continued to explain that the two dead young men were not well-liked by anyone, and that it was only the matter of time before they received their dirt naps. He told a grisly story about a young girl that they raped, she turned out to be the witness's younger sister. I then knew that the spectator had contemplated what he was now seeing. He wanted the two kids dead, and he did not care about the third body, or me. I was his savior, and even though I did not do what he thought I did, it didn't matter to him either way."

"I take it he walked away."

"No," I said, "he told me to find Jay's vehicle and get rid of it. He said he would take care of the rest. I pleaded with him that it was not his problem; he seemed more than happy to deal with it. He pulled out his driver's license and pointed to his name and address. He then described the fact that I knew exactly who he was and where he resided. He explained that he was in just as much trouble as I was since he was a witness, and many others knew about his grudge with the two dopers. If he turned me in, it would be his word against mine, and he did not want to deal with that scenario. He then advised me to ditch the car and disappear. I was told never to return, and he would cover up the mess. I did as he wished. I have many disturbing thoughts about the entire situation; I was young and naive and didn't want to go to jail for a crime that I did not commit."

"What happened to Junior's body, and what did you do with his vehicle?" Dean inquired.

"To this very day the whereabouts of his corpse remain a mystery. I returned his transportation to his home and discarded the keys," I said as I turned my head from Dean trying to hide the shame.

"Would you like me to drive?" Dean asked changing the topic to something less terrible.

"I will drive until we drop off our knight in rusty armor," I joked and patted the hood of Old Rusty; it was as if the metal machine was our friend. "Sounds like a plan. We should head back to the real world, whatever that is."

"Yes, the real world: a world of drug fiends, thieves, liars and misfits," I chuckled out loud, "I can't wait to return." I opened the passenger side door for the aching old gent and closed it behind him. I walked around the back of the beast, paid my respects to Frank and his family, and hopped in. As we drove into town the silence was overwhelming. We were both struggling in our own heads with the details of the past twenty-four hours. It was urgent that we arrived home soon and achieved rest. We were both deprived of sleep, and hallucinations were just around the corner. Before we could do anything the first stop was the hospital. I had to make sure that my friend in blue was still living in reality. Then we would return Old Rusty, make one final stop at Frank's to retrieve my transportation, and head to Dean's homestead where we would wrap things up.

CHAPTER ELEVEN

We arrived at Dean's house and departed our vehicles as if we were athletes that finalized a marathon. Every muscle in my body screamed as it was utilized. By the groans leaking out of Dean's mouth, it was evident he was having similar issues. We approached his stoop and fell upon a swinging bench. After a few moments of taking it easy, Dean stood up.

"Get off the stoop and come join me for refreshments," Dean demanded. "Oh, water would be excellent," I remarked as I leapt to my feet and dashed under Dean's arm as he held the door open. The place cried out with loneliness. After snooping around the living quarters, I found a small end table that held about twenty random photographs. Each photo had its own unique frame and Frank was in every one of them. A walk around the room proved that there were no other pictures… not one. Why would an old man such as Dean only have photographs of one person?

"I have some sausage and crackers to go with your water," Dean entered the room with gifts.

"That is more than wonderful," I graciously commented and immediately reached for the food. "Why do you have so many pictures of Frank?"

"I know that it looks creepy, but it is not how it seems. A few days ago, I had a rather intense dream. Frank warned me that you would be calling." The meat and crackers leapt out of my hand and landed upon the floor.

"You spoke with him?" I inquired. After Dean discovered the distraught look upon my face, he took a few steps back before he tended to my question.

"It was nothing more than a dream," he responded.

"Something isn't right here." I kept turning my head in every direction. "What are you keeping from me?"

"Terry, you must relax; have a seat," he tried to persuade me to sit as I pushed him from me. "I am not going to hurt you."

I drifted over to the table that was loaded with Frank's face and kicked the legs from underneath. The wood wailed as it crashed to the floor. The breaking glass chimed as it shattered. My foot swept through the wreckage only to discover a picture that was familiar. I knelt down and removed the photo from the mess. Frank was standing before the garden of pain with his left arm wrapped around my shoulder. The pictures taken of me were few; everlasting proof of my existence was something I was not enthused about. Frank begged for one picture to remind him that there were good people in the world.

"What is going on?" I questioned.

"After I dreamt about Frank, I couldn't get his image out of my head," as Dean spoke, he sat his aged bones on the chair that was next to the broken end table. "The photos were all in a box that I dug up from the cellar. I was obsessed with his face; I had to see him. The night vision was so real."

"Then it was real!" I shouted out my philosophy. "You had a conversation with Frank, and you wait until now to mention it. I know Frank; I know he swore you to secrecy, now you need to come clean. How much of this nonsense did you already know about before I entered the equation?"

"I meant you no harm; I had to keep quiet."

"Speak up and tell the truth," I made eye contact. "We bonded over our last day. Don't you deny it," I said as I waved my finger in his direction. "I understand about being loyal to Frank; it is time to be loyal to me."

"Yes, I will tell you, as long as you promise to hear the words with an open mind," he said. "I have never seen anything like what I experienced with you and that is the truth. On rare occasions, I heard stories from the mouth of Frank. I paid close attention to what he said, for I knew he would not repeat a word. I've known Frank all my life. We hung out in this very backyard as infants," as he spoke, he pointed out one of the windows.

I moseyed over and peered through the pain of glass as two babies were seen frolicking upon a blanket. There were two ladies sitting close by, and another child playing in the distance. The third child was of male gender and looked to be no older than five or six.

"Who was the older boy in your childhood?" I interrupted to pry into the past. Confused, Dean sat on the edge of his chair.

"Who are you referring to?" he asked. I made my way back towards Dean.

"When you and Frank were young, there was an older boy. His hair was dusty blond, and it was cut short."

"How would you know about that?"

"I observed it outside the window. There were two babies, two mothers, and a boy playing by himself in the back. He was scampering around the big oak tree in the yard."

"I'm not sure what to think right now. I thought you only saw things in your dreams," Dean said as his face looked puzzled.

"That is what Frank thought. You only know of me through his stories, so anything that I kept from him, he obviously kept from you." During Frank's final days, we had a short conversation about me seeing visions and not dreams. He was told that it was a new source to gain information, however, that was not completely true. I had always seen things during my time of being awake and was too embarrassed to even let him know.

"We can talk about me later. Finish your story." I said.

"I knew that Frank was different. When we were teenagers, he started having convulsions. He made me promise that I would not tell anyone. Not until our early thirties did I hear him confess his other life," Dean paused and sucked in some air. "We were at a bar and when we returned home, I noticed that Frank was bleeding. When he saw me staring, he covered his nose as if to make it look as if it sprung a leak. It was dark outside, but I witnessed the blood seep from his eyes."

"That is quite interesting," I interrupted. Dean nudged my words away, for it was his turn to reveal secrets.

"He denied the entire episode. About two months later, I found Frank sprawled upon his bathroom floor with small cuts covering his skin. He lay in a gigantic pool of his own blood. He then had to come clean. That was the first time he told me about his life that he hid so well."

It was funny how the table turned for us. Now Dean was the one being interrogated when not so long ago I was the one under fire.

"After the bathroom incident, it took ten years before I witnessed another one of his ordeals. He learned to hide them better, but they were beginning to take over his life. He no longer could hold them off while he darted to a place of loneliness; he then disappeared. He wrote however, he gave no return address." Dean glared at the Frank scenery that was covering the wood floor. "Until today I have never let those precise words out of my mouth. I would have done anything for Frank, and I still would. When he came back from his hiatus, he was somehow different. He was gone for about six years, upon his return he regained his stamina and had a better grasp upon his life. He had control once again. That is when he decided to teach me."

"Teach you what?"

"His life without seeing it for myself," Dean held both his hands out in front of him while he shrugged his shoulders. "I know everything that he as ever encountered, yet I have witnessed nothing. What you showed me tonight is by far the most action I have ever been involved with. I can only believe what he told me was true, and I do. My job was to let him vent. I was the only human that he could say whatever it was he needed to release from his inner mind and there would be no consequences. I was aware of you because you were a great impact on his life. He filled my ears with five years of stories before you physically entered into his life. I knew about you and Junior before we met."

"You what?" I flayed my arms in the air as I headed for the back door. "Lies, betrayal, what is the point of all this nonsense? Is it to cause pain?"

"I wasn't trying to hurt you, I was protecting."

"Whatever, that sounds like Frank," I said and stormed out the door.

Dean made his way towards my escape route.

"That's because it is Frank. Don't you get it? All I am is his damn messenger!" He turned and disappeared back inside his house as I roamed the backyard.

The fairy tale was never ending. I walked around the yard; someone was feeding me memories, for I saw the young children playing around the oak tree. The infants were now toddlers, and the older boy was still present. The boy was a stranger, however, I was certain he had a sad story. It appeared as if every ghost that sought out my brain had a tragic end to their life. I really didn't care about the boy and wanted nothing to do with him; I ignored him as I made my way around to the front of the house where Dean was resting upon the stoop.

"You know that you also stretch the truth, words from your own mouth," Dean pointed out.

"It doesn't matter how many times I lie to someone, it always pains me to find out that someone is doing it to me."

"The secrets were not meant to harm you in any way, just like the ones that you hold," he said as he motioned for me to have a seat next to him. "I had direct orders to not let you know what I knew. I was to play stupid and let you handle whatever lay ahead for us."

"Did you know what was going to happen at his house?" I asked as my head grew closer to his.

"I knew of no details. I was told that you would be contacting me and that it would turn out to be a trying time for both of us." He tilted his head towards the ground as if he was embarrassed.

"How is that possible?" "How is what possible?"

"If you were warned of me coming and also told that something was going to happen, then that would mean that Frank knows the future."

"I get what you're saying," Dean responded as he raised his eyebrows. "How is that possible?"

"I have no clue, but it tells me that my whole life is already planned out for me," I squawked and stood from the step. "Tell me everything that he said to you, word for word."

"It was a dream; I don't remember my dreams the way you remember yours. What I told you is the gist of it. He did not go into detail, and he did not inform me that we would be going to his house. I don't think he knew exactly what was going to happen, but he must have expected something to happen; I bet he had a feeling. Just like the ones you have. He is obviously aware of Junior and his connection with you, therefore, since his demise, he must have discovered that something was amiss. Merely because he knows you, he knew that you would become involved."

"How much time passed after the dream before I contacted you?" I was trying to figure out the reasoning for Frank's ability to predict the future. I've seen strange and unexplainable events, however, to my knowledge I had never seen the future, only the past.

"The following afternoon I received your phone call," he admitted. "So, to rationalize the situation, I was thinking about calling the evening before, so he somehow collected my thoughts. He was bound to know that Junior would be contacting me. He can't see the future; he can invade thoughts and put two and two together."

"That actually makes sense, after the last couple of days I will believe anything."

"What exactly do you know about me?" I inquired.

"I know that you gave a great man the strength to continue living in a world of darkness. The first day that he saw you in his dreams was the first time I had seen him smile in quite some time. Frank was at his wit's end; he had given up on humanity altogether. He was a broken man. You showed him a chance to teach. He looked upon you as a student, someone who could learn from him, learn not to make the same mistakes as he did. You have told me that Frank did not know about your splitting flesh, but he knew. He knew everything about you. All the secrets you kept from him he already knew. He was a part of you, how could you not see it?"

"I know that he was inside my mind, only because I was also inside his. I did not choose to let the information in. For the most part, I ignored the truth and continued living in denial," I gazed at the wrinkled face that was enticed by my every word and realized how pathetic I really was.

"Is everything all right?" Dean asked with concern pouring from his lips.

"No," I said politely, "I am not who you believe me to be. Frank knew many things about me without anyone telling him. I possess the very same power, and I was in his mind more than I was in my own. I used Frank so I could verbally release my anger. It is an uneasy task to hold bitterness inside; eventually it finds a way out. I found that I was leaking quite often, especially when I had a few cocktails. I had to find a source that would allow me to vent."

"Then you came upon Frank."

"I sought him out," I thought of my memories. "I saw his house in my mind. I then followed the map in my head. The part that no one knows, not even Frank, is that I had the map when I was very young. I used to draw it in the dirt as a child."

"You knew of Frank as a child?" Dean asked with a shocked look that accompanied his words.

"I saw his face in my dreams and I would see silhouettes of him when I was alone. It was not until I grew older that I discovered that the images in my head were actually real. Once that conclusion was present, I went to find him. I did not know he had a daughter, and I did not know they were buried in the garden. I am puzzled by the things I don't know. I realize that I have a lot to learn."

"I think we all have a great deal to learn," Dean stated.

"That would be a true statement," I commented. "It's funny how neither Frank nor I told our secrets to each other even though we both knew of them."

"Do you see anyone else in your visions?"

"I see a various number of other characters; it is only the prominent ones that receive my attention. I've seen Frank so many different times that it became impossible to forget him. I have seen other people more than once, but nowhere near the amount of Frank. I also have other maps, but if I disregard them, they eventually disappear."

"Wouldn't that be considered a missed opportunity? And why didn't you seek one of them out instead of contacting me?"

"I don't believe that I missed out on anything except more pain that I didn't need at the time. Frank had a different feel than the others. His appearances were welcomed and comforting. The others gave me a creepy sensation and were not comforting in any way, plus Frank was a living, breathing, human being while everyone else I see is presumed to be a spirit," I answered part one. "I contacted you merely because you were connected to Frank. When he told me about you, I acted as if I was shocked."

"You knew about me?"

"I knew of you only because you were in Franks thoughts. I didn't know anything else, I promise," I tried to regain trust between us. "I know that there is a great deal of information that you are hiding from me, just as I am hiding from you. The only thing that makes me deal with the mistrust is the fact that the secrets are kept to protect and not to torture. I know that you are not lying to me to benefit yourself. My secrets are of the same purpose of yours. As we communicate, we will divulge the words that we have been hiding and everything will become clear. You must understand that I do not know everything, and I am not trying to convince you that I do."

"I do follow what you are saying, yet I am still very confused."

"I think we should head back into the house so I can clean up my mess and you can take some time to clear your head." I came up with a plan. Dean nodded as he stood and held open the front door.

I separated the pictures from the broken frames and stacked them neatly upon the table. After the trash was discarded, I took a seat in Dean's chair. I slowly browsed through the portraits, and the many faces of Frank brought on a jealous moment; it seemed unfair that Dean was able to speak with him. Since my youth, Frank was a fixture in my mind.

There was so much about him that I misunderstood. It was shocking to hear about the events Dean informed me of. He spoke of blood leaking from Frank's eyes and a pool of his own blood forming from hundreds of small cuts upon his flesh. Those were incidents that were shared in my life, and it seemed odd that we did not discuss them with each other.

Dean lived a tougher life then what was alleged. He listened to Frank pour his darkest secrets into the air. The only thing that he could do was trust that what he heard was the truth. The respect that he had for his friend was enough for him to believe. Frank had some obscure stories to spill, and they were hard to accept as factual no matter who you were. Dean was very robust to be able to fill his head with such disastrous tales and not leak a word of them. Frank released his demons verbally onto Dean's ears, however, Dean was trapped with the fact that he could not share the information with anyone. He had to live with it in silence. That did not seem fair, but it was common knowledge that life was not fair.

I found myself staring at my reflection in the bathroom mirror. The image screamed for a thorough scrubbing. I removed my soiled clothing and all the cuts and bruises upon my flesh were revealed. It was going to be difficult to conceal the damage, but the marks had to be hidden. It was becoming more and more problematic to cover the abrasions after an incident and excuses were in short supply. I wore long sleeves and pants in the summer, and swimming in public was not acceptable. It did not matter what strangers thought of my scarred skin, however, there were many concerns about what those close to me thought.

It was impossible to scrape the dirt and blood from my body, for the pain was overwhelming. I tried to relax as the warm water ran down my flesh and to the tub below. Even though my skin would come clean eventually, it was my mind that would forever be tarnished. I turned the knob, and the water slowly lessened until the flow was stopped. I put the dirty clothes back onto my bruised flesh, defeating the purpose of the shower.

I left the room for bathing in the past as the kitchen became the place to dwell. I made every movement with care, because the goal was to not disturb the gentle man that rested at the top of the stairs. Dean's age was unknown, but I was certain that after the last couple of days, he had aged ten years. Frank's age was also a mystery; age was not important to me. It did not matter how long a person roamed the world, what was significant was what they learned as they meandered. There were ten-year-olds that have lived more than a sixty year old human; age was based on experience. I may have been in my early twenties, yet in my non-reality I was reaching a hundred.

"Feeling any better?" I immediately asked as Dean sauntered into the pantry.

"As good as I am going to, I presume," he smugly admitted. "How about you?"

"I'll live to see another nightmare."

"I see you made yourself at home," he commented as he saw my wet hair. "I'm glad, but you should have borrowed some clothes."

"Yeah, I know it kind of defeats the purpose; it was more of a relaxing experience than anything else."

"My nap was the same idea," Dean touched my shoulder gently. "I'm sorry I just disappeared. I am happy that you stuck around."

"You seem surprised."

"I just thought that you would have left. I am glad that you find it comfortable enough to stay here."

"Look at me, if anyone sees me like this, I will have to tell some outrageous tale that I don't want to tell. I will wait until a late hour before I head home, if that is all right with you."

"We still have quite a few things to talk about, so you are welcome to stay as long as you wish," he said graciously. He then grabbed a container of water and headed for the stoop. The day was glorious, and it would have been absurd to sit inside and waste it. I followed Dean and had a seat next to him.

"So, where do we begin?" I asked.

"You know more than what you say you do. Did you know that there were bodies in the garden?"

"I have kept information from you. That does not mean that I know everything. I was not aware of the bodies. If I did, I wouldn't have agreed to go to the house."

"Yes, you would have," Dean corrected my words.

"Yeah, I guess you're probably right," I snickered back at him. "Anyway, tell me what you know."

"Frank told me his secrets in confidence; his stories were for me to hear, not for me to repeat. I believe that you understand that I can't break my silence, even for you," he discussed his loyalty and I did understand. "I will tell you his stories if, and only if, I feel it will help you with your life. The cuts that you seem to have were also a large part of Frank's life. They appeared during stressed times, or as you would say: when he was weak. He did not ever figure out exactly who or what caused the tiny pests, he learned that if he stayed strong, he had some control over them. It took him most of his life to gain the little control that he had. The honest truth is that he told me he was hoping you would discover the secret of the tiny devils and let him know how to stop them."

"So, he did know that I dealt with the unwanted lesions."

"He mentioned to me that he saw you bleeding one day. He also mentioned that it was a rare occasion for you and that fact made him glad. He knew how horrific it was to watch the cuts appear and have no clue why. He only wanted you to be safe. Are you bitter about his demise?"

"I don't know. It seemed so sudden. I just wasn't ready." "Is anyone ever really ready for death?"

"I suppose not. Frank was the man that kept my mind involved with sanity. Now he is gone, and my emotions often run rampant," as I spoke I could not face Dean. I was embarrassed of my feelings towards Frank's demise and felt that my thoughts were selfish.

"There is nothing wrong with a few bitter feelings about your mentor's death. We all knew that his time was coming to an end. I am damn sure that you have many unanswered questions. That is why he advised you to contact me."

"It doesn't matter," I quickly remarked and rose to my feet. "He's gone, and here I sit, face to face with the only man that knows the stories that were in his head. Of course I have unanswered questions, but to have you tell me his tales does not seem like the right thing to do."

"Why do you feel that way?"

"You may be aware of the acts Frank had done, however, you don't have answers. All you have is stories and I have a million of my own. What

I need is long gone; it died with Frank," I peeked at Dean to see if he comprehended my mad thoughts.

"I realize your point and agree, for his stories were all I received. He did not speak of the torment that cursed his mind. He only told what he saw, not what it did to his mind. The answers that you search for are in his deepest thoughts, and I do not contain that information." He looked at me with sadness painted upon his face. "So, what do we do now?"

"Enjoy each other's company and the beautiful day that surrounds us," I reached over and slapped his shoulder. "Why don't you go make some sandwiches and we will have a picnic in your glorious backyard. We will continue to converse, and the day will be one of splendor." Dean nodded his head in agreement as he slowly rose from the stoop.

"We will need to find a table and some chairs," Dean said.

"You know what? Why don't you find an old blanket and we will have an old fashioned picnic." Dean nodded and headed back into his domain. I wandered to the exact spot where the babies were playing from my earlier visualization. Dean returned with a bedspread; there was an amazing expression frozen upon his face.

"You have something on your mind?"

"Not really, I was just speculating why you chose this particular location." "It just seems like a good place to rest," I replied.

He realized that there were ulterior motives, yet he kept quiet. We set out the quilt and fueled our deteriorating brains.

"What is on your mind?" I asked. "I'm just confused."

"Confused about what?"

"About you," he said.

"I understand that you're old and your mind wanders, so you are going to have to be more specific," I chuckled.

"Hey now, no geezer jokes are necessary. When I was trying to take a nap—"

"Trying?" I immediately interrupted him.

"Every time I drifted off, I saw nothing but horrifying things," he paused to keep himself calm. I could definitely tell that he was agitated. "I saw people jumping from the dirt trying to grab my legs. I saw Frank and his family being tortured. I saw your skin peel from your face. How do you deal with your life? I was always upset with Frank because he did not let me help him with his troubles. Now I completely comprehend his reasoning and agree with his methods."

"So basically, you are blaming me for your dreams."

"I know that is how it seems. You must trust me when I say that was not what I meant. I was the one who volunteered my time for you. If you remember, you warned me about the after affects and begged me to leave. I blame myself."

"I will forever feel guilty about what I let you see. I could not have accomplished the task without help. Even though I expressed deep concern for you to vamoose, I desperately yearned for you to stay. My life scares the crap out of me, and your company was greatly appreciated."

"How do you deal with the dreams?" he asked.

"I have dealt with nightmares my entire life. When I was a young child, I would sleep walk; I was trying to escape my world. My mother would jab a butter knife in the top of the door hinges to prevent them from opening, otherwise I would stroll outside. As I grew older, I discovered that I bore a unique gift."

"And what would that be?"

"I found out that I had the ability to control my dreams." "How can you do that?"

"Once I realize that I am dreaming, the outcome becomes changeable. When I wake from a dream, there is the ability to go back into slumber and continue at the exact spot that I left off. There are secrets that are released through my night visions. If I don't comprehend what my dream was trying to get across, there is the power to go back and view it all over again; I also retain the memory of it, therefore I am able to pick it apart scene by scene. It is an aid to better understand what my brain desperately wants me to know. The subconscious of a human is a mighty powerful tool that unleashes itself throughout the night."

"Therefore, you have the ability to calmly rationalize the story," Dean commented.

"Exactly, and that trait helps discover what needs to be accomplished when I wake. The power is not completely mastered. I am getting closer each and every time my eyes close."

"Do you think it would be possible for you to teach what you know?" "Not necessarily. Like I said, there is a long way to go to gain complete control; therefore, I must teach myself before anyone else." "What exactly do your dreams reveal to you?"

"Over time I have discovered that the spirits I see while awake have the power to manipulate me while I sleep. When weary, I am vulnerable and don't have the willpower to fight off the demons that reside in my head. The same scenario goes for when in slumber. My eyes close and I become an open target for the dead. As a child, I was not aware that the visions were not my own, but as the world spun, I realized that somehow the dearly departed found a way to confuse my thoughts. This particular theory is one that is hard to believe, therefore it is important that my thoughts are kept to myself. If people think I am insane, they may try to lock me up, and that could be a deadly situation for me. Being locked away would add stress, and once stress comes into play, I become…"

"Weak and vulnerable," Dean finished the sentence.

"Weak and vulnerable," I repeated his words. "The past few years have shown many new traits to my supernatural capabilities. I believe that not everyone I know is of the living."

"What exactly brought you to that conclusion?"

"Many different scenarios. There was one incident that made me aware that my reality was much different than most people. I was visiting one of my friends who had been taken to the afterlife way sooner than he was expected too. As I walked through the field of buried bodies, there was a particular area that I was drawn to. The name on the headstone was familiar. The past two years or so, I have met him enough times to know where he worked, where he lived, and that he was a middle-aged man with no family."

Dean did not say a word; the wheels spinning in his head could be heard in the silence. He was thinking about everyone he had come across throughout his long journey of life. He did not have to explain what he was contemplating; it was apparent.

"Let me get this straight," Dean addressed me as he turned his body in my direction. "You cannot tell if a person is living or dead?"

"Not if they don't want me to, I guess." "Do they know that they're dead?"

"I'm not sure about that," I said. "I am only beginning my journey for the answer to that particular question. I have only recently discovered the gravestone, so it is relatively new to me. I've gone to the man's house after his grave was discovered. The house was empty and quite eerie; there was a feeling that gave the impression of someone else in the room, yet no one appeared."

"Do you believe that he was the one you felt?" Dean inquired. "Absolutely, I truly believe that the roaming spirits have to figure out their own powers. When my time comes to seek another realm, I will have to do the same. All the knowledge that I have achieved thus far will no longer be any use to me. So, when the ghost's house was barged into, he was not prepared. He was scared of how I would react, so he hid. On the other hand, as you said before, he might not have known he was dead. Therefore, he was hiding because he was confused. He did not take the opportunity to converse, so nothing was learned." I finished speaking and sighed loudly.

"How is it possible for you to hide your life from others?"

"It's not possible; I've been slipping," I referred to my carelessness. "Only recently I have been telling the wrong people about what I witness. That was the main reason that I decided to contact you. I felt that it was necessary to talk to someone, and it had to be someone who would keep quiet. Since you were referred by a man that I trusted, you became my best bet."

"Why do you believe that you told the wrong people?"

"I have a problem that continues to drag me into situations that I would normally run from. Since Tina and I ended our romantic ties, I have been desperate to feel what I felt with her." I paused for a brief second. "After many attempts of trying to replace Tina, it became apparent that love was never meant to be forced, it has to come naturally, and that was the one thing I was not letting happen. My feelings were forced upon women, and my stories were leaked to gain intimacy. Unfortunately, what took place was the exact opposite. I was building a wall between myself and everyone else in the world. My life is so abstract that when my tales reach a pair of human ears, it startles the owner and pushes them away. Another disastrous habit that I picked up was drinking. Once my mind became intoxicated, the truth soared through my lips, received by anyone who was present, which was certainly not the crowd that should be let in on secrets."

"That sounds horrible," Dean recited.

"It is a sad premise; humans only know how to deal with a problem by adding unnecessary drama. It is a way of life."

"I think you are onto something. People like to believe that they are humble, honest, caring individuals, but the fact is: that is not true. When an opportunity to talk behind someone's back becomes present, I don't think any human can walk away from that."

"That is correct," I nodded at Dean as I spoke. "No matter how much someone bitches about backstabbers, I believe that we all do it."

"Do you?"

"Of course I do, I am human. I am not proud of myself and have talked crap about people when they were not present to stand up for themselves. Sometimes I do it on purpose to sabotage a certain relationship. It doesn't make my actions right, but if I need to cut the strings with a fellow person, I do whatever it takes. Even if becoming an intolerable creature is what has to be done." I saw Dean looking at me strangely. "I do not hurt or reveal secrets about the people I care for. If I become friends with a certain individual and I announce my loyalty, that is what they get. I am loyal if I like the specific person. If I have doubts about a friendship, I cannot be trusted."

"Do you like me?" Dean asked so he could be sure his secrets were secure. "I would never do anything to harm you. You and Frank are unique gentlemen, and I would not tarnish your reputations." "I believe you. Do you trust me?"

"Yes," I simply stated.

"You are quite an honest person. You are even open about your deceitful ways."

"It is the only way I am able to live with myself," I admitted.

"Frank had a much different mentality than I do. For years I argued with him about his way of treating people. I thought the complete opposite. I believed that the only way to make it in this cruel world was to have respect from your peers. Frank said that the only people that deserved respect were the ones that you truly loved. He said a stranger's opinion meant absolutely nothing to him. It took me decades to realize that he was correct. It doesn't matter what somebody thinks of me if I don't care what they think. It may be a hard concept to grasp, but after I understood, my life was much easier to get through, simply because I wasn't trying to impress anyone."

"That is the key. You must live your life for you and no one else. If you are happy with the person you are, that is all that matters. If you are secure with yourself, your loved ones will respect you. Strangers' opinions mean absolutely nothing. I know that is the way I should live, but I am far from it," I added my thoughts.

I felt that most humans lived an unimportant life and the only way they felt significant was when they were sticking their nose where it didn't belong. I have tried to call people out when they were acting a fool, but the positive impact that I hoped for was not achieved. It was impossible to tell someone of their wrong doings and expect them to take your words to heart. Instead, they would reverse the role to add negative impact upon myself. Even though I would spill my thoughts so I could help make them a better person, I was only adding fuel to their fire of ignorance. It was difficult for anyone to hear bad comments about themselves. I had learned that if there was tension between two people and honesty was not the best policy, the only appropriate act was to walk away.

"Anyway," Dean interrupted the silence, "we have both seen tragedy, yet here we both sit, alive and well."

"Alive anyway," I laughed out loud. "All we can do is grow from our experiences and let our lives play out." Dean motioned his head in a vertical movement that proved we were on the same page.

"What's up with your hair?" Dean asked changing the subject entirely. My hair hung halfway down my back, bangs and all. I figured that Dean would be bringing it up at some point, since he was old; my appearance seemed to irritate aged people.

"When I was young, I hosted a mullet on the top of my skull. I was not allowed to have long bangs, therefore, I grew out the back and decided that when I became old enough to make my own decisions, I would then let my top hair graduate to the length of the back."

"So, it was grown out of spite?"

"It started out that way however, once I grew it out, I liked it and kept it for myself. As I became older, I discovered that I was immediately judged by strangers." I tugged upon my ponytail as I shared my thoughts. "I was refused employment by many different companies merely because my hair was lengthy. The problem irritated me so profusely that I went back to reasons of spite. It was decided that if respect was to come from any given person, that person would have to know the inner me. The whole scenario of other humans not approving of me simply because I let my hair grow long angered me so much that I sat back and judged myself."

"And what did you find?"

"I found myself to be a revengeful human being and I was not proud of myself," I rubbed the sweat from my brow and coughed quietly. "At that point I quit caring about what other people thought. My entire life, up to that point, was spent on trying to impress others. Once that trait was lost, I then began to live my life for myself and was then able to try to find the real me."

"Who is the real you?"

"I am still searching. His hair is long." I then saw a person standing behind Dean. It was the child that was observed earlier; he waved.

It was obvious that my attention had drifted from my talk with Dean however, he did nothing to interfere with the dazed look in my eyes. The boy from Dean's backyard was older than he was the last time I saw him. Was it the present version of the child, or was it a figment of my imagination? The past times he appeared there was eye contact between us; the older version showed no sign of acknowledging my presence. My focus changed to the old man who showed signs of boredom upon his face. He was not aware we had a visitor.

"We have company," I spurted the words out of my mouth. Dean was taken by surprise by the sudden outburst.

"Do we now?" he questioned. "Yes," I said simply.

"Who seems to be with us?" Dean asked as he shifted his body towards me. "Someone I know?"

"I don't know the answer to that question. The last time he paid a visit his age was different."

"Do ghosts age?"

"That is also a question that I don't have the answer to," I said as I waved my finger at Dean. "Frank's daughter looked as young as the picture I saw of her. The photograph was taken during the last year of her life, so her appearance did not age. She had no eyes, so I assumed that she looked exactly as she did on her last day of life. Her mannerisms and her wisdom seemed older than a ten-year-old. She did mention something about her mind growing, but not her body."

"What I am getting from you is that you have a lot of the answers you search for, yet your lack of confidence does not allow you to realize them."

"And the shrink emerges," I said egotistically.

"I am talking as a friend. I don't think a person can learn from their mistakes if they don't realize that they're making them."

"So what exactly are my mistakes?" "You don't believe in yourself."

"Do you believe that I see someone?" I questioned as Dean stared blankly into the distance. "He has blond hair, light freckles amongst his cheeks, a scar just above his right eyebrow and he is most likely in his early teens. He seems distant to his surroundings."

"Are we playing a game?" Dean asked a bizarre question.

"What kind of game would we be playing?" I replied with a transient calm.

"I feel like you are messing with me," he said with seriousness printed upon his face.

"You stared directly at Junior; you watched him disappear right before your eyes. How can you not believe me?"

"It is not an easy ordeal to accept," he calmly spoke.

"Yet it is my life, and the reason why I stand before you today," I waved my arms with frustration. "The stories of Frank and what you went through with me have to be enough for you to trust that I am not deceiving you."

"I do not think you're deceiving me," he quickly found his backbone. "I think that your mind is playing tricks on you."

I became irritated with the words that seeped from the old mouth. I finally spoke of what my mind displayed and was instantly denied the gratification that someone of the living would trust my word. He was the only living soul that I expected to trust me; another disappointment to deal with.

"I think that you're hiding the truth from me. I think you can't handle what I see, so you have fallen into denial." Dean hung his head low as the words left my mouth. "Who is the boy?"

"I did know someone that fits that description; he disappeared many, many decades ago."

"How long ago he died does not matter."

"I didn't say he was dead; I said he disappeared." "He's dead," I stated. "How in the hell would you know?"

"He's right here in front of me!" I screamed and waved my hands with frustration. "You think that I am so crazed that I must make up characters to feel a part of something?"

"Tell him hello," Dean snapped as he stood up and walked away. We were both overwhelmed by what was taking place. Dean was a fragile man and whatever the young boy's story happened to be, it was obviously a sad one. I decided to leave Dean alone with his memories. He had to face his fears and decide whether or not he wanted to involve himself with any more uncomfortable situations. In the meantime, I finished what was left of the food. The boy did not wander away; instead, he began to acknowledge me. He sat and observed my every move; it was unnerving. I gathered the remains of the picnic as the boy disappeared without a trace. The most practical reasoning was that he was searching for a better way to grab my attention. He required my assistance and surely would not give up so easily; he'd be back. A quick glance around assured that there was nothing left for Dean to pick up, and I headed back indoors.

Once inside the domain, I brought the used utensils into the kitchen where the quiet created an uneasy sensation. I said Dean's name aloud from my mouth, but there was no response. A nervousness began to slither through my veins. My rapid heartbeat set the pace as I searched the entire house very quickly; it was empty. Immediately the stoop popped into my head, and a mad dash brought my shaking body to another deserted site. I plopped upon the bare stairs and a queasy sensation overtook my bowels as I discovered Dean's truck was missing. *He left me alone? Why would he do such a thing?*

CHAPTER TWELVE

After dealing with the disappointment of being left on my lonesome, it was time to see how credible my ability to see spirits really was. Ghosts appeared to me quite often but on their own merit; it was the right moment to see if I was able to conjure up a spirit upon my own will. It became obvious that the last sighting of the apparition was more than likely the best place to begin. I returned to the great oak in Dean's backyard and sat next to the massive trunk. My legs crossed, lids shut, and head pointed down as all thoughts drifted towards the mystery boy. I took deep breaths through the mouth and long exhales out the nose. My mind was more than ready, unfortunately, my tactics didn't do the job that was desired.

With despair, I uncrossed my legs, opened my lids, straightened my neck. My abilities were falling short. As the mighty oak grasped my attention, my head began to swim and my eyelids gained a pound or two. Without warning, my back slammed onto the grassy ground. While I was unconscious, there were images of a boy dancing throughout a wide variety of backgrounds; it was more of a shadow than an actual person. The shifting scenes were vivid and quite creative, as if out of the mind of a young child. The images were peaceful.

With no warning whatsoever, the harmony ceased, and all hell broke loose. The shadow of a boy turned into a large, monstrous figure, the lovely background reformed into hectic scenes of doom, and my demeanor grew ugly. I shook the horrible images from my thoughts as consciousness returned. My eyelids opened and there stood the boy with a somber look upon his face. He stretched out his hand and moved it toward my head. With every inch he moved, my heart beat twice as fast. I turned my head and rammed my eyelids closed. I was still a coward. An intense heat erupted from the top of my skull. My eyes opened, but it did no good. I was blind to the world. My brain was twirling in my cranium, and my outlook on life was dark and depressing. The blood flowing through my veins began to boil and the pain was so intense that once again dreamland set in.

The boy's life was shown as the darkness of unconsciousness washed over me for the second time. He was often alone, and it appeared that his family was extremely distant. The hallucinations came quick and disappeared in the same fashion; it was difficult to retain the information. There was one piece that stuck with me: a map to a small, wooded area that was unoccupied by human life.

My palms were sweating, and my body trembled as the boy reappeared under the great oak tree, then came the sound of a vehicle approaching. After further investigation, I discovered that Dean had returned, alone and empty handed. I watched him enter his domain, and all became intensely quiet.

A few minutes passed as I decided to roam to the front of the house; Dean was found sitting upon the stoop sipping some steaming liquid. I kept out of sight and noticed that he couldn't take his eyes off of my vehicle. *At least he was thinking about me.* As I hid from his sight, a slithering menace caught the corner of my eye. With no thought whatsoever, my hand thrust down and seized the garter snake by the head. The commotion was enough to give away my location, and Dean was soon standing over me. My free hand took ahold of the tail as I mentally prepared to put the serpent to sleep forever. Dean looked at me with sympathy in his eyes.

"You going to take its life?" Dean asked.

"No," I said as I dropped the serpent to the ground. The snake gave me an odd look before it slithered away.

"I think he was saying thanks," Dean chuckled loudly.

"Yeah, whatever you say," I said with an aggravating tone behind my voice as I walked right by the old man and headed for my car.

"You gonna leave without letting me explain?"

"What's good for the goose is good for the gander," I recited.

"I deserve that. I wish you would let me explain."

"I don't know where you went or what you did. As far as I know, you went to the authorities and now you are trying to keep me from leaving before they arrive."

"I need to talk with you," Dean stated. "You know damn well I did not turn you in."

"I don't know anything," I glared at him with confusion dripping down my cheek. He turned from me and headed towards the porch motioning me to follow. We both knew that we had to converse with somebody. It only made sense that we spoke to each other. After arriving at the front of the house, we both sat upon a step. My mind went on a journey back to the last moment of Frank's life. I held him on his stairs and now I stared at his best friend, worried about the experience repeating itself.

"I am not going to die here on the steps," Dean opened the world of silence and let his words sweep the air.

"Is it that obvious?"

"It is as if your face is playing the movie that rings out inside your head," he answered. "I am a miscreant."

"Why is that?"

"I should not have left without informing you first," he admitted his mistake. "I am having a great deal of trouble handling your life. I don't think that I can take any more."

"Then why did you stop me from leaving?"

"I needed to tell you, I couldn't just let you storm off."

"So that's it. Nice to meet you, now get out," I revealed the anger that was growing inside.

"It doesn't have to be this way. I am not kicking you out. I can't see any more of what you see," Dean spoke as he held a blank expression upon his face. "The boy you speak of was a neighborhood outcast. It was believed that his father was abusive to him and his mother. The mother was so miserable that she lashed out at her son every moment she could get. The boy was scared and had no one in the entire world to go to for help."

"His name was Eric," I announced.

"Yes," Dean said with a surprised look. He began to edge himself away from me. He was doing a horrid job of concealing his distress. "I'm not adjusting to the fact that you talk to ghosts. It was much easier to deal with when it was only stories. The actual sight of them is eating its way through my brain."

"Did you see Eric?"

"No!" He shouted as he raised his hands. "With my own two eyes, I was aware of Junior and that was enough proof for me to believe anything. The visions of disappearing wounds on your skin made me pinch my own. I was right there in the middle of chaos, and I had to conjure up all my strength to keep my heart beating. You were going through a great deal, yet you showed no signs of shock. How is it possible to numb yourself from the entire picture?"

"It is not possible," I stared directly into the eyes of the innocent. "You did not have the pleasure of joining me in the woods. I was not calm and cool; I was a shaking mess. One can only run with a clouded mind for a short time. Eventually, sanity will find its way through. I react moment to moment. When someone is with me, I tend to be more in control than when I'm alone."

"Your initial reaction is to stay cool so your friend won't freak out," Dean pointed out what he thought was the obvious.

"I just do what I do. I don't contemplate on why. I know where Eric is," I paused and let Dean sigh. "I can do it alone, but I think you should help."

"More digging I presume?"

I chuckled, "I would like to know Eric's story; you seem to be the man for that."

"How do you know where he is? And is he dead or alive?"

"As far as I know I mostly see them when they're dead. I have a map in my head, and I can visualize everything in its surroundings," I said as I took a deep breath. "I am not sure why or how I get the maps."

"So we are going on a whim?" Dean finished his question and stretched his creaking bones as he anticipated my answer.

"I guess so," I said with a grin formed with my lips. "Conversing with you has shown me that I am trying to keep the knowledge away. I am not absorbing the information that is fed to me; I block it out and store it in the cellar. It is the moment in my life that I learn about my curse, so I can discover a way to defeat it. I do not wish for you to torture your brain any more than you already have. I truly hope you decide to go on one more quick adventure. It is not far from here." Dean sighed, a great sigh and then his sight shifted to the sky.

"Where is he?" he asked.

"In the forest past your backyard," I said. "You know exactly where?"

"I can find him; it won't be a problem, however, I am not sure exactly how far in the woods he is."

"The woods aren't that big, so it shouldn't take too long," he said, keeping the conversation flowing.

"That means you're coming?"

"What choice do I have? It's time to act like a man and help a friend," he said with a poor excuse of a smile.

"It's nice to have a friend again," I replied as I nudged his knee with my fist. "I will gather some supplies, you sit and rest."

Dean stayed put on the porch and watched as I scurried around his property. The old man desperately required a time out. After a few minutes of searching for the right supplies, I regrouped with Dean. He looked up at me with his weary eyes, and his hostility was apparent. I was aware that there were many other things he would rather be doing, however, he would provide assistance; that was the kind of guy he was.

"Are you ready?" he asked.

"I think the question should be: is Dean ready?" I reworded his inquiry.

"I am as ready as I will ever be," he said as he unhurriedly lifted his creaking bones from the hard surface.

"We should have enough daylight to accomplish our task as long as we move quickly," I informed the reluctant helper.

"From the shovel, I am assuming he is buried in the woods," Dean commented.

"That is what I believe," I simply answered.

"That's it; you are not positive?" Dean asked as he began to follow my lead.

"It will be fine, old man, trust me," I recited as I peered over my shoulder to grin at him. "All I want from you at this point in time is to tell Eric's tale."

As we walked I heard Dean's heavy breathing over the light sounds of nature, so we reduced our pace. As we grew closer to the woods, a sense of enlightenment nudged at my brain. My mind was clear, as if what we were about to do was the correct idea. My speed once again decelerated, for the frail man behind me was falling back.

"I apologize for my sluggishness," Dean said sincerely.

"No need for apologies here," I responded as I turned my head towards him. "We have plenty of time."

"My mother was an absolute angel. She had the biggest heart ever to be in a human body. She was the kind of soul that cared deeply about others and spent most of her time pleasing them. Not sexually," Dean specified his words and I giggled. "You remind me of her; of course, you are far more crude than my mother, yet you both try to keep the people around you content. You don't do it for personal gain either; you do it because you don't know any other way. It is completely natural and one of the most beautiful gifts in the world."

"Well thanks for the unpolished complement," I interrupted to express my thoughts.

"I don't mean anything bad with my words," Dean explained himself. "Anyway, I was trying to make a point."

"Sorry, go right ahead."

"Eric was a sad young man with no one to show him affection. Naturally my mother could not bear to see a child in such pain. She began to invite him over for lunch. That grew into dinners and the dinners grew into breakfast. He was a well-known person in our household. He barely spent any time at his own house, and nobody blamed him. He acted as my big brother; he protected and watched me when my mother had other duties to fulfill," Dean paused as he wiped a tear from his eye. "He was five years older than me, and he was a great help to our family. Everyone enjoyed him and hated when he had to leave. His dad beat him often; he tried to hide the bruises, but we were all aware. No one in my family had the heart to talk to him about it, for they knew that it was hard for him to deal with."

"How long did he hang around?"

"My mother started caring for him when he was five years old; I was newly born. He disappeared when I was ten, so he was part of our family for a decade."

"So, he just magically vanished one day?"

"My ninth year he wasn't around as much. I overheard conversations that discussed the fact that Eric's parents were upset about all the time he spent at our house. I was nine, so I don't remember all the details, plus I didn't know that many specifics at that age," he stopped talking long enough to take a gigantic breath of air. It was obvious that he was in pain, however, he would not admit it. "I remember asking my mother where Eric had been, every time I asked, her eyes would tear up. I didn't know then, but I know now. It meant Eric's life was troubled. I turned ten shortly before Eric stopped visiting. When it was proven that he was missing, the neighborhood grew restless. The entire town blamed Eric's father, and the rage grew until Eric's parents had to move out of town. The mystery of Eric's disappearance was never solved. Most adults believed his father took his life, unfortunately there was no body for evidence. Everyone was aware of the beatings, but without Eric, there were no bruises for proof. So, sadly, we went on with our lives and left Eric in the past. Thanks to you, I am now sure that he has been suffering all these years."

It finally surfaced: the reasoning for Dean's unannounced car ride. It became necessary for him to have time alone. He had been dealing with the question of what happened to Eric his entire life. Not knowing the outcome of his dear friend had been eating at his insides, and receiving closure was not as easy as one would think.

"I feel like a complete fool right now," I verbally shared my humility. "It has nothing to do with you," Dean responded immediately. "In actuality, it is probably good for me to get some closure."

"It's difficult to hold on to pain for such a long period of time. Sometimes an answer can lead to guilt and regret, however, it is necessary to discover the truth."

The next few moments were spent in silence. Eric had been following us the entire way; it was unusual for a spirit to be in my sight for such an extended amount of time, but then again, there was nothing usual about my life. Our trek had been going on for about forty minutes or so, and Dean was none the wiser that we had company. My body began to tremble, and my stomach became furious. As a thick fluid gushed from my mouth and on to the dirt below. Dean did all he could to ignore it, however, his heart would not allow such a selfish act to be committed.

"Anything I can do for you?" he calmly asked as I plummeted to my knees.

"I put some water in the pack that you carry," I informed him of the necessity to rinse my mouth. Dean approached with the bottle of clear liquid.

"By your actions, I tend to think that we are close." "I was pondering on the same thought."

"I thought you knew where to go, but you seem to be guessing."

"I do know; you'll have to give me a second to collect myself so I can arrange my thoughts!" I snapped back at him. "I'm sorry about losing my cool; this is very painful, and it is difficult to concentrate. Please be patient and I will find the exact spot."

"Sounds terrific," Dean said sarcastically. "I am going to get off of my feet while you figure things out."

"Thanks for the understanding," I replied as my head shook back and forth with frustration. My temper was close to erupting; everything was irritating. The breeze upon my face was pissing me off, the sounds of nature made me want to scream for mercy, and the fact that the puking went on and on and on was infuriating. Dean was aware that I was struggling; he gave me plenty of room to do what was necessary.

There was another presence among us. My eyes focused upon Eric as his head pointed upward. Looking high up in the trees an old friend ("old friend" being sarcastic) was perched on a limb with an aggravating smile plastered upon his face. My eyes met his, and we stood motionless. Eric continued to move through the thicket; I decided to leave Junior by himself and follow the boy. With every step, the feebleness of my body grew stronger and stronger. We moved away from Dean, who was sitting against an oak tree. As we left his sight, he followed. A few feet further, Eric pulled a Houdini and vanished just as a rustling sound invaded the background. With a quick glance over my shoulder I spotted Dean staring into the thicket next to him. With a sudden twist of his neck, he gave me a look of pure desperation and bolted past me, disappearing into the woods.

After moments of screaming for the scared elder and receiving no response, I verbally ordered him to sit and wait for assistance. I was doubtful that he would comply with my demand. Then I felt a presence directly behind me.

"I was so wishing that you had left me forever," I said to the ghost lurching over my shoulder.

"You think because you freed that pitiful old man from my prison that my use for you is null and void?"

My perception of Junior's power was masked. Could he physically harm me? Was he wanting me dead or was it essential that I remained alive? Either of the questions had no true answer and it was important that I proceeded with caution.

"Whatever it is that you need from me, you will receive nothing without a fight," I said.

"You act all strong and mighty. I know deep down you are cowering."

"My days of fearing you are in the past. Why are you here?"

"To be honest, I am here for many reasons, most of which do not concern you. The fact that you are using your unique gift and following the map in your head is one of those reasons. The more you use your powers, the more like me you will become," he said with a snicker.

"I have hatred burning through my veins. It is the fuel that keeps me moving and able to run from the likes of you. I have the power to see right from wrong and that is the one difference between us that will never change."

"Hate is exactly what leads to a life such as mine," he smirked as he spoke. "Your hatred for the common human is what will bring you to me."

"Get out of my face!" I shouted as my emotions took precedence, and my fist swung at an image of my imagination. "If you are going to do something, do it now, otherwise leave me be. I have more important tasks to deal with." I stormed off in a huff to locate Dean.

It was time to find the old man and make sure he was still among the living. Eric was aware of what I had to do and disappeared so he would not be a distraction. Twenty minutes passed and it was starting to seem like an impossible mission. I shouted Dean's name through my lips over and over to no avail. My head began to swim, and my face plunged into the dirt and leaves under my feet.

"I have seen you in that position far more than I wish to," Dean's voice flowed from his mouth and into my ears like beautiful music. I spit leaves from my mouth.

"What a glorious sound," I recited.

"I am glad to see you in one piece," Dean said. "What did the junior prick want, and why can I see him and not Eric?"

"I am guessing that it has to do with what they've learned during their time of demise. I believe that I may hold the power to see each and every spirit at any given moment, however, I have yet to learn how."

"Why do you think that?"

"It's not that I think, it's more that I just know. It's difficult to explain; some of my dreams lead me to feel that way."

"I am only beginning to understand the power of dreams," he shared his remembrance. "The night vision I had of Frank still remains fresh in my memory. I really do think that it was more than a dream."

"Like I said before, it probably was. As you are finding out, each life is filled with certain abilities to be learned. If they are not worked on, nothing becomes of them. If I ignored my habits, which I did for many years, I would not have met Frank, nor would I be in your company now."

"It's all about digging into unknown thoughts," Dean thought out loud. "Precisely," I roared out. "Even you must admit that there have been thoughts in your head that you have overlooked. Sometimes thoughts do need to be ignored, and I am not speaking of immoral ideas. I am speaking of the topics that that make you sad, therefore you block them out. I know that it is difficult, but you need to fester upon those thoughts that involve Eric. He wants us to know something, and he has an unusual manner when Junior is present. I am starting to accept that they are connected somehow." "That is insane!" Dean surprised me with a sudden burst of emotion. "No, never mind that rash explosion. I am overwhelmed by all the coincidences. I am not sure how many more I can endure, for the world already seems quite small."

"I agree it is a little creepy. I am wondering when we find out that you are my father."

"I would believe that," Dean said as he exploded with laughter and rolled amongst the leaves. I joined him and we giggled our way away from the drama, at least for a few moments.

"We should get this job done," I said to Dean as I noticed that Eric had reappeared.

"You have the knowledge?"

"We must dig," I answered, "right there." I pointed to where I saw Eric waiting.

Dean did not hesitate or ask any more questions. He was finally learning to trust what I said. He seized the shovel and commenced the dig. I was not planning on letting him do any more grunt work, yet he was determined in what he was doing. Moans and groans sounded from the hole that Dean dug; he was bound to finish, and the spade never slowed until it hit something other than dirt. The sound was strange and like nothing I've ever heard. It was not metal on wood or metal on metal. Dean tossed the digging tool and pounced to his knees, using his bare hands to dig the rest of the way. After a few moments of free hand digging, the old man leapt out of the trench.

"Son-of-a-bitch!" he exclaimed.

"What in the hell is going on?" Dean tried to calm himself down as he made his way towards me. He crouched down breathing heavily.

"I pierced his skull," he said emotionally.

"What?" I asked. "So, he is not in anything whatsoever?"

"Obviously not," Dean's voice bled with pain. He then shook off his distress and proceeded to uncover the rest of Eric's bones. I began to provide my assistance.

"You have done enough. This is my calling," Dean said as he reached out and held my arm. "Find something to carry his remains."

"All right, I'm here if you desire assistance," I responded as he nodded to confirm that he heard me loud and clear. I emptied out the sack that I brought. The supplies were meaningless to us since we already fulfilled our mission. I set the sack next to Dean and watched as he carefully swept the dirt from the bone. Dean stopped moving and I drew closer to peer over his shoulder. His filthy hands held bones that resembled a rib cage. Stuck between the ribs sat a knife. Dean looked up from the disastrous sight, and a tear ran down his cheek, leaving a trail upon his dirt-covered face.

"It is an ordinary butter knife," he sadly described the utensil. "Stabbed with the dullest tool possible, what a horrendous way for a child to leave the world of the living. I guess this was most likely the doings of his father."

"I'm not sure that is entirely true." "Of course you don't."

"I have a feeling that Junior has something to do with it."

"He wasn't even born when it happened," Dean informed me.

"I am aware of that, but he knows about it," I said as I held the bag open so Dean could discard what was left of Eric.

"He doesn't know shit about it!" Dean expressed his opinion with a boost of passion. "He is here because you are here. He has a connection to you and no one else in this area."

"I know that. All I am saying is that I have a feeling that Junior, or someone he knows, was involved with the death of Eric. If you have learned anything from the time spent with me, it should be that my feelings mean something."

"Why don't you ask Junior?" Dean urged me to look where his finger pointed. I did; and there stood the spawn of Satan.

"I see that you have found my father's treasure," Junior's voice erupted into the air.

I cocked my head at Dean; he nodded and mouthed the words *I'm sorry*. It wasn't the first time that I didn't want my outlook to be accurate. The thought of Jay Sr. stabbing Eric was grizzly at best. He was older than Frank and Dean by only three years. That meant that he was about thirteen years old when he took the life of another. It did make sense now that I knew how young Junior was with his first kill. Dean seized the sack that carried his dead friend and marched away. He headed for his home; he was done dealing with the nonsense.

"You know what?" I questioned the unholy ghost. "He wasn't even your father. He was a delusional human that kidnapped you from your parents and manipulated your mind into killing them. He is nothing to be proud of."

"A father is someone who teaches and protects their child. He taught me how to be strong and how to provide for myself. Blood means nothing to me. He was my father," Junior explained himself. "He did not manipulate my mind; I lent him my brain, and I asked him to fill it with his wisdom."

"You both are very sick individuals. Even in death you are a piece of work," I expressed my opinion. "I can only hope that this was your father's first kill."

"That may be, and it may not, it doesn't pertain to you."

"Obviously it does pertain to me!" I screamed out into the air and pointed towards the fleeing old man. "Eric came to me because of the bullshit your so-called father caused. I am connected to the disaster your life feeds on. I am the one that must clean up the messes that you and your horrible acquaintances caused. You say that it is none of my business, but we both know that the universe will not allow you to keep secrets from me. No matter what you do or what you have done, I will find out and I will be expected to fix it!"

"You need to see yourself for the piece of work that you are," he responded to my outburst.

"Flattery will get you nowhere. I am now going to leave you. Leave you alone with your retched self."

"No matter where you go, I will find you." "I am sure you will," I recited.

The journey back to Dean's was a slow one. Weariness was my enemy and had to be fought off every second. The soreness throughout my body made every step short and light. As I reached the destination, the sun began to set. I approached the great oak in Dean's backyard and noticed a large pile of dirt sitting next to a freshly dug hole. Hammering sounds from the nearby shed pulled me in its direction. Dean was inside the shed constructing a rectangular box; he looked like death warmed-over.

"Every time my mind would drift to the days of Eric, I would see him playing around that tree. So, I decided that he should be properly buried underneath it," he explained his actions and they made perfect sense.

"Could I assist in any way?"

"Like I told you before, you have done enough. This is my ordeal. Please relax and I will talk to you when I am done." Dean was desperate to feel pain; he felt that if he suffered, it would bring him closer to Eric's spirit.

Relaxing, under the circumstances, was easier said than done. Waiting for Dean to finish his job was excruciating. It was not an everyday experience for me to let someone do hard labor while I sat and did nothing. I understood that Dean had to accomplish his task alone, but it was not simple to allow. The minutes seemed like hours as my eyes burned holes through his antique cuckoo clock that rested upon the wall. Finally, the back door creaked and I heard Dean pulling himself through the doorway. Once he came into view it was obvious that he was in dire pain and required rest. His expression was stern and full of frustration; he was about to blow, and I was in range.

"Anything I can do to help?" I asked a naïve question.

"Yes," he said with a glum tone to his voice, "you can take your crazed life and take it far, far away from me." His eyes overflowed with liquid as he slid his tired, bruised body down the wall. He hugged his knees and bawled like an abandoned child.

"If you would be more comfortable alone, I would understand that."
"Honestly, being alone would probably not be the best thing for me right now."

"I will stay as long as you wish me to," I responded and rubbed my hand down his filthy back. When I was stressed with the thoughts and memories of what my life portrayed, I wanted nothing more than solitude. My desire to be left alone was not shared by other humans; most people required company during moments of insanity, even though I did not comprehend why. I knew that I was the odd ball out.

As I sat up against the wall, shoulder to shoulder with Dean, it became clear that no words were going to provide comfort, so we let the silence invade and wallowed in our sorrows. After a few minutes the sounds of sleep drained from the aged mouth to my right. His weight shifted onto my arm as pins and needles affected my hand immediately. The man required rest, and a little discomfort on my part was not going to interfere with his well-being. My eyes closed, and I joined Dean in another reality.

During my time of sleep, I was well-known for walking, so it wasn't too surprising when my eyes opened to the sight of the great oak. After assuring myself that there was nothing strange in the air, I returned to the house to locate the owner. Searching high and low and coming up empty, I peered through the kitchen window to make sure both vehicles were present. They were. The scene around me appeared to be drama-free, yet my mind began to think irrationally. My life was filled with disaster; behind every door there was an obstacle, and the very second I decided a situation was serene was the very second that all hell broke loose. It became impossible to relax as my body started to tremble. I yanked open the front door to the home and kicked the screen door into the fresh air by my foot as I screamed with hatred and fury.

"What in the hell are you doing?" Dean demanded an answer as he sat on the outside steps staring at his broken door.

"Oh, you're safe," I said while winking at him. "Just follow along." Dean stood up, shaking his head.

"You have lost it, my boy." He then disappeared into his home. "Wait!" I shouted, "I have a plan." He did not come back, and his footsteps faded as he made his way up the stairs. He was correct: I had lost my mind. It wasn't the first time and it definitely would not be the last. The gibberish flowing from my mouth did not intimidate Dean one bit; he had witnessed a different reality and was a different man than he was before I came hurdling into his life. I was convinced that Junior was close and was trying to act wild to pull him out into the open. However, my plan was not well thought out, and should have been run by the old man first. Dean was tired of my schemes and wanted nothing to do with an unrehearsed idea; I did not blame him for his reaction.

The inside of the house was filled with creaks and moans as I heard Dean roaming room to room. I was not certain exactly what he was up to. We had both seen unexplainable events the last couple of days, and sanity was becoming distant. The stairs creaked as Dean made his way down them; I waited patiently upon the porch. The wood door that blocked my view of the inside of the house sprang open, and a determined man with crazed eyes and a shotgun in his hands whizzed by. Quickly getting out of his way, I followed close behind as he ventured towards the backyard. Once we arrived next to the oak tree, I asked what his intentions were.

"I am going to shoot the son-of-a-bitch," he replied with wickedness shooting from his eyeballs. He was on a mission, and I had to talk some sense into him.

"You can't shoot him, he is already dead." He turned quickly toward me, "So you say."

"What the hell does that mean? Are you calling me a liar?"

"You have made it quite clear that you have been known to stretch the truth, what makes this any different?" He pierced my eyes with his own. "Of all the ghosts that you say you see, why do I see him and none of the others?"

"You saw Frank!" I shouted back at him with retaliation. "That was a dream," he explained.

"It wasn't a dream, that is how it starts. When your mind is resting, it becomes open to other realms. That is the easiest way for a confused spirit to make contact with one of the living. He came to you and force-fed you a message. It was really him."

"Then why has he not visited you?"

"I don't have all the answers, neither did Frank; you know this. The only reason that I think he did not make contact with me is because my dreams are filled up. There is a waiting list for the dead souls to torture me. He probably didn't have the time to wait. He knew that I was coming to see you, so he took the initiative to tell you what was to come. I am damn sure that if he had the chance to speak with me, he would have."

"For not having any answers you sure seem to know things."

"I am guessing," I replied. "I look at the situation and come to a sensible solution. My thoughts are not entirely correct; they are educated guesses."

"Educated," Dean mumbled. "What kind of education are you referring to?"

"It is my life! I am going from all the details I have learned along the way."

"I am sorry; I am not trying to rile you up. I am confused, and tired of not knowing."

"Once again, welcome to my life. I am also sorry. I didn't want you to have to deal with my personal issues."

"I recall," he said.

"I accept your apology, and hope that you understand that I want no harm to come to you."

"I do," he simply quoted.

With all honesty, I was fearful. Watching a man lose sight of reality was a disaster waiting to happen. Observing a man lose his sanity while holding a deadly weapon was a dangerous experience. I could not take my eyes of his shaking hands as the cool night air blew directly through me; the world was spinning, and I was still. Dean continuously vanished and reappeared before me as my lids bounced up and down. There was a shadow behind my old friend; the sun had set, so I was certain that it was Junior. My fingers became a vice and were used to hold my eyelids open. I fought wooziness and gradually regained my strength. I craved to witness the next scene and not wake up somewhere strange with more questions upon my mind.

A gust of wind instantly brought back memories of the other night.

Dean shrugged when the wind began to blow. "Here we go with this deviant again," he said. "Don't be a fool," I spat from my mouth.

"Yeah," Junior replied to my words that were meant for Dean. "Don't be a fool, Dean. Go ahead and blow my brains to the ground. What are you waiting for?" As he taunted the scared old man, he grew closer to Dean's vibrating back. I could sense the terror that was pouring from the old gent's eyes. He could feel the spirit approaching.

"Go into the house, Dean!" I demanded. He did not heed my warning. His fear could be smelled from miles down the road; his tracks had become frozen. I composed myself and sheltered my friend from my foe.

"It is of perfect sensibility that you tell me of your wanting," I said. "So calm, so charming," Junior invaded the airway with sarcasm.

"You think that the upper hand is in your court. Your thoughts are more preposterous than you wish them to be. I am deceased; I no longer breathe your air, nor do I bathe in your ignorance. The realm that chose me has granted me a power unlike any other. I will have the chance to fulfill my every thought, no matter how gruesome it may be, as soon as I master the strength."

"So all of this," I spoke as I motioned towards the great oak and its newly found friend, "all of this is a way for you to stall?"

"In a matter of speaking, I did not plan this. Unfortunately, you are discovering that a certain gift has been given to you. You have the ability to communicate with the souls that find you. I will find the key to your demise, and I will certainly take pleasure in bringing you to my realm."

"This is absurd; you are accomplishing nothing but filling my ears with nonsense!" I let my words be heard from afar. I turned my back towards the mischievous deviant and shoved the old man towards his home. "Don't argue with me; just do as I say. Earlier this evening I let you be by yourself. I now demand that you return the effort," I pointed to his house. Dean put the rifle at ease, bowed his head, and nonchalantly moseyed away. With my body still turned away from Junior, my composure was refocused.

"Now what?" the annoying spirit questioned my actions. "Are we going to talk some more, or would you prefer we play a game?"

My eyes squinted as my stare turned deadly. I was no longer looking at him, I was piercing a hole directly through him. The hatred made the blood rush through my veins in a panic. The rhythm of my heartbeat was erratic and on the verge of exploding. If he was still a human, I would have ripped his head from his body. All his horrible deeds were flowing through my mind, not allowing the opportunity to think straight or wise. My next actions were not clear. As the plan was being created inside my head, my attention was drawn to the squeak of Dean's back door.

"I believe you have other duties to tend to at this time," the wise-cracking dead man spoke as he disappeared from which he came.

Dean stood buck-ass naked with both arms held straight out before him; both middle fingers stretched into the night air. I stood wide eyed, desperately holding back the chuckles. I hadn't seen a naked man over the age of sixty. The sight was rather humorous, and the fact that he was extremely pissed off and out of his mind only enhanced the comedic nature. The funny emotion shortly turned to pity. I felt the worst sense of guilt that I had ever had the displeasure of borrowing my mind to. It was all the fault of one naive soul, and that soul happened to be me.

Dean halted from flipping the birds and fled back into his private domain. The war that was going on in my gut had erupted into a nuclear battle, and I released the soldiers from my innards. The sounds of destruction were leaking through the cracks in Dean's door, and it became obvious that his rage was releasing. It was in my best interest to not make the situation worse. His reaction was brought on by the notions I allowed him to see and be a part of, therefore my presence would be like adding gasoline to an already prominent fire. I sat upon the dirt and waited for the sound of silence to invite me in.

The racket from inside the house subdued and the night was still. The silence meant that Dean's rampage was over, and that was scary in its own right. He could be lying dead on the floor. A deep breath of the night air filled my lungs as I turned the doorknob into the house. There was a click as I pushed the wooden obstruction inward; it was forced in by some other force and in a split second I was shoved from the doorway and forced to the ground.

"Are you alone?" the fearful old gent questioned. I was thrilled to see that he found some garments.

"I believe that he will leave us alone."

The old man crouched down and sat himself upon the stairs. He was still shaking from his last disastrous moment. I pulled myself close to him and continued to lie on my back. The cool, rough ground felt fantastic upon my bruised, stiff back. I then reached out my bleeding hand and grabbed a hold of Dean's ankle.

"Why are you bleeding?" he asked.

"I have no clue whatsoever," I answered. "I think it would be best if I try, once again, to clean myself up." I began to lift my aching body from the dirt, and then I felt pressure amongst my shoulder.

"I think we should talk," Dean said with a serious tone in his voice. "I would like to make this conversation as quick as possible."

"It sounds as if you are trying to get rid of me," I snickered.

"I just want to say what I have to say," I nodded as he stressed urgency with his hands. "I understand that the reason you have graced me with your presence is because you were at your wit's end, and believed that I may be someone to vent to. After experiencing a fraction of your life, I understand what you came for. You have shown me that most of the things I believe in are untrue. You have unraveled my reality and now, I am a seriously confused individual." He lifted his hands in the air, "I do not blame you, or resent you in any way. My point is that I have only endured two days of your reality and I have had enough. You have spent your entire life dealing with the dead, whether you like it or not. I commend you for your strength; even though you asked me not to.

"Anyway, Frank told me that you were different. He wished that he was more like you," as Dean spoke, he noticed my eyes rolling. "Someday, hopefully soon, you will understand what he meant. Until then, you must fight your demons off. By demons, I mean your lack of self-worth. You are not worthless, and you do not bring anyone harm. Those who have been hurt had their reasons for helping you. One day you will see yourself through the eyes of those who saw you the way Frank did."

"Are you one of those people?" I interrupted with a question. "Absolutely," he answered briefly. "The problem that I am having is that I am too old to go through such a drastic realization of what life is. I can't handle the truth. I will do whatever I can to help you along; even though I am scared, I am here for you. You only have to ask."

"You know damn well that is not going to happen." "And maybe that is the best for both of us."

The air did not get thick from tension. Actually, the air appeared perfect. We both were aware that there was no other way. My time with Dean carried every emotion of man, it was a roller coaster ride the entire two days and, unfortunately, it would not be forgotten. I respected Dean for his honesty, loyalty, and his tremendous courage. He was a wise old man, and I was certain that Frank was dying to get me to realize it. Dean saved my life a number of times, and it would not be taken for granted. The last couple of days changed us both.

It came to the moment of my departure. Deans' one hand was sandwiched between the two of mine. We stared at the pupils of each other and cracked a slight smile. There were no words to be said that weren't already known. There was nothing easy about walking away from the man in front of me however, the sooner I left, the sooner he would be able to get back to reality. I turned and walked away from my new friend. That was the first and last time that we would unite as two living beings.

The trip home was one that carried a great deal of sadness. The mission to confront another human and bleed my dark, dismal thoughts did not go as planned. Instead, it opened up a whole new field of guilt. It was a privilege to come face to face with such an extraordinary man. It brought great pleasure to know that Frank had such a wonderful human being to assist him through his miserable moments. The friendship that they shared was one in a million. They were both extremely fortunate to have had each other in their lives; I was awfully jealous of what they shared, however, I was honored that I had the opportunity to experience their friendship.

I arrived at my residence and was hesitant to depart my vehicle. I didn't know what was going to take place in my future. The extreme menace identified as Jay, also known as Junior, was definitely going to continue tormenting my ridiculous lifecycle until he was able to receive closure. How he was going to make that happen was a mystery, nevertheless, it was a conundrum that would bring senseless pain to my well-being.

Before I left my means of transportation, I spotted a young girl standing before my humble abode. She was staring directly at me with a stern expression printed upon her youthful face. I did not recognize her, and the fact that she stood outside my domain by her lonesome was a mystery. I instantly knew that she was not a normal child by the sensation that imbedded my being. My head shook with disgust for the distress from the past few days, since I had no time to heal and it was apparent that the presence of the girl was another difficult ordeal that was going to impact my life.

I gradually released my body from the metal machine as a familiar sensation of pain gained attention amongst my flesh. Lesions began to appear and the bodily fluid that coursed through my veins drained onto the cement foundation from which I stood. The small child stood before me with a mischievous grin planted upon her face, and then she ceased to exist.